MORE THAN
THAN
LEGEND

A BOOK FOR THE WHOLE FAMILY

The fiery glow of the "Door of the Sun" weakened and began to waver across its counterpart on the canyon wall.

How eerie it seemed.

The clue to a long lost secret was vanishing away right in front of them—slipping right through their fingers.

MORE THAN LEGEND

DARYL N. PATTERSON

CABIN BOOKS
PARADISE, CA.

This book is a work of fiction. Names, characters, places and incidents are either the products of the author's imagination or are used fictitiously. Any resemblance to actual events or locales or persons, living or dead, is entirely coincidental.

Published by Cabin Books
Paradise, California 95969
Printed in the United States of America

Additional copies of this book may be obtained from Cabin Books

ISBN 0-9646761-2-5

EAN-13 978-0-9646761-2-1

Library of Congress Catalog Card Number: 2009908188

First Edition: January 1996

Second Edition: January 2010
First Revision: October 2016

cabinbookspublishing@gmail.com

To my Family,
May Life Always be an Adventure

My Thanks to Family and Friends for
Their Support and Encouragement

TABLE OF CONTENTS

MORE THAN LEGEND

1

IN THE HIGH SIERRA

October 2, 1793

I t all began with the quest for power, and ended shrouded in mystery. After two hundred years the intriguing stories that had been told over many a lonely campfire eventually became legend.

High in the gleaming peaks of the *Sierra Nevada Mountain Range*, the discovery of an unusually rich deposit of gold held the potential of financing the overthrow of Spanish power in the West, but that hope was short lived. *Captain Camino* and those that joined him found themselves in a tragic situation. They were trapped. Escape seemed improbable, due to the fact that they were boxed in by hostile Indians. The miners had come to call this place the '*Oro de Cañon*,' the Canyon of Gold. But what good was the gold now, what could it buy? There was no more food and the men had grown weak. It was only a matter of time.

The Chief of the Pohono Indian Tribe could no longer control the renegade band who trapped not only the miners, but also his own daughter and grandchild within the confines of the steep-walled canyon. He pleaded with *White Feather* to leave, but she declared her love and loyalty to Captain Camino, and her determination to stay by his side to the bitter end.

A tear ran down her cheek as she relinquished her infant son to her sister, realizing she may never see him again. But he had to be taken to a place of safety.

Captain Camino removed the golden medallion from around his neck and separated the inscribed disk into its two halves. He concealed one of these in the blanket beside his son. The infant was too young to understand the Captain's last words: "All this is your inheritance if you return to me. The medallion shall show you the way back."

Later that day the assault again ensued. Arrows hissed through the air driving them back. A cry from the far ridge was followed by an avalanche of immense boulders and rock, sealing off the *'Door of the Sun,'* the only known access into the legendary 'Canyon of Gold.'

Silence now crept into the canyon for two hundred years, waiting, waiting—waiting.

May 25, 1993
TUOLUMNE COUNTY, CALIFORNIA

As the early morning dawn crept silently down upon the Purple Hills from the mighty Sierra Nevada Range and lofty peaks flushed pink against the far blue sky, long unexplained events began to fall into place.

The dark outline of the *Obelisk*, a sharp piercing spire that dominated over the river basins inspiring Indian lore and stories of forbidden trespass, now became visible high in the bold-faced granite peaks. Among these jagged sentinels, ages of time had revealed the riches of eternity. The Stanislaus River roaring with velocity, flowed from the high mountain snowfields to share its gift with a younger land. Sitting at the base of the Great Range, the Purple Hills seemed to flow down into the Central Valley and vanished into the vast alluvial sea.

The pink flush of the high mountain peaks began to fade, revealing in increasing light, a sleepy little town at its feet,

Columbia. Once a roaring camp of the Gold Rush, it now lay quiet in the shadow of those memories, reminiscent of a lawless and adventurous time.

From the earliest of times according to some early inhabitants this gold rich area had been known as A'ora. Subsequent settlers were puzzled by that name. It did not seem to be of Indian origin, but probably from the Latin word, *Aurora*, that depicted a golden sunrise. However, they soon realized that there was more than just a golden sunrise here. In the Gold Rush of 1849, the local rivers were found to be laced with golden sands. Miners coming up out of Mexico synonymously named a nearby camp, Sonora, after their home district. The name *Aurora* had all but vanished except for historical references found in the local archives.

Thick brush grew around many of the old abandoned mines and the decaying head frames that still remained aloft overlooking the town. The rhythmic beating of the stamp mills that had crushed the ore day and night were now silent. These were now a mournful monument to the miners who long ago worked here.

Just east of *Columbia* was a jagged battlefield of distorted limestone and marble bedrock, over thirty feet deep, that had been laid bare and cut into by hydraulic monitors. These white eroded formations, now intermixed with the Chinese Tree of Heaven were a habitat for a variety of wildlife. Miners in their quest to find the illusive hiding place of precious metal had left no stone unturned as they painstakingly scraped and polished these rock formations to remove the rich gold bearing soil.

Among those miners were thousands of Chinese workers brought in as an economical source of labor. Although gone, they left their mark as evidenced by the small townsite nearby called Chinese Camp and by the various kinds of trees and plants that still flourished here. Remnants of stacked rock fences that crisscrossed the countryside also attested to their hard labors.

More Than Legend

Hiding the scars of yesteryear's mining hostilities were clusters of oak and scrub pine, with an undergrowth of chaparral and manzanita that dotted the rolling Purple Hills.

Many of the residents of Columbia were descendants of the original gold miners. The others were ones that had fled the rat race of the big city. Daily life here was usually slow and simple; and hospitality could generally be found at every door.

Yet, a dark secret still hung over the land, a mystery generations old. How was it possible that these mountains could hide such a momentous secret for so long? Could there still be a hidden intrigue working within these shining peaks?

Gunshots sounded in the distance as Bryan cautiously pulled an increment borer from a tree and carefully slid the core into its plastic tube. That made forty samples; and end of the line. Hearing a vehicle racing off, he wondered what had happened. It was rare to hear gun fire so near the sleepy little town. Opening his notebook, Bryan indicated the distance from the previous tree and its approximate girth and height. His class project was now nearer to completion.

Slapping the hard bound notebook closed, he poked it into his shoulder bag and stepped over to the edge of the canyon bringing the depth of the Stanislaus River into view. Bryan glanced up river as his thoughts turned to the mysterious dark *Obelisk* and the piercing peaks of the high country. As he thought about the Obelisk, Bryan wondered if this ominous spire was really more than just an astonishing landmark, but perhaps the key to the greatest mystery of them all, the *'Legend.'* His thoughts probed the stories and speculations of Indian lore, and its connection with the legends of hidden gold. Nevertheless, there were never enough pieces of the puzzle to sort things out. Turning, he could see a lone hawk flying over the river looking for fish. It was now time to hike back to town, which was about three miles through the woods and up to the main road.

In The High Sierra

Bryan Anderson was sixteen years old, eyes brown, hair black, and was about five feet eleven inches in height. He did very well in school; but things at home were not as they should have been.

His father, Tom Anderson, who was of medium build with fairly wide shoulders and light brown hair, continued to struggle in his endeavor to establish a mountain pack service, a dream he always had. But the reality of that dream was found to be frought with obstacles and unforeseen circumstances. Business was often sporadic, and bills weren't always paid on time. And despite the beckoning beauty of these mountains, there was the *'Legend'* and a certain mystique that pervaded over the region. Partially due to the fact that so many had disappeared in these mountains or had strange unexplained accidents, such as Bryan's own father. Three years previous he was caught in a freak landslide that nearly buried him alive. Though remarkably recovered he now walked with a slight limp.

In the balance financially was also one hundred and sixty acres of virgin timber land acquired by his grandfather back in the 1920's, and their present home which sat in one corner of the property. His grandfather conveyed it to his son, Bryan's father, after passing what he called the "age of productivity." Bryan's father, Tom, had big ideas for that land in conjunction with his high country pack service, yet there was a black cloud that had descended upon that tall timber. The White Pines Timber and Mining Company with greedy eyes exerted much pressure to acquire it, but his father flatly refused to sell. There was the possibility that if he defaulted on the taxes, they would get it anyway, and as it was, he was already behind in his payments.

Bryan's mother, whom he hadn't seen in a couple of years, left to pursue a career and a better way of life down in the city. For the most part the pain of that experience was gone, but it still managed to surface from time to time. Bryan's father habitually buried himself in his work; but Bryan still felt the hurt and was left with a feeling of distrust for the whole gender. He was told that time would heal all; but the wound had not gone away. It was difficult to cope without understanding why she left. There were yet many questions left unanswered.

As he finally approached the main road leading into town, Bryan could see the line of jagged peaks thrusting upwardly above the oak treed foreground, reminding him of a colossal picket fence that discouraged wanderers from approaching. Why did the mountains keep calling him? Was there something waiting?

After climbing the bank and mounting the road something bright red caught his attention. Fresh blood? It certainly looked like it. From a small puddle, a trail of blood led along the edge of the pullout and ended near a set of tire tracks.

"Huh, what is this all about?" he wondered recalling the shots and the vehicle that had sped off earlier. Was there a murder? With the body being carried off? No, Bryan thought, stifling the mental pictures that flashed through his mind. Probably just an accident or something. But two shots?

Crossing the road and taking a shortcut across the grassy rolling terrain toward home, a change of thought came to him of how the school year was almost over and that scenario called "summer" would soon be here.

He approached his home of many years, a brown medium-sized house built partly of log and contemporary construction, well shaded by large pines. To the left and further back was the barn and a small corral where Midas and Thunder, two of his dad's prize pack mules were kept. Midas was a brown "bell mule," the one trained to take the lead in a pack train. Without such a leader, the other mules would not easily budge. Many of the old timers preferred white 'bell mules,' but they had become very rare.

As Bryan proceeded up the driveway he heard barking from the rear of the house. It was Graffiti, their golden retriever who was tied up by the feed shed, which indicated that his father must have left. Graffiti was an appropriate name because he was always leaving his signature wherever he went.

In The High Sierra

Climbing the moderate slope to the porch, he bounded up the steps, turned left and opened the screen door. Which at that time of the year was the only door in use. Having dropped his pack on the kitchen table, he glanced around the dimly lit room to hear only the tick of the wall clock. Discovering a note on the table he picked it up and found it was from his father. It indicated that he had gone to Coulterville on business and wouldn't be back until late. Bryan crumpled the note, thinking about the numerous wild goose chases his dad had made in the past. But he had to give him credit for not giving up.

Feeling a little hungry, he turned toward the refrigerator. Suddenly, he heard a loud popping and the backfiring of a vehicle approaching from down the road. As it grew louder he knew it must be Joshua Knight. His assumption was verified as the noise rounded the corner, and an old Jeep with faded green paint proceeded up the driveway. Graffiti barked anxiously at the noisy intruder.

Josh was tall, lanky, and blonde haired. He chewed the most dreadful green gum; and was usually inseparable from his baseball cap. They were very close friends, more like brothers.

For the last week, Josh had been tinkering on his older brother's abanboned Jeep. The vehicle came to a final stop with one last bang! Josh swung himself out of the vehicle as Bryan stepped out of the house.

"Say Buddy, how do you like my new limo?" exclaimed Josh.

"Ha! I'm surprised you didn't get arrested for disturbing the peace," laughed Bryan. "How did you finally get it started?" he questioned.

"I borrowed Mel's jump starter, and with a little perseverance it finally kicked over."

"Well great," happily responded Bryan. "Come on in, let's get a bite to eat."

Entering the house, Josh noticed Bryan's pack lying on the table. "Say, did you finally get all your samples for your project?" asked Josh.

7

"Ah, yeah," answered Bryan as he pulled the cold cuts and cheese out of the refrigerator. "Matter of fact, that's where I just came from. But I still need to read the cores and plot the data."

"Hey Buddy, time is almost up, next Tuesday is it!"

"I know, but I needed these to complete my study," replied Bryan as he laid out the slices of bread and piled on the mystery ingredients. "Oh, listen to this. When I was way out near the river collecting samples, I heard a couple of shots and then a vehicle sped off. Well anyway, after I hiked back and got up on the road, I found blood on the ground and a trail of blood spots."

"Really? Sounds like foul play to me."

"I kinda wondered that myself. Let's ask around and see if someone else has seen or heard anything."

"How can you possibly eat that?" objected Josh.

"It has taken years to perfect the technique," laughed Bryan.

Scooting down into a chair, Josh continued the conversation, "I can't wait till school is over."

"Yeah, I suppose. But what's there to look forward to? It's the same old thing this summer. It's not that I don't mind helping my dad with the pack trips. He needs a good wrangler and all, and frankly I enjoy being out there, but I feel tied down with no time to strike off and do anything on my own. I guess I just feel restless. Say, maybe you can join us for a few days this year?" proposed Bryan as he sat down.

"I would like that, but I hear my brat cousin Tammy is coming up this summer, so I'm not sure how much free time I'll really have."

"Sorry to hear that."

"You're telling me. She's a real hand full. Smartest in her class and I think it has gone to her head."

Bryan slid further down into his seat, "I wish, somehow this summer could be different."

If only Bryan knew how different this summer would really be and how it would change his life and those around him, forever.

2

THE FORGOTTEN TRAIL

L ater that evening with the sound of chirping crickets filtering through the screen door, Bryan began the tedious task of laying out each tree core set and comparatively measuring the ring spacing. Next it was necessary to plot the locations of the new trees on his linear base sheet, from which he would overlay the other sheets and transfer the locations. Each sheet represented 50 years of growth which was designated by a vector arrow showing direction and magnitude of ring distortion. After plotting the new cores, he lined up the sheets of paper from the present on down to the year 1750. Then something became very apparent. Somewhere between the years 1750 and 1800 there was a major ring distortion among several trees that gradually faded away. It was undoubtedly due to the fact that the tree canopy had naturally grown back together.

What am I looking at? Bryan pondered as he sat on the edge of the table. Could it have been a fire or something? There was no sign of burn in the rings he recollected. It would have showed up at the beginning of the distortion he thought. There must be a precedent to this, but what today would be similar? Looking at the 1900 to 1950 cross section, Bryan spotted two areas that had similar distortions. One was off the main road a short distance and the other about a mile in.

"What I need to do is go out there and see if there is anything that could clue me in to what is causing these distortions," he stated to himself as he leaned over the table to get a closer look.

For a fleeting couple of seconds he pondered once again the blood along the roadway. It bothered him. Quickly his thoughts lapsed back to his project that was laid out before him.

His dad came in a few minutes later, visibly tired, declaring he had lined up the necessary horses for this year's pack season. He also mentioned having briefly talked with a certain professor, who was asking numerous questions about the local rivers and the historical nature of gold mining in the area. There was a strong possibility, that he could be stopping by in the next day or two to get more information.

"Sounds like another gold chaser," surmised Bryan.

His dad was still talking as he went into the kitchen to find something to eat. Evidently because of the drought, the price of feed had gone up. He sat in the kitchen for a while longer, thinking about the day's events, and finally announced that he was taking his weary bones to bed after catching himself nodding off. Bryan soon followed suit.

Early the next day after chores, the two boys and Graffiti headed out in Josh's Jeep, which intermittently backfired as they drove along the winding dirt road out of town. Bryan, feeling a little embarrassed slid down low in the seat. Graffiti sitting in the back seat pretended to be just one of the boys, cocking his head back and forth trying to pick up on their conversation. Nearing their destination, they pulled into the wide spot along the road adjacent to the woods, which was in close proximity to the beginning of the tree borings, and the location where Bryan had seen the blood.

"The blood was right over there," pointed Bryan as they bailed out of the vehicle.

"Where? You sure you weren't just imagining things?" questioned Josh after a brief look around.

Bryan squatted down low and surveyed the scene. "It was right about here. Someone has covered it and stirred things around."

"Why would they come back unless they were trying to hide something?" reasoned Josh.

"That's right," agreed Bryan standing up.

"Look here, a footprint, the heel has little squares in it," spotted Josh.

"That could be from anybody," commented Bryan. "We better get going."

After putting on their packs they were ready. Dust flew, as they scampered down a fifty-foot bank and into the woods. Graffiti, barking excitedly took the lead.

"We are getting close," informed Bryan, looking around with some vague recollection of where they were.

After walking for another minute, they worked their way into a small void in the forest growth and found the two particular trees that he was looking for, number 7 and number 8, respectively.

Josh spun around in his tracks. "Looks to me, like an ol' road ran through here some years ago."

Bryan was silent for a moment as he studied the growth patterns of the trees and brush. Squatting down he could see dead brush overhung by densely growing small to medium-sized pine trees. Old rotted stumps almost buried in pine needles told the rest of the story. "Josh, I think you're right, it definitely runs in a strip to the north," he confirmed. "I'll write this one down as an overgrown logging road."

Bryan and Josh immediately set out for the next site winding their way over rolling terrain, and crossing through small drainages containing pockets of Canyon live oak. Dry leaves crackled underfoot as they worked their way in and out of the ravines.

"Keep an eye out for an old oak tree whose limbs almost touch the ground," informed Bryan as they topped a grassy rise and leveled out.

11

It wasn't too much further when they spotted the old oak, dark and twisted. Just past the tree, and through a stand of tall grass was the next site. After verifying that they had the correct set of trees, they began their investigation.

"There doesn't seem to be anything here except the visible height difference in the trees," said Josh looking north.

To the south was a small open meadow and along the east and west flanks were tall Douglas fir and ponderosa pine surrounding the elongated site. Spreading out, the boys filtered their way through the trees and brush that bordered the location, looking for anything unusual. Graffiti, keen eyed with panting tongue, immediately took the lead, thinking perhaps they were on some kind of quest or at least some kind of new game. After covering the outer perimeter, their attention focused on the center of the site which was densely overgrown with a vigorous growth of manzanita. After a few minutes of frustration in crawling through the overgrowth without any discoveries, Bryan slipped out into the open.

"See anything?" half-yelled Bryan.

"Not a thing here," voiced Josh a short distance away. Suddenly there was a loud swat! "Ow!" yelled Josh.

"You all right?" questioned Bryan.

"Yeah, I got hit in the head by a branch, and it clean shot my cap back in the bushes somewhere."

"Oh no! I'd never thought it possible that your cap could ever come off," teased Bryan.

Josh grumbled something as he crashed back into the bushes in search of his hat. Suddenly the popping and crackling stopped.

"Say! Buddy! We got something here," called out Josh.

"What is it?" questioned Bryan as he made his way toward Josh's voice.

"Well, for one thing, there's an old broken wagon wheel and what looks like a hand hewed log."

"An old wagon wheel, wow, that's great, it definitely proves that something happened here," said Bryan ducking under branches as he neared Josh's location.

"This old log is rounded, but flattened off on the top, perhaps being part of a wall or fence," guessed Josh.

"Here's a corner, must be what's left of a cabin," further speculated Bryan dropping to his knees and following the wood along the ground to a point where it angled.

"This area must have been cleared, homesteaded, and abandoned many years ago. Say, I wonder what stories this place could tell?" wondered Josh.

It was thought provoking to Bryan. Sitting down, he faced Josh who was looking far away, as if he were looking back into the past.

"We may not know what happened here in the past, but what does it mean for us today?" pondered Bryan. "These two sites are not natural processes of the forest, but appear to be caused by manmade defoliation. This indicates to me that the tree deflection in question between 1750 and 1800 should also be some kind of human activity."

"How much further in is this next site?" questioned Josh.

"Oh, about another mile or less," replied Bryan. After a pause of thought he continued. "To really prove my hypothesis, two more sets of cores need to be taken, one let's say —a thousand feet north and another—a thousand feet south of the original cross section. That should do the trick."

"That kind of reminds me of Mr. Krasnik's 'scientific method' that he keeps trying to pound into our heads," commented Josh.

"I don't know how scientific this is, but when I mentioned this project to him he looked at me sideways," chuckled Bryan. At that Graffiti got up and nudged Bryan under the arm, prompting him to get up. "Okay Graffiti, I get the message, time to hit the dusty trail."

Venturing further out toward the river canyon, they finally arrived at the mystery site, respectively trees number 36 through 38.

"We're here," announced Bryan as he flung his arms upward.

"Strange place," commented Josh. The area was dark and heavily timbered, much more so than the rest of the woods. Even Graffiti did not like this place. It was foreboding, ominous, and creepy.

"Well, let's have a quick look around anyway," said Bryan. The wind stirred the tops of the trees as they began their investigation.

A thorough search back and forth through the area revealed nothing out of the ordinary, except that the heavily timbered section appeared to run in a strip running roughly parallel to the river canyon. Why? Could it be topographical or climatological? Bryan didn't think so. They collected the two sets of cores and scrambled back toward town, as food now became their top priority. Both were very quiet as they hiked back, pondering the day's finds and the blood that had been on the roadway. Reaching the Jeep, they threw their packs in the back, jumped in, and headed down the road.

"Say, Josh, let's fix a quick lunch and then make a visit to my grandfather and see what he knows about any homesteads that may have been out this way," proposed Bryan as they passed the old dilapidated city limit sign.

"On one condition, I get to make my own sandwich, if you get my drift," grinned Josh.

"There you go again! Trying to slam dunk my sandwiches!"

"Nooo! It's just that I don't believe I have the strength to toss one of them up to a hoop," laughed Josh.

Once at Bryan's, the boys made a couple of tuna fish sandwiches and settled down for a few contemplative minutes. Bryan finished his sandwich, and with mouth still full, grabbed his pack and pulled out the cores they had taken that morning.

Separating the cores into their respective sets, he proceeded to carefully lay them out, one by one.

Josh got up and put their plates in the sink. "My uncle must be right—its going to be a bad fire season," he said looking out the window toward the far dry hills.

"Uh, huh," replied Bryan completely absorbed in counting rings. After a pause he continued, "You know, Josh these cores are basically identical to the original set. Look here, see that sudden, sharp deflection in the rings?"

"Hmm, yeah."

"And another thing, remember how the trees were bigger and taller along that strip? Think about it, when that area was logged off, say back in the 1880's, that strip may have been too small to harvest. So, after many years the timber along that strip would be significantly older and taller than the surrounding area. I think what we may have found is an old trail or road that was cut through there."

"Is this the oldest of all the sites so far?" asked Josh.

"Yes, it is, except for a couple places that seem to be related to lightning strikes. That puts us back about two hundred years. All the others were during and after the Gold Rush, but this one is before and its major."

"That's interesting, a forgotten trail, but to where?" pondered Josh.

"Obviously up the river, but my mind keeps drifting back toward the old stories about hidden gold, and the 'Legend,' " replied Bryan.

"The 'Legend?' This is got my adrenaline pumping, how can we find out more?" excitedly wondered Josh.

"Let's walk over to my grandfather's and question him, as we had planned. He knows a lot about Aurora, Columbia, and the old stories," replied Bryan. Agreeing on that, they further decided to walk the short distance into Columbia rather than causing an ugly scene by driving in. Walking out of the driveway, they proceeded down Italian Bar Road, over to Main Street, and into town.

3

GRANDFATHER'S REVELATION

Many of the old established businesses along Main Street were still in their old original red brick structures. Rustic iron frames and metal shutters gave the buildings a definite old-time nostalgic appearance. Seemingly ageless, they had weathered the riggers of time since the Gold Rush of 1849, when money flowed abundantly from the mines, and it seemed it would never end. Plank and brick sidewalks still fronted many of the old buildings. Brick soldiers marched in the rugged masonry walls, breaking the monotony, creating decorative patterns wherever possible.

Aged Honey Locust trees lining the street would provide much relief from the coming hot summer days. Visible down the side alleyways, grew pockets of the Chinese Tree of Heaven which grew profusely in many of these out of the way places.

Old timers sat on benches here and there, under the building overhangs talking about the way it was. The old City Hotel, a two-story landmark made up of brick and decorative woodwork stood tall along Main Street. It's ten foot tall doors with multiple panes of glass and polished brass lanterns set off the building's historical character. Passing the Golden Rule Saloon, the sound of a rambling piano issued through the swinging doors, and a large ornate, yellow and black sign advertising sarsaparilla was visible out front.

Ferguson's General Store was located on one of the busiest corners in town. This brick and iron faced building was accessed through a double door, which when opened, announced entry by the jingling of a small bell. Foot traffic echoing on the hardwood floor truly gave it an old-time or "country" atmosphere.

Down the street was the Mountain Bakery, still using the original brick oven. From the open doorway, beckoning odors would drift up the street early each morning searching for customers.

Toward the far end of the street was the now silent, two-story brick Wells Fargo Building. A balcony with wrought iron railing extended out over the brick walkway with matching hitching posts at ground level. Inside, posters and advertisements on the walls gave glimpses into the historic yesterday of stagecoaches, bank robbers, and the Pony Express. In its heyday, over a million dollars in gold dust was weighed out upon the large gold scales that now sat on a counter along the north wall. Above the counter on the rough masonry wall was a poster advertising for Pony Express riders. "Orphans preferred," they had to be, "skinny, wiry, and willing to face death daily"—all for $60 a month.

Across the street, only the walls remained of what was once the hub of the town, the Assay Office. Small trees and grass now grew inside its perimeter, where miners joyously confirmed their fortune or went flat broke.

Tucked in and around the narrow streets were also many "hole in the wall" businesses. Visitors were attracted to these small distinctive shops by their marble entryways, wall mounted kerosene lamps, and colorful groupings of flowers.

Nearing the Candy Kitchen, the boys noticed, Dark Shadow, a local older Native American man who always seemed to be lurking around town. That nick name seemed to fit him as he was always hanging out in the shadows and silently watching.

His long black hair, ragged clothing and crinkled hat seemed to place him back into the ancient past somewhere. There was something about him that was peculiar. He reportedly would disappear into the mountains for weeks at a time with no food, nothing.

Turning left onto a side street, the boys crossed to the opposite side and proceeded to the fourth house, where Bryan's grandfather lived. It was small and weathered, set on a rock foundation with a covered porch and a short wooden railing along the front. Plants in clay pots decorated the way up to the front door. Bryan banged loudly on the door so his grandfather could hear.

"I hope he doesn't have one of his lapses of memory today," said Bryan.

After a moment, Mr. Anderson shuffled up to the door, unlatched it and opened it part way. "Who's there?" he inquired with raised voice.

"It's me and Josh, Grandpa" replied Bryan.

"Oh, Bryan, I thought maybe it was George, come on in. What are you boys up to today?" He asked as he shuffled back in and dropped into his rocking chair.

The small room was decorated with old paintings and photographs. Scattered about on the hardwood floors were round hand braided rugs. A pendulum clock sounded off rhythmically along the side wall. Stepping across the room, the boys seated themselves in two wooden chairs.

"Well, we were hiking across the plateau over toward the river and found what appears to have been an old homestead. We wanted to know if you recalled any places out that way?" asked Bryan.

"Yeah, there were a few. When I was your age or perhaps a little younger, there were about four or five, but they're all gone now, have been for fifty years or more. Like the old Julius place, it was a two-story Victorian with two barns, but it all burned down and was never rebuilt. Those land grabbing vultures from White Pines have gradually run everyone off!" answered Mr.

Anderson with some fire in his voice. He then paused as he fell into a sea of recollection as many of those old memories returned.

After a moment Bryan collected his thoughts and proceeded to explain his theory about the two hundred year old trail.

"Well, you're certainly into the right era when most of the old stories and legends had their beginning. Back when the Indians were the only residents and early Spanish explorers came searching for riches and fertile lands. I've heard all kinds of stories over the years, some you have already heard me tell many times. When I was a young man, I used to gobble up all those stories, but as time went on, they became just a mere passing curiosity."

Pausing again, his grandfather's mind drifted far off somewhere while he rocked back and forth, and the floor creaked in rhythm. Behind him sitting on the fireplace mantle, Josh noticed a black and white photograph showing two men displaying a significant catch of fish between them. They were standing next to a creek with numerous, jagged, odd-shaped peaks in the background. Josh figured that one of those men must be Bryan's grandfather.

"I'm sorry boys, what were we talking about?"

"The old stories," reminded Bryan.

"Oh yes," he responded, pausing for a moment. "Back in the twenties when I worked at the *Eagle Shamut Mine*, the commonly told tale by the old miners was about a fabulous gold discovery made somewhere up in these mountains, but it was mysteriously hushed up and never heard of again."

"Is there any clue to who made the discovery if it were true?" asked Josh.

"No, except that about forty years ago some archaeologists from the University investigated a couple of sites in the area and claimed that the Spanish had at least a minor settlement established here. They couldn't tell much, but by the few items found, burned and buried, it appeared that something devastating may have happened to them."

"Then perhaps the gold is still hidden up there somewhere," pondered Bryan.

"Many have thought so and looked. Some found nothing or never came back at all. Years ago, on one of the streams up here, I can't remember for the life of me which one, but anyway, after a heavy storm, bones could be found, I mean human bones, washed down from who knows where. But it hasn't rained like that since Truman was president."

He leaned over toward the boys and continued, "I had an Indian friend. We grew up together. Keep this which I'm about to tell you under your hats. I have never told anyone this before, not even your grandmother when she was alive."

"My friend's name was Riverhawk, his hair was long and black, and I could see fear in his eyes as he spoke. The Indians of old held a closely guarded secret that was never passed on, only warnings. No one today knows exactly what that secret was. He warned me not to go up into the canyons in search of gold or anything else for that matter because there are those who are watching. Anyone venturing too far would not return."

"I asked him for specifics of where and when, to kind of work him around; but he wouldn't divulge anything more at first. However, he did say this: 'Never let your right hand guide you into the mountains.' "

"Wow, I wonder what that could mean?" questioned Josh finally letting his breath out.

"I don't know, never had a clue," replied Mr. Anderson as he lapsed back to rocking again.

"Thanks, Grandpa, that was interesting. Do you need anything today?"

"No, I'm fine. Have you heard from your mother lately?" quizzed his grandpa.

"No, I haven't," Bryan responded slowly.

"If I were your dad, I would go right down there and hog tie her and bring her back!" he exclaimed. Bryan said nothing to this.

Grandfather's Revelation

"Well, take care Grandpa, I'll be back in a couple of days," said Bryan as they made their way out the front door.

"Your grandfather can really get riled up at times," said Josh as they scampered out of the yard and down the street.

"Must be the Irish in him," winked Bryan.

4

THE SPANISH MAP

A s they approached Bryan's house they noticed a brown sedan parked on the opposite side of the road about two hundred feet north of the driveway. Two unrecognizable men sat in the car arguing, not loud enough to ascertain their conversation, but their hand movements indicated that there was no agreement between them. Their discussion abruptly stopped when they noticed the two boys walking up into the driveway.

"I wonder what that's all about?" questioned Josh.

"I don't know, looks suspicious to me," answered Bryan.

Nearing the house, they saw another strange vehicle, a gray four wheel drive Toyota Land Cruiser parked up near the house.

"Looks like you have company," observed Josh, "I'll catch you later, and we can talk about this further."

"Okay," agreed Bryan.

Josh fired up the beast and quickly made his way down the road and around the corner. As Bryan neared the front door he heard voices coming from the dining room. Entering the house, he found his father and another man standing next to the table, peering at something laid out in front of them. The stranger dressed well, yet casual in appearance. He was a small man with dark eyes and a striking black mustache. He also showed signs of partial balding which he tried to comb over.

The Spanish Map

"Bryan, I want you to meet Jim Burke; and Jim, this is my son, Bryan," introduced Mr. Anderson.

"Glad to meet you, Mr. Burke," responded Bryan.

"Happy to meet you also, Bryan. I was asking your father a few questions about the general geography of the area."

"Oh, you must be the professor that dad mentioned he had met over in Coulterville," remembered Bryan.

"Yes, that's right," confirmed the Professor.

Bryan's attention was now drawn to the object on the table, an old parchment map sewn onto a leather back. A couple of books had been placed on its edges to weigh it down, due to its tendency to curl.

"I don't know, Jim, this old map is showing me rivers and mountains that seem familiar, but they don't run in the right directions," Mr. Anderson commented as he studied the map.

The professor turned to pull something out of his briefcase when suddenly he grabbed his side in pain. Reaching for a photo copy, he set it next to the original, pretending nothing had happened, but the strain in his face showed otherwise.

"Show me what mountains seem similar to you," asked the Professor as he handed him a marking pen.

"Well, these peaks here look like the Three Chimneys and over here could be Burst Rock, and to the northeast by its outline maybe Eagle Peak, but they are all wrong in relationship to one another."

"This is the one that is bugging me, right here in the dead center of the map, as if everything is tied to it somehow," pointed out the Professor.

"You got me. I don't have a clue," answered Bryan's father.

"What is this map supposed to show?" asked Bryan, who was dying of curiosity. "I notice some Spanish words and a few symbols spotted around the map."

"From what I can decipher, after finding this map in among some old documents hidden at old *Fort Santa Domingo*, I believe that this may well lead to some kind of old mining operation," replied the Professor.

The mention of an old mining operation caught Bryan's attention, but he also noticed that when the Fort was mentioned, his dad flinched. Why?

The Professor continued on, "I'm more interested in it for its historical and archeological significance than anything else."

The Spanish words *Oro de Cañon* appeared at the top of the map. Bryan thought to himself, 'Canyon of Gold.'

"Jim, I can't say this map fits this area, but it might further south in the Palisade Range. Sorry, I can't help much," sighed Bryan's father.

"Well, okay, but if you should think of something, call me collect. Here is my card with the phone number on it," requested the Professor. He rolled up the map and put it in his brief case. They could tell he was very disappointed.

"I sure will, Jim," replied Tom Anderson as he shook the Professor's hand.

"Nice meeting you too, Bryan," said the Professor as he grabbed the brief case and headed out the door, unconsciously holding his side.

As the screen door clapped shut, Bryan turned back to the table to notice that the Professor had accidentally or on purpose, left the photo copy of the map laying on the table.

Fabulous, thought Bryan, I can't wait to study it further, but before he could lay a hand on it, his father came in.

"Bryan, you've been gallivantin' around all day, time to feed the animals and finish any homework you have," he ordered.

"I'll get right on it," said Bryan looking at the wall clock. "Dad, what do you know about this Fort Santa Domingo?" questioned Bryan.

"Nothing! I don't know a thing about it!" burst out his father in a final tone as he picked up the photo copy and put it in a desk drawer as if ending the subject.

Bryan was a little taken aback by his father's reaction. Had he hit an old wound? Proceeding out of the back door and over to the corral, he contemplated all the events of the last two days.

The Spanish Map

"Well, Thunder, do you have any words of wisdom for me today?" asked Bryan. Thunder shook his head and cocked his ears. After feeding the animals, Bryan slid down against the bales of hay and sat there for a few minutes enjoying the solitude.

Life is so full of strange events. How does one know which way to turn or go at times? he questioned in his own thoughts. For a fleeting second his mother's face entered his mind. Shortly, Graffiti came in and found Bryan sitting there, breaking his train of thought.

"Graf, you been out chasing the quail up on the hill again, haven't you? Guess you're hungry too?" asked Bryan as he got up and headed across the yard. Reaching the back porch, he poured a bowl of food for the dog and checked his water.

Dinner that evening was unusually quiet as they sat across the table from each other. While doing dishes after dinner, Bryan watched the pink to purple alpine-glow deepen in the mountain heights as the sun slowly set. How many times had the sun dawned and set upon these mountains—forever? And what was he—just a moment in time.

One of the mules brayed, and out of the corner of his eye he noted that a light came on in the barn. His dad was either checking on the animals or inspecting the pack equipment.

Remembering the map, his curiosity was again rekindled. After wiping down the table and counters, he retrieved the photo copy from the drawer and disappeared into his room. Switching on the light he set the map on a small table by the window and pulled up a chair to begin his investigation.

The map was basically a twelve inch square, showing rivers, the vague outline of mountain peaks and ridges, Spanish names, and various unknown symbols. He did notice that notations and symbols seemed to favor the streams branching left from the main tributary. As the Professor pointed out, the sharp peak in the center seemed to be a significant reference point. It could match maybe two or three peaks in the area, but his dad was right, as a whole, the relationship of various mountains depicted did not match anything local. A bit of disappointment came over him in the realization that this map may in no way be a clue to the 'Legend' whatsoever.

" 'Oro de Cañon,' where can this be?" he muttered to himself. What were the meanings of these other Spanish phrases? "Caudad matallco—I have no idea. Aguilas volar donde–aguilas, eagles–eagles fly. Where Eagles Fly, yes." But he realized that was too vague to be of any help. Eagles hadn't flown in these mountains for decades. "Cielo erratico, no sabe. Sol de la puerta—Door of the Sun. Wow, sounds mysterious." Bryan next focused on a symbol next to the 'Door of the Sun,' a semicircle with radial lines like sun rays, with some kind of pointed object extending up through the bottom line. "Where have I seen this before?" Perhaps in a book or at a museum? This symbol must represent the 'Door of the Sun,' but what is that pointed object in the bottom? he pondered.

Bryan also noted two X's, one adjacent to the first Spanish phrase and the second to the right of the 'Door of the Sun' symbol. The first X and unknown Spanish phrase was located along the river toward the bottom of the map. That would be the logical place to start, if the correct river could be found. And from there it would be just a matter of following up the series of river forks to the last designation, the 'Door of the Sun.'

"Wait till Josh hears about this! He'll flip."

Bryan jotted down the unknown Spanish phrases to be looked up later and returned the map to the desk drawer. Freeing his mind from this quandary, he decided to go out to the barn to see what his father was working on.

5

THE ILLUSIVE CLUES

Next day after chores, Bryan set about to complete his school project. His basic idea was to tape three sheets of illustration board together and hinge them to sit on a display table. The summarized tree profiles showing ring distortion would be laid out from the center section to the right. On the left panel, he thought, would be the ideal place for the labeling. Bryan printed in large letters: hypothesis, conclusion, and so forth with the appropriate statement under each. From these statements he decided to draw bold lines and circles around the different ring distortions. After accomplishing this, it became apparent that the theory and proof were still not well enough illustrated. What could he add?

Stomping at the back porch diverted his attention. "That blasted mule!" yelled Mr. Anderson dusting himself off. "There's going to be mule-burgers in your future!" he yelled again looking toward the corral. Coming in with an aggravated limp, his dad had a smirk on his face.

"What happened?" asked Bryan.

"Midas, caught me off guard and kicked me. I flew clear across the corral."

"You hurt?"

"No-o. You know that beast, it's a game with him. It was more like a push than a kick."

"Ha ha, Midas has the touch," laughed Bryan. His dad chuckled too.

"Say, what's this here, looks like a doctor's office with all these EKG's?" asked his dad.

"It's my school project, which I have to turn in on Tuesday. But I still need to somehow better illustrate why things happen the way they do," answered Bryan.

"It looks impressive, but probably what you need is just a simple illustration showing how trees lean and grow toward the open sunlight," suggested his father.

"Yeah, and at the same time showing the eccentric ring growth. That's a smart idea, thanks dad," replied Bryan.

"I wish I was smart enough to get us out of debt," he commented. At that the phone rang, and Mr. Anderson limped into the next room to answer it.

"Hello. ... Yeah. ... What! ... Really? He was here yesterday, in the afternoon. What happened? ... No! How is he? ... Okay, I'll keep my ears open. I'll see ya."

"What happened?" begged Bryan who was hanging on every word uttered.

"Well, it appears that Professor Burke, sometime after leaving here yesterday, was run off the road near Jamestown by Woods Creek. He received some cracked ribs and bad bruises, but I guess he'll survive. He's still over at the County Hospital. Evidently, the Sheriff believes there is foul play afoot—most of the Professor's things were stolen. The only thing the Professor could remember was that the vehicle was a brown Chevy sedan," reported his dad.

"Really! Yesterday there was a car just like that parked across the road, while the Professor was here. There were two men in it arguing," stated Bryan excitedly.

"My goodness, I better call the Sheriff right back, and I want you to tell him exactly what you had seen," directed his father.

Later that day, Bryan couldn't hold it all in any longer, he had to tell Josh. But since there were no phone lines out that way, he decided to walk the mile and a half to his house located on the road to the marble quarry. The older home, sadly in need of a paint job sat down amongst a variety of trees off the narrow road. Josh's Jeep was parked under an oak tree on the north side of the house, which was a good indicator that he should be around somewhere. Half way down the driveway Bryan spotted Josh carrying straw into the chicken house. He silently approached the doorway.

"Josh! I'm glad I found you home, I have news that your dying to hear!" suddenly spoke Bryan as he stuck his head into the doorway.

"Bryan! News? I'm what? Oh no!" answered Josh, half startled. Grabbing his chest he fell against the wall and slid down onto the hay. "I'm dying? Why didn't you tell me sooner?"

"Josh! This is serious."

"Ha ha, laughed Josh as he rolled over. "Say, you almost made me swallow my gum."

"If it's that awful green stuff, please do," replied Bryan.

Getting down to business he began to relate the highlights of Professor Burke's visit and the mystery of the old Spanish map, and finally concerning the Professor's accident.

"Wow! This is like one of those mystery novels, except this is for real," commented Josh.

"There's something going on all right. Those two men we saw parked in that brown car by my house, I believe were the ones that forced the Professor off the road and stole most of his belongings," added Bryan.

"Really? Which included the Spanish map I suppose," stated Josh.

"That's probably what they were after in the first place. It was in his brief case as I recall," added Bryan. "If you think about it, here he was driving up and down the foothills asking questions and flashing that map around, and I suppose somewhere along the line these modern day desperadoes became interested in this 'Canyon of Gold.' "

"Just like us," commented Josh. "But they have the map."

"Well, we do too, the Professor left a photo copy at my house. But my first inclination is that the map may not be for this area," responded Bryan.

"However, the Professor must have had some kind of clue of where to begin looking," thought Josh.

"I don't know what on the map would be such a clue," pondered Bryan.

"I can't get over today, but I'd like to come over tomorrow after school and look at the map," said Josh.

"Okay, we'll reconvene our investigation tomorrow," agreed Bryan as he waved goodbye and headed back up the driveway toward home.

He wondered though, what is this whole thing about anyway? Maybe absolutely nothing. Perhaps just a bunch of tall tales dreamed up years before by bored miners sitting around a pot bellied stove through the long winters reminiscing about the "good old days." But the old trail they had discovered and the Spanish map seemed to be real enough. Why then, hasn't someone found this place by now? What did his grandfather say about "a closely guarded secret" and those that would be watching? His eyes scanned the silent distant peaks, wondering what secrets they really did hold.

Next morning, Bryan packed up his project and transported it to the school auditorium, where he set it up before the beginning of his first class. As he glided through the crowded hallways he could sense the heightened excitement and laughter among the students in anticipation of summer vacation.

At lunch time, the boys met at the library to look up the unknown Spanish phrases. Finding a Spanish dictionary, they grabbed a vacant table in the corner.

"Caudad matallco, is the first one," whispered Bryan as Josh began flipping through the book.

"Let's see—under caudad—nothing. No such word," informed Josh as he started to flip to the next word of that phrase, matallco.

The Illusive Clues

Stopping, he placed a finger on a page and moved it down through the various words to finally reach the bottom of the page.

"Well?" questioned Bryan.

"Nothing by that spelling, but wait, matalon is very similar. Its meaning is—an old worn out horse," reported Josh.

"Ha!" responded Bryan.

"That can't be right," added Josh. Opening the folded paper, Bryan gave Josh the next phrase.

"Cielo is—the sky, and erratico—I hope is here. Yes, it is—to wander, wandering," announced Josh.

"Sky wandering," voiced Bryan.

"I know, Wandering Sky," blurted out Josh drawing sour glances from across the room.

"Okay, but what kind of clue is that? It doesn't tell us a thing," whispered Bryan.

"Another dead end," agreed Josh just as the bell rang and everyone began departing for classes.

After school was over, Josh waited for Bryan at the far end of the benches where the school buses would pull up.

"Well, that's one day less of school," commented Josh.

"And seven more to go," added Bryan as they headed down the hill into town.

Nearing home, Graffiti on seeing their approach began barking anxiously, eager to be set free. Going into the house through the back door, they headed into the kitchen to get a cold drink. Wasting no time, Bryan retrieved the map from the desk, and in a covert sense of action slipped into the bedroom closing the door behind them.

"This is it," introduced Bryan.

"Uh, interesting—rivers, mountains and other strange looking shapes," commented Josh.

"Notice the Spanish phrases that we looked up at the library," pointed out Bryan.

"Yeah, 'Wandering Sky,' 'Door of the Sun,' and down here are the others," agreed Josh as his eyes trailed down the map.

"Now, Josh, what do you see that would be a clue to this map's true location?" questioned Bryan.

Josh first looked close at the various aspects of the map and finally drew back to look at the whole thing.

"Well, I see one thing, that's like, 'not seeing the forest for the trees,' as they say. The river itself is the clue."

"What? There's lots of rivers along this range," pointed out Bryan.

"Yeah, but how many rivers have three branches in close proximity to one another?" explained Josh.

"Wow! You're right, that's genius. I only looked at each individual clue, not at the whole," responded Bryan.

"You have any maps?" asked Josh.

"Somewhere, wait, the one on my ceiling," said Bryan as he grabbed the chair and set it under the map.

Standing on the chair, he pulled the tacks loose to bring it down. Setting the large map on the table, they again became silent as they studied the various drainage systems on the west flank of the Great Range.

"It's not the San Joaquin or the Kings River, the forks are all staggered," observed Josh.

"Nor, the Calaveras or the Mokelumne Rivers, the branching is basically singular," added Bryan.

"And the Merced doesn't seem to have the right number of branches either," pointed out Josh.

One by one, the various rivers were eliminated except for the Stanislaus, which they in a hopeful way left for last.

"If that doesn't beat all, there are only two forks that are close together—only two," responded Bryan in a disappointed tone.

"I don't know, if you ask me, this so-called mystery map isn't worth the paper it's printed on," grumbled Josh.

"I'm beginning to think so too," agreed Bryan with a sigh. After a moment of thought, Bryan folded the large map and put the photo copy back in its place.

"It appears we're back to square one," said Josh after a moment.

"Yeah, I guess. Let's think more about this later," replied Bryan dismissing the subject.

"Catch you tomorrow," said Josh as he grabbed his pack and headed toward the door.

"They're supposed to be grading our projects so I heard. See you there, Josh, bye," replied Bryan. What next? Chores! Always chores!

For the rest of the day he mulled over various aspects of the old map. And that night, Bryan had an unusual dream. He dreamed he was a Spanish explorer, dressed in leather and armor. Facing the mountains and the numerous deep canyons ahead, he wondered which way was the way to go. There must be a sign somewhere. Suddenly there was an earthquake. Bryan woke to find his dad shaking the bed.

"Wake up Bryan! You'll be late, let's go!" said Mr. Anderson.

The Spanish explorer swung his legs out of bed, it was hard getting up with so much armor on, but it had to be done. Ha! Who was he kidding? Getting dressed and a bite to eat, he was off to school, another day to rise up to and conquer.

The day went quickly, and about mid-afternoon during science class, they were dismissed to put final touches on their projects. Bryan stepped back from his display to see what a first time impression of his exhibit would be like.

"Bryan, you have one of the most original projects I've seen in years," said Mr. Krasnik approaching with his clipboard.

He couldn't help but notice the bandage on the right side of his forehead. It stuck out like a sore thumb.

"It came together a little better than I thought," replied Bryan.

"I noticed that in your conclusion, you state that you found an old trail along the south side of the river canyon."

"That's correct," confirmed Bryan.

"It's possible too, that this phenomenon may have been caused by extremely high winds. Locally they've been called the *'Mono Winds'* that come down out of the Nevada side of the mountains. The Indians believed that the wind dwelled far up in amongst the highest peaks. Old Mr. Connors who lives down by the Parrots Ferry Bridge, told me about an experience he had while camping with a couple of his fishin' buddies up in the canyon, one dark night. He said it was initially very calm, all you could hear was the crackling of the campfire, then all of a sudden a distant boom! way up somewhere in the high country echoing down through the canyons. They could hear trees being hurled to the ground, crashing with great force. He described it to me as being kind of eerie, how you're able to hear it working its way down from thirty miles away. Once it reached their camp it filled the trees with a powerful gust of wind, growing ever stronger, breaking branches and blowing dust everywhere. Gradually it passed and continued down the canyon," related Mr. Krasnik.

"I would've liked to have seen that myself," commented Bryan.

"I don't want to take anything away from your project, Bryan, but maybe that's what you've actually run across out there. Those winds can take a very narrow and selective course at times," furthered Mr. Krasnik.

"It's possible I guess, but because it parallels the river so precisely, I think I'll stick with my original conclusion," replied Bryan.

"Okay. Good project, interesting project, Bryan," was Mr. Krasnik's final response as he edged away.

Was he right? There was always the possibility that it could have been caused by some freakish natural event. What a bummer, seems like everything is going amiss. Looks like the 'Legend' will always remain just a legend, he thought.

After a half hour or so, Bryan swung by his exhibit one last time, before going to his final class. Rounding the corner leading to his project, he stopped short when he saw Mr. Krasnik looking close at his display. Jotting something down, he quickly disappeared, glancing around as he went. Bryan thought it a little strange, that he would come back and look at it again.

By Thursday, Bryan was feeling kind of glum. The last two days seemed to just drag by. After school, he stopped at Ferguson's General Store to pick up a soda.

"Bryan, you look kind of down and out. Summer is just about here, you should be jumping for joy," said Mr. Ferguson.

"Yeah, I know," responded Bryan with a forced smile. "Say, by any chance have you heard anything about a shooting a couple of days ago, just east of town?"

"Shooting? No-o. Was there one?"

"I don't know exactly."

"No-o. I haven't heard a thing. By the way, have you heard from your mother lately?" asked the storekeeper.

"No, I haven't," he calmly answered as Mr. Ferguson handed him his change. Why does everyone have to keep asking me that; don't they know by now? he thought to himself.

His feet echoed on the hardwood floor as he headed for the door. The bell jingled as Bryan went out. Then remembering something, he stopped and turned back to the store to peek back inside. On the wall next to the window was an old yellowed fishing map that had been there longer than he could remember. But why look? It wouldn't be any different anyway, just another disappointment. On the other hand, what the heck.

Stepping over to the map, he located *Columbia* and the Stanislaus River. Running his finger along the black line that represented the river, he came to the *Forks*, three of them.

Wait! try that again. That's right, but how can that be? A lump formed in his throat. Could this really be the path to the "Legend" after all?

Bryan hurried home to get to the bottom of this. His dad was leaning over the table preparing a supply list for an upcoming pack trip when he came in.

"Dad, I have a question for you," said Bryan.

"Oh? Okay, what is it?" asked his father straightening up.

"Maybe you can settle a small controversy. How many forks does the Stanislaus River really have?" questioned Bryan.

"Well, there are actually three, but only two now flow into the river. About thirty years ago, the Middle Fork was diverted through a tunnel to the powerhouse over at Donnells," answered his father.

"So, current maps should only show two forks of the river coming together," concluded Bryan.

"Yes, but in doing so they ended up ruining the fishing and most of the wildlife. There's still a lot of hard feelings, about how they pushed that project through," reflected his dad.

"Huh, that's great Dad," responded Bryan.

"What?" questioned his father with surprise.

"I mean, that settles the issue of how many forks there are," answered Bryan realizing his unconscious departure.

"Oh, by the way, looks like Saturday I'll be leading a three-day pack trip to the limestone caverns above the South Fork and returning on Monday. Because of school, you'll have to stay behind this time," said Mr. Anderson.

"That'll be fine, actually I have some follow up work on my project I would like to investigate," replied Bryan.

"Okay, but be careful, use that Anderson head of yours to keep yourself out of trouble," his father warned. His dad was always good at applying psychology, using family pride as a guard against acting foolishly.

"You got it, Dad," confidently replied Bryan.

After putting his school things in the bedroom, he wasn't sure what to do with this new found knowledge, but one thing was for sure there was a two-day window of exploration open. That's what he had to do, plan! plan! plan! The 'Legend' beckoned!

6

CRAZY JOE

Friday couldn't have come soon enough for Bryan. Meeting Josh at school, he proceeded to relate excitedly concerning the discovery of the missing 'fork' and his strategy for the next step.

"You're really taking this seriously aren't you," replied Josh who was slow to recatch the enthusiasm.

"Absolutely! It has to be real, there are so many pieces of the puzzle. We just need to put it all together somehow, starting with this first one," reasoned Bryan.

"I don't know, the evidence is still pretty thin to be convincing to me," commented Josh.

"Okay, if we find a positive, undeniable clue, will you believe it then?" proposed Bryan.

"Oh, I suppose, but I have my doubts," replied Josh. "Nothing ever seems to happen around here."

Saturday morning, a cool breeze rustled the leaves as the pack train picturesquely mounted the first hill on its trek to 'Cave Country.' Bryan waved as his dad disappeared over the horizon. There were yet a few things to button up before he could leave. One was to finish organizing his pack. Graffiti, was wise that something was up and wanted to make sure he was not forgotten. After about twenty minutes, Josh finally arrived in his mechanical wonder, coming to a screeching halt.

"You ready to hit the dusty trail?" quizzed Josh as he mounted the front steps.

"Just about, come on in," answered Bryan holding the screen door open.

"Did you make a copy of the map?" asked Josh.

"Uh-h, yeah, I traced a rough copy last night," replied Bryan coming back into the front room. "Let's see, canteen, food, compass, binoculars, and the map, that should do it," continued Bryan as he rummaged through his pack.

"Where do we begin?" questioned Josh as they headed out the door.

"Based on the premise that this is the same river as shown on the map, and the evidence we found of an old trail—" pausing, Bryan locked the door. "What we need to do is follow the river east from above where we first discovered the trail. And from there search for the first site indicated on the map," he continued as they loaded their gear into the back of the Jeep.

"Ha! Graffiti is already in the seat," pointed Josh.

"Yeah, but there's no seat belt back there," commented Bryan.

"Oh yeah, since when do dogs have to be wear seat belts?" smirked Josh.

"Well, the law states that all passengers must wear seat belts," teased Bryan. Josh grumbled something as Bryan picked up on the previous discussion. "Once we get past the 'Forks' it gets tricky, because all we know is to veer left."

Getting on their way, they proceeded along the old dirt road out of town. They soon passed a poster of 'Smokey the Bear' mounted on a gabled Forest Service sign marking the boundary of the Stanislaus National Forest. At the bottom of a steep grade the road made a sharp hairpin curve to the right, from which a faint roadway veered off in the opposite direction. Josh followed the Jeep trail for about a mile along the south side of the canyon until it became impassable. After parking the vehicle among a group of trees, they headed up canyon with Graffiti taking the lead. Part of their route was along an old logging railroad grade. As they progressed easterly the bluffs rapidly closed in and the roar of the river became more discernable. From a clear vantage point, they paused to look back down river.

"Josh, do you see that thin tree line coming up the canyon from where we took the cores in the heavy timber?" pointed out Bryan.

"Yeah, I see it, looks like a thin backbone," replied Josh.

"It's an amazing sight. Our eyes in a way have been opened to see it. I doubt if anyone else has paid much attention to it, nor has any idea what it means," said Bryan.

"Woo. You ever had that feeling you were onto something big but didn't know what?" realized Josh.

"Indeed I have—look, it's pointing the way!" exclaimed Bryan.

As they neared the river the roar got louder and louder. After several minutes they reached the south bank of the raging Stanislaus River. It was approximately one hundred feet across to the opposite bank. Just upstream coming into view was the white water of a prodigious series of rapids, called the Narrows. A faint fishing trail meandered its way along the river, through scattered clusters of oak and pine, no doubt used by the occasional fisherman looking for that illusive, undiscovered fishing hole. The higher mountain peaks could no longer be seen as the deep river canyon now swallowed up everything in view. The morning air now grew warm as the sun rose high above the cliffs. Dust flew as they hiked on the powdery sections of the trail. In places distorted rock outcroppings ran down the canyon walls to finally dive into the river. Deerflies buzzed from the thickets that were nestled in the hollows. Noticeable along the water's edge were young willows waving to and fro in the gentle breeze. Ocassionally a fish could be seen jumping out of the river. After about half an hour of walking they stopped to rest on a fallen snag that was all broken up among a group of large boulders.

"Have you ever been fishing up this far?" asked Josh.

"No-o, for some reason my dad always stayed clear of this area. We generally went up to Lost Lake or Bourland Creek," replied Bryan as he petted Graffiti who walked back to join them.

"Many years ago, I remember that we came up this way looking for crawdads along the creek openings," recollected Josh. "You know what my uncle used to catch fish with? Crawdads. He would keep them in a can with whiskey in the bottom. The fish really love 'em."

"Really? Crawdads? Have you tried eating them?" asked Bryan.

"Me? no way, those pincers give me the creeps," Josh replied.

"Me too," Bryan laughed. Have you ever watched them underwater? They are very territorial, defending their own area of the stream bed from intruders."

"It is kind of interesting to watch their antics," replied Josh.

"I guess in many respects people have been territorial as well, defending their land and way of life; but in our time it seems that there's nothing good that remains," commented Bryan.

"So, what are you trying to say? There are no more lands to explore or adventures to seek," asked Josh.

"Well, maybe just one more," smiled Bryan as he scooted off the tree trunk.

Continuing east along the river, the course grew rough and rocky. Twisted oak trees secured themselves in the rocky crevices and provided little shade. After passing a shale outcropping the walls steepened and closed in. Suddenly there was an explosion of rock and earth crashing down the slope behind them, generating a great plume of dust.

"Woo! We didn't start that, I don't think," spoke Josh.

"No, but someone or perhaps even an earthquake may have," declared Bryan.

"Let's move on quickly out of this steep area," suggested Josh as he glanced up and down the slopes ahead.

Picking up the pace, their eyes were now constantly scanning the heights above. After a couple of minutes, another thunderous rock slide breaks loose just behind them, this time closing off the trail completely. Their return path was sealed off. The roar of the river returned as the slide subsided. Graffiti who was about seventy-five feet ahead had his gaze fixed and ears cocked toward something high above them.

"There's someone up there!" whispered Josh loudly.

"Apparently so. Shh! Listen!" agreed Bryan.

There was the sound of loose grating rock coming from somewhere up on top of the cliff. Graffiti barked once. The sound moved off and could no longer be heard.

"Is someone trying to warn us off?" questioned Josh.

"It's possible, but why would they block the trail from behind and not ahead?" reasoned Bryan.

"I don't know, this is mighty strange ," commented Josh.

"Let's get a move on, we can't stay here," replied Bryan.

Were the stories true about those venturing into this mountain wilderness? He began to think so.

The rough terrain soon gave way to gentle grassy slopes and scattered white oaks as the canyon opened up.

"I'm glad to be out of there," commented Josh, looking back over his shoulder.

The grass swayed in the gentle breeze as they ventured on. Several deer trails crisscrossed, leading down to the river; undoubtedly a prime watering location for animals.

"Bryan! I think I see someone. I keep getting a glimpse of something red through the trees to the right," warned Josh in a hushed tone.

"Red?" questioned Bryan as he looked around without stopping. "If there is, don't let them see you looking, just keep going."

"Did you see it?" asked Josh.

"I got a glimpse of someone, but who could it be?" wondered Bryan.

Their path now led them to a small knoll thickly covered with a mix of oak, pine, and cedar.

"Stop! Listen! Someone's behind that rock," concluded Bryan.

Graffiti ran back to their position with ears up, growling, and barking.

"Quick! This way, fast!" ordered Bryan.

Running through the trees for about three hundred yards they came out into a clearing and suddenly stopped. There before them was an old weathered miner's shack. There was no way to get around it. The boys looked at each other and then cautiously continued forward. The old shack looked like something that time forgot with its severely weathered rough-sawn wood, spotted with flattened tin cans, missing window panes, and a bent stove pipe. Old metal barrels and rusted mining equipment were scattered about, half hidden in the weeds. Curving right, the river canyon opened up beyond the shack.

As they approached to within one hundred feet, an old man with a shaggy beard, tattered clothes and crumpled hat, stepped out from the shack holding a double-barreled shotgun. His expression was of one being startled. Graffiti began to growl, prompting Bryan to put his hand on his head to try to quiet him.

"You boys better stop right there! No trespassers are welcome here! I don't know how you got this far, but you better head right back!" yelled the old prospector.

"We were only hiking up to the Forks. We didn't mean to trespass on your property," spoke up Josh.

"You're not coming through here! Now git!" he warned.

"But Mister, we're trying to trace an old trail up to the Forks," explained Bryan, chancing this knowledge would help their plight.

"Trail? I told you! Git!" he replied as he raised the shotgun over their heads and fired both barrels.

Crazy Joe

Boom! The reaction of the double shot threw his shoulders back. Losing his balance he fell backwards over a small keg landing on his back.

The two glanced at each other, Graffiti was long gone. Frozen in place they didn't know whether to run or see if the old man was all right. After a second, he didn't move. Cautiously they approached to where the old man was lying. Bryan took the gun, checked it, and hid it in one of the empty barrels. They grabbed the man by his upper arms and raised him up. He immediately started to come to.

"O-o-oh, what happened?" were his first words.

"You fired your gun, fell backwards and knocked yourself out," replied Bryan.

"You boys still here!" he flamed out.

"Well yes, you might have been hurt or something," explained Josh.

"Aren't you boys afraid of me? Don't you know who I am? I'm *Crazy Joe!* Everyone has heard of *me."* he announced.

"Crazy Joe," repeated Josh, "I may have heard that name somewhere."

The old miner seeing that the name didn't seem to phase them, continued on. "I'm mean, ugly, and I eat rats!" he exclaimed.

"Boy, we better get you down for a good home cooked meal," was Bryan's response.

Josh put his hand over his mouth to keep himself from laughing. The old man was startled, he could not seem to scare them as he had others in the past.

Getting up he asked, "Where's my gun?"

"You're not going to shoot at us again are you?" asked Bryan.

"No, I guess not," he grumbled.

"It's in the barrel over there," pointed Bryan.

Fetching it out of the barrel, he headed toward his cabin.

"I don't understand how you got past the goat," questioned the old prospector.

The boys looked at each other. "Goat?"

"No one has gotten by it before. I don't know how you did it. Didn't you see it?" the man continued.

"There was something up on the cliff above us and then something followed us here, but we couldn't see what it was," answered Josh.

"Just look over there," pointed Crazy Joe. On the edge of the clearing was a goat, colored bright red. "I painted that goat red as a warning to others to stay away. I don't want to be bothered!" he exclaimed.

The two thought to themselves, he truly must be crazy, painting a goat!

"We're sorry Joe for disturbing you, we'll be on our way up river if you let us go through," said Bryan.

"Ah-h," he grunted, "you can go through this time, but don't come back through here again, my aim might be better next time. You can go back by using the pass that cuts over the ridge, you'll see it, about half a mile further up," Crazy Joe ordered.

"Thanks," returned Bryan.

Near the cabin they noticed a number of different kinds of old mining devices that dated back to the times of the Gold Rush. Easily identifiable was the Cradle. Appropriately named for its size, shape, and motion. Water was poured over the gravel while the Cradle was rocked back and forth separating the heavier gold to the bottom. The Long Tom, was a long box in which a miner using a hoe would work the gravel toward one end, while removing the larger rock called riddlings. The fines containing the gold would then fall through a sieve and be collected below.

"Oh, one more thing, how is it that you know about the old trail, it took me thirty years living up here to finally notice it?" he called out.

Turning around to answer, Josh explained. "It was during a class science project that it came to light."

Crazy Joe

"Huh? "Well, just the same it leads nowhere, it fades out as you reach the Forks, where the trees thin out," informed the old prospector.

"Thanks for the tip," replied Bryan as they headed east further up the river.

Realizing that Grafitti was lingering behind, Bryan called him to catch up. He quickly came tearing up the trail to resume the lead.

Glancing back, they could see Crazy Joe leaning against the cabin rubbing his head as he watched them go. A short distance beyond the shack were several excavated pits, some new, some old, covered with old timbers and boards. A number of them were partially filled in. Scattered amongst the spoils were rusted, rotted metal fragments, and charred pieces of wood. Also, becoming visible behind the cabin was a tunnel driven straight into the canyon wall. The entrance was blocked by a wooden door secured by lock and chain. Running vertically above the opening was a large quartz vein.

"For a minute there I thought we were goners," said Josh.

"He may pretend to be crazy but I don't think he's a fool," commented Bryan.

"Why is he trying to keep everyone away? What is he hiding? Has he found gold in that old mine?" questioned Josh out loud.

"From what he said he's been here for a long time and probably hasn't found the big one yet, but he may be convinced that he'll hit it any day," theorized Bryan.

"Looking at his apparel and living conditions, it would seem that he hasn't hit pay dirt yet, but anyway, maybe he just want's to be a hermit. No! Why didn't I think of it before, what if he's a criminal hiding out from the law," conjectured Josh.

Bryan stopped dead in his tracks. "Woo! You know something, you could be dead on!"

"There's a couple things that doesn't jibe. The absence of recent mine tailings, and the area in front of the mine was overgrown with low grass, except for the well-worn path to the mine itself," recalled Bryan.

"Well, if he isn't mining, what's he doing there?" questioned Josh.

They glanced at each other, but there was no answer. Continuing on they were silent as they contemplated how close of a shave their encounter with Crazy Joe may have been.

Advancing further, the canyon widened to nearly a quarter of a mile across. Visibly ahead, about three-fourths of a mile was the apparent junction of the Forks, where the mountain slopes were noticeably laid back due to the convergence of the river canyons. In just a short distance, a narrow ridge descended the steep south canyon wall. Rounding the point of the ridge, they stopped to peer at a rough trail that ascended the inside of the brushy ridge.

"This must be Crazy Joe's pass up through here," pointed Bryan.

The small drainage course meandered up through the manzanita brush and rock. Steep at first but becoming more gentle further up.

"Not exactly a freeway is it?" commented Josh.

"No, but it may be our best ticket home," soberly reflected Bryan.

Turning their attention easterly again, the course along the river became more or less straight in its approach to the Forks. Granite peaks were now coming in and out of view, as the various drainages were passing through a visual alignment with the high country, including the ominous *Obelisk*.

"Well, here we are at the threshold of a great mystery," declared Bryan.

Coming to a sandy bank over looking the converging streams, a school of fingerling trout darted upstream. Finding a level rock to sit on, the boys decided it was a good place to stop for lunch.

"Well, you're right, there are three separate canyons coming together here," observed Josh as he removed his pack.

Crazy Joe

"It seems we have confirmation, including what Crazy Joe has graciously contributed," agreed Bryan. "But I wonder, how did Crazy Joe come to realize the existence of the old trail?"

"Over the years, I guess he must have stumbled upon things that led him to that conclusion," replied Josh.

"Well, the fact is he did figure it out. We can't be all crazy, can we?"

"You almost got me convinced," replied Josh pulling an apple out of his pack. "Let me see that map when you get a free hand."

Bryan threw a few morsels of food to Graffiti, then pulled the folded map out of his pack and handed it over. Josh unfolded it while he held the apple clenched in his mouth.

"The first X and the unknown phrase 'caudad matallco' is just below the Forks, so it would have to be between here and Crazy Joe's," pointed out Josh.

"But the question is, what are we looking for? Some kind of marker or landmark?" pondered Bryan.

"I guess without knowing what the phrase is saying, all we can do is search the area and look for any and all clues," reasoned Josh shrugging his shoulders.

Bryan nodded in agreement as he finished his sandwich. Looking across to the north side of the river they noted how the bluffs came right down to the water's edge, giving little chance that anything on that side would be of any significance.

As the boys spread out to begin the search, Graffiti went into search mode, with ears up and tongue out. Bryan climbed down the bank to the river's edge and searched among the boulders, while Josh began to look through the tall grass and the scattered brush along the cliff. Hugging the rocky canyon wall, scattered bay trees were gnarled into the protruding rock, giving off their distinctive odor. Gradually they worked their way downstream to a point just out of sight of Crazy Joe's.

Bryan climbed back up the bank and could see the disappointment in Josh's face. "If anything was here, it's not visible now," he said.

"I guess after so many years, landslides or floods could have wiped out the signs of almost anything," answered Josh trying to be optimistic, but failing.

"Probably so, but we still have the course that leads up to the North Fork," encouraged Bryan.

"Looks like time is about gone today, we better start heading back," said Josh glancing at the descending sun over the high bluffs.

Bryan agreed, the North Fork would have to wait for another day. It was a short hike to the ridge trail, and not long before they had ascended the meandering drainage course through a thick stand of manzanita. The drainage depression soon disappeared into the bulk of the mountain. Crossing a gentle ridge, a faint path contoured its way through Chamise brush along the folds of the mountain. Topping out at about two hundred and fifty feet above the river, the trail began a slow descent. Coming out from behind a tall jagged rock chimney protruding from the brushy hillside, Crazy Joe's cabin suddenly came into full view. The boys ducked down behind a portion of the rock outcropping to peer down upon this strange site.

"Look, there's that red goat on the other side of the shack," whispered Josh.

"I wonder what it is with that goat? Old Joe was sure miffed that it let us get through," replied Bryan after a moment of silence.

"Ironically, it was almost as if that goat directed us here." commented Josh

"Yea-h. Josh, look at all those craters or pits down there that are scattered all over the place. That's kinda odd if you ask me. There doesn't seem to be any activity in the mine, but he's dug up everything outside, is that crazy or what?" pointed out Bryan.

"Hey, sounds like a Crazy Joe to me," returned Josh.

"There's a mule over on the other side of the shack in a small corral that I didn't notice before," observed Bryan as he raised up and peered over the edge again.

"Well, with shots being fired and all the commotion its no wonder," answered Josh.

"Speaking of shots, we better hit the dusty trail before we hear some new ones," suggested Bryan.

Slyly gliding back into the brush they rambled along the trail until it began to descend to the river below. Josh suddenly stopped in his tracks and stretched his arm out to prevent Bryan from continuing on.

"Listen, someone is coming," warned Josh in a loud whisper.

In silence they could hear hurried, muffled footsteps coming toward them.

"Quick! duck down in here," ordered Bryan.

Sliding off the trail and down the side of the hill into the manzanita and buckeye, Bryan put a hand over Graffiti's muzzle as they waited. The footsteps got louder and occasionally a faint voice could be heard. After a moment, words became discernible: "—pick up the trail in the sand but we must hurry."

"I'll tell you one thing, if that goat shows up again, I swear I'm going to blow it's head off—" spoke a second high-pitched voice. Soon the voices faded away in the distance.

"Did you hear that first voice?" asked Bryan. "I'm certain I've heard it before, not just once either, but where?" wondered Bryan, breaking the silence.

"It does seem vaguely familiar, yet I don't know. I wonder though, if these two guys could be the same ones who were tailing the Professor? But did you catch what that second fella was saying? He's packin' a gun," anxiously responded Josh.

Bryan gave him an acknowledging quick glance. "Let's go while the coast is clear."

Climbing up the bank, they were back on the trail again. Picking up the pace as they descended, they were now several hundred feet downstream of where the canyon had closed in.

Crossing the wet seepage from a nearby spring, something in the corner of Josh's eye caught his attention. "Bryan, wait. A footprint—looks fresh."

Bending down on their knees to get a closer look, it did appear to be very fresh, the imprint was still moist. Graffiti sniffed the print and ran on.

"Note the squares in the impression of the heel," pointed out Josh.

"Squares? Hmm, that's right, it's the same heelprint that you had seen near the blood. Detective Knight, you have a good eye," replied Bryan.

"Bryan, I don't know about this. I think we have jumped from the frying pan into the fire on this one," commented Josh as he soberly reflected on these events.

"Josh! Things are just now getting truly exciting, the clues, the events, we are at the threshold! Can't you feel it? The mountains are calling, we can't give up now! That is, I can't give up." responded Bryan as they continued their course up through the trees.

"I'm not saying I'm not hooked on this mystery, its just I think we should proceed with some degree of caution," explained Josh.

"I totally agree," said Bryan.

After locating the Jeep, they were soon on their way after a brief but fruitless search for other vehicles. The sun was soon to set with shadows growing ever longer. Above them birds were flocking to find a place to roost for the night.

Arriving at Bryan's house everything seemed to be fine until Graffiti jumped out of the vehicle and proceeded to run around the north side of the house. Sniffing the ground, he whirled around in a circle and ran toward the back of the house, barking. The boys quickly followed, finding the dog on the back porch, barking at the door.

"What is it, Graf?" asked Bryan in suspense.

"Look Bryan, the door is cracked open. I thought you locked it before we left," pointed out Josh.

"I did. Somebody may still be in there. Graf go check it out," commanded Bryan as he opened the door.

Crazy Joe

Graffiti rushed in barking, running from room to room. The boys after a few seconds followed. It was for the most part dark inside except for a few stray beams of sunlight flickering on the walls. Graffiti ran back into the dining room and gave one last bark. Evidently no one was present.

"Oh no! Look at this!" exclaimed Bryan.

The dining and front room area was a disaster. Items and papers were strewn all over the floor.

"Somebody sure tore through all your stuff. I wonder what they were after, and what they took?" questioned Josh.

It took a moment for Bryan to get over the shock. "Well," sighed Bryan, "let's look around, but don't touch anything yet."

"Detective Knight on duty!" replied Josh.

After checking the other rooms they found that nothing else had been disturbed.

"Either they found what they were after and left, or they were scared off," reasoned Josh.

"If I ever find out who did this, they'll be dead meat," angrily responded Bryan as he stooped down to pick up a broken ceramic figurine. "This was my mother's."

"You still miss your mother don't you?" asked Josh.

"Yes, but it's something I don't like to admit," he confessed.

Josh stepped over to view the rest of the room. "They went through everything clear around the room, except for the small cabinet next to the desk," observed Josh.

Bryan wheeled around. "That would mean they found what they wanted before getting to it. The desk. The map! They were after the map!" concluded Bryan.

"Okay, if that's true it'll be gone," said Josh.

Making a thorough search through the drawer and all the papers on the floor, it could not be found.

"Well, it's gone, and it was evidently the only thing they were after," established Bryan.

"Who knew about the map, besides us and your father?" asked Josh.

"The Professor of course, but there is a possibility that the two men we seen out front that day—the ones who followed the Professor here, may have thought he left a copy," speculated Bryan.

"That could be. We may have even passed those same two guys on the trail earlier," agreed Josh.

"I think, we've had enough excitement for today, I'll clean up this mess tomorrow," said Bryan. "I guess I better report this to the Sheriff before I disturb anything."

"That's probably a good idea." Josh agreed as he stepped toward the door, leaving Bryan to ponder the day's events in silence.

7

METALLIC CITY

onday had come and gone. Bryan's father had returned with the group of spelunkers, and was already working on preparations for his next pack trip. But best of all, it was the last day of school and 'summer' was knocking at the door.

After Mr. Krasnik's apparent glowing praise of Bryan's project, he surprisingly only gave him an average grade. Josh was happy enough with a similar grade on his miniature greenhouse project, but Bryan was positively miffed. Seeking an explanation from Mr. Krasnik, he found that he had made himself unavailable.

Laughter filled the hallways as students rushed around, getting their yearbooks signed and excitedly making plans for the summer. For most there was always next year.

The next day, Bryan was off with his father on a six-day pack trip to Aspen Lake with the five members of the Laramie family. Grabbing the pommel, he swung himself up into the saddle. It was a welcome change to be with his father for a few days, to ride the saddle again, hear the grunt of leather, and to daydream. The inner fire to solve the 'Legend' was still there, but he felt it could wait for a few days.

That evening while sitting around the campfire, his dad was telling his traditional campfire stories about the early explorers and the Indians that had roamed the Sierra many years before. Between stories, Mr. Anderson would strike up his harmonica, playing some of the old ballads, western tunes, and songs that were conducive to a sing-along. The whole Laramie family was caught up in the moment, laughing and enjoying themselves.

"Mr. Anderson, did the Indians ever go on the warpath like they show in the movies?" asked the youngest of two girls.

Her older sister laughed causing a temporary distraction. She pointed at the marshmallow about to fall off her younger sister's stick.

"No, not quite as dramatic as Hollywood would have us believe. And nothing like the Indian wars that were fought in the Southwest. However, there are stories and legends of things that may have happened here," he answered.

"Legends?" questioned the girl's mother.

"These mountains are filled with stories. But what has commonly been called the 'Legend' around here, deals with the discovery of an extremely rich gold strike. The strange thing about this mythical discovery, according to legend, was that soon after its discovery it was hushed up, never heard of again. Old miner's tales and Indian stories speculate on what happened," Mr. Anderson explained.

"Tell us some, please," they begged.

As his father began to relate one of the stories, Bryan gazed into the dancing flames, mentally drifting back into that era, when the land was still wild and unknown. How could an explorer find anything up in these rugged canyons? It would virtually take a life time of searching. There were however, native inhabitants of these mountains that had hundreds of years of opportunities to make such discoveries. Perhaps through the sharing of information something significant could have been learned.

Coming to the present, his dad was completing one of his stories. "Additionally, there was an intriguing statement told to me in confidence by a dying man some years ago."

"Tell us," they reechoed, eating up every word.

"He said this: 'The place you seek is above the heads of mortal man, it cannot be found, the door is closed, the light has vanished,' " recalled Mr. Anderson.

"That could have many meanings," replied Mr. Laramie.

"Indeed it could," agreed their guide.

As the night air turned cool, the visiting family decided to turn in for the night. The fire had burned down and the coals burned brightly. Only Bryan and his father remained.

"I never heard that story before," mentioned Bryan.

"It's not as colorful a story as the others. I seldom tell it, but it has always mystified me. I guess that's why I've never forgotten it," his dad replied.

"Who was it that told you that story?" questioned Bryan.

"Oh-h, what was his name? Ke— Ke'-ma, if I remember right. The proper term nowadays is—Native American. But anyway, back in my younger years I took a job installing a fence on an adjacent piece of property next to the Reservation. During the days I worked there, I chatted with him off and on. Others on the Reservation warned me, he was kind of loco, 'don't listen to him, he just rattles on.' They said he was from the 'old tribe.' They had too many secrets. Like—'they had something to hide.' But he had some interesting things to say, especially about the way things used to be. Then one day he became very sick. Said he was 'on his last legs.' That's when he related to me those words, and after a few days he was dead. I've never forgotten that old man, it was like he had a story to tell, but he wouldn't betray what he really knew. Perhaps he did leave a clue, though," concluded his father.

"That's interesting, I'm glad you remembered that," said Bryan. Changing the subject, he continued on after a pause of thought. "You think we'll ever hear anything from Mom?"

His father sighed and looked deep into the glowing embers. "Bryan, I wish I knew, we can only hope," he said as he threw a stick into the fire pit. The hoot of an owl echoed through the lonely woods. "Time to turn in," decided Mr. Anderson as he got up.

Most everyone was already in bed as Bryan strolled over to his bed roll and slid into his bag. A gentle breeze whispered through the forest. The stars were so bright that they seemed to hang in amongst the tops of the pine trees. How could they appear to be so close, but yet be so far? They must represent a challenge, he thought to himself as he drifted off to sleep. For without them there would be nothing out there to beckon, to seek, to dream.

By midmorning of the next day they had arrived at Aspen Lake, and began setting up a more permanent camp. The oval shaped lake was about half a mile across, surrounded by a mix of fir and aspen trees. Carved into many of the old gnarled aspens adjoining the lake, were names and dates going back to the 1880's. Most of these were attributed to Basque sheepherders moving their flocks through the area.

It was interesting to consider how different cultures, appearing and disappearing through time, dwelling in the same region, could coexist without overlapping, or did they? pondered Bryan.

After settling in and setting up tents, Mr. Laramie and his twelve year old son tried their hand at fishing down at the lake, while the rest of the family lounged around, reading. Tom gave the novice fishermen a few tips on mountain lake fishing, the use of dry fly lures, and casting.

There was plenty of time to waste, chores were light, and the evening meal wouldn't be for another two hours. Bryan decided to hike up on the ridge to a rocky crest, that overlooked the green rolling forests and the Purple Hills below. Turning to the east was the granite sentinels, the monoliths, including the *Obelisk*, all of which looked so much closer and monumental. The towering pinnacle looked shorter and wider at the base. The shape of the summit had also changed from a slender point toward that of a triangular buttress. Volcanic breccia appeared to ring the buttress like multifaceted jewels on a crown. It was amazing how much a different viewpoint could change the perception of a reality.

A mild up canyon breeze sprang to life bending the spindly summer grass scattered among the exposed rock outcroppings. A pair of peregrine falcons could be seen circling in the canyon below.

What was it that the old Indian had said? "The door has been closed." Could that be the same door as in the "Door of the Sun"? Had it been closed, so that no one could find their way in? In the warmth of the sun it was easy to daydream and ponder.

After being refreshed by the grandeur of the scenery around him, he returned to camp to get things organized for the evening meal.

After the meal was prepared, Mr. Anderson rang the triangle and as tradition would have it, yelled, "Come and get it!" Everyone seemed to be extra hungry that night as they devoured every morsel prepared.

Again it was campfire time, which was always one of Bryan's favorite parts of camping out. The subject that night was bears. After a song, his father began relating a few amusing stories about the mountains' furry inhabitants. Starting off with the incident at Ostrander Lake in Yosemite. It involved a mother bear and her two cubs who were trying to snag a camper's food sack. It so happened that it was suspended from a tree limb that hung out over the lake.

"Now, how do you think they would get the sack?" Mr. Anderson asked. Everyone fell quiet thinking, and only the licking of the flames could be heard.

"I know! I know!" excitedly spoke up the young boy. "The cubs just climbed out on the limb and got it."

"N-o-o, the limb was too small to support their weight, they would've fallen and probably got hurt." After another thoughtful pause he went on. "This is what they did: the mother bear sent the two cubs up the tree above the limb and they in turn, jumped out and tried to grab the pack on the way down, landing in the lake."

"Ha ha," they laughed, "did they ever get the sack?" they asked.

"No, after quite awhile they gave up." After some other humorous stories, his dad finished up with some sobering examples of how bears can also be unpredictable and dangerous.

As in the past Bryan's father would have him tie a rope in the brush somewhere out beyond the lighted perimeter of the campsite, completely hidden. At his signal, Bryan would jerk the rope causing the brush to bend making crackling sounds as if something was approaching.

"Ah! What was that?" they nearly panicked. Their eyes were almost the size of saucers.

"Ha ha, don't worry, you're safe here," laughed Mr. Anderson.

"Mr. Anderson! you're unbearable," said Mrs. Laramie. Everyone laughed.

"Tomorrow is another day in paradise, I'm turning in," said Mr. Laramie. The others soon followed.

"Say Dad, have you ever run into a fella who lives down on the River by the name of Crazy Joe?" asked Bryan.

"Crazy Joe? You ran into him?" asked his father.

"Yes, the other day," he replied.

"Stay away from him, he's unpredictable. I haven't seen him in a long time, but he's sure a strange bird," answered his father.

"Is he actually mining there at his place?" Bryan asked.

"I don't know, but that old mine I understand has been there a lot longer then he has. Come to think of it, he's been seen prospecting up some of the side canyons just above his place. So perhaps the old mine has played out," he responded.

"That red goat he has is about the strangest sight I've ever seen," commented Bryan.

"Ha! the goat" he laughed. "Sometimes that horny beast comes sneaking up and charges from behind and knocks people for a loop. I guess it's been effective, everyone steers clear of the area. It didn't chase after you did it?" his father asked.

"No, it just seemed to follow us. It never did charge us directly," he answered.

"What were you boys doing up that direction anyway?" Mr. Anderson asked.

"Well, according to my tree cores there was a trail heading up river, so we tried to follow it, and that's when we ran into old Joe," explained Bryan, being careful to conceal the whole truth.

"Mmm. You haven't been bitten by the gold bug too have you?" smiled Mr. Anderson slapping him on the shoulder.

On Sunday they returned to Columbia. Bryan was filled with renewed enthusiasm and new ideas to share.

Mid-morning of the following day a discernible banging noise drew closer. All the ears of the animals in the corral and Graffiti, perked up, they knew what was coming. As Josh turned the corner a passenger was visible next to him, a girl, busily chewing gum. She appeared to be a little younger than Josh, had long, very light red hair, and a few scattered freckles.

"Hi Bryan, I want you to meet my cousin, Tammy," introduced Josh. "And Tammy this is my best buddy, Bryan."

"Hello Tammy, I almost forgot that Josh said you were coming up," greeted Bryan. At the same time he remembered what Josh had called her: "my brat cousin." He couldn't help but notice how her hands, arms, and face were so terribly white and untanned.

"Hi," she replied cocking her head. "Josh said you guys are working on a totally awesome mystery," she replied.

"Well yeah, but let's keep this quiet, okay," emphatically requested Bryan, who was somewhat taken back by this strange creature from the city.

Tammy searched Bryan's handsome face and warm brown eyes, but she didn't know how to take his air of authority. "Oh, it's a secret then," she said putting her fingers over her lips, kind of smirking.

"That's right. Josh, there's a couple of new clues that we need to discuss," said Bryan turning his attention to him.

"Good, otherwise it seems we're at a dead end," replied Josh.

Bryan waved them over to the barn. "I have hidden the map up in the loft," quietly spoke Bryan.

Climbing the short ladder, they stood in the hay loft with bales of hay stacked along the right side. A square framed opening looked out through the back of the barn into the woods beyond. Bryan pulled a wooden shim out from between two rough sawn beams to reveal the folded map.

"From now on this will be the secret hiding place, I don't trust leaving anything in the house anymore," said Bryan.

"Okay, but what are the new clues?" asked Josh.

Bryan proceeded to relate the words of the old man and the story that surrounded him as it was related by his father. As well as his knowledge of Crazy Joe.

"Can I see the map?" asked Tammy.

"Sure, but be very careful, it's the only one we have," nervously answered Bryan.

After she unfolded the map, Josh pointed out the various features of the map. "This is the only Spanish phrase that we haven't been able to decipher, right here by the X," pointed out Josh.

Tammy squinted as she looked close. "Mmm. Parts of these letters could be missing. It's like a seam ran across here or something," she observed while still chomping on her gum.

"Well that could be, it was traced from a photocopy," said Bryan.

"What letters look incomplete?" questioned Josh as the two boys gathered on each side of her to gaze at the map.

"M-e-t-a-l-i-c-o, metalico," spoke Tammy as she slowly reconstructed the word, letter by letter.

"What could that mean?" asked Josh.

"Well, metal is the base word and i-c-o makes it more like—metallic," she slowly responded.

"You know Spanish pretty good," stated Bryan.

"I've had three years of Spanish," she bluntly answered.

"Tammy, look at the other word," coaxed Josh.

"C-i-u-d-a-d, ciudad, wait, ciudad is a town, a village or a city," she finally realized.

"You would certainly pick up on that," Bryan remarked.

"Okay, the phrase correctly rendered then is, Metallic City or Town," concluded Josh.

"Metallic City," repeated Bryan.

"The city part of that must refer to a camp or something," figured Josh.

"But what is it that's metallic?" asked Tammy.

The two boys looked at each other.

"Are you thinking what I'm thinking?" asked Bryan.

"Crazy Joe's! All that metal dug up in those pits," Josh exclaimed.

"Yes, Crazy Joe must be sitting right on top of it. I wonder if he realizes what is there? This fits right in. And the old mine has been there longer then he has," added Bryan.

"Wow, what a breakthrough," realized Josh.

"Thanks to me!" Tammy reminded them.

"For a girl, you did all right," replied Bryan.

"For a girl!" she protested. "For that I ought to punch your lights out!"

"Ah-h, I think what Bryan meant was that he was just surprised how quickly you were able to come up with the answer," interceded Josh. He now realized there may be a little friction between these two.

"I'm not so sure," she replied.

Bryan had to bite his tongue, or he was afraid he would say something regrettable, and offend Josh. He wondered how these two could be related in any way.

"We need to verify that this site is truly the Spanish camp, and if it's true, ye ha! 'Canyon of Gold' here we come!" excitedly exclaimed Josh to get their minds back on track.

"Josh, you make me laugh," said Bryan finally breaking into a smile.

"When can we go?" asked Tammy.

Josh and Bryan exchanged glances.

"I don't know if that's such a good idea, there's a lot of crazies running around these hills," responded Bryan.

"Hey, I'm cool, Josh is supposed to be watching out for me anyway," she pleaded.

"Well, okay, but you have to do exactly as you're told," insisted Bryan.

"Yes, General!" she replied snapping to attention.

Bryan glared at Josh.

With excitement running high, they decided to take off immediately. After buttoning up a few loose ends, they packed up some food and threw a flashlight into the sack, and were off. Graffiti could not understand why he had to be left behind to guard the house. By noon they were hiking up the 'ridge' trail, and it wasn't long before Crazy Joe's cabin became visible below them.

"Looks quiet down there," observed Josh as they peered over the rock outcropping.

"His mule is gone, he might be out prospecting for the day," theorized Bryan. "But we better wait and watch for a little while to make sure."

"Don't forget he's got that shotgun," reminded Josh.

"Say, where's Tammy," asked Bryan.

"Huh? She was just here," answered Josh.

"Oh no, look! That stupid girl is climbing down the bank below us, she's going to get us into a royal mess," said Bryan stumbling over his words.

"Tammy! Tammy!" called Josh as low as he could.

"She won't listen," concluded Bryan plopping down against the rock.

"I guess we'd better go after her," said Josh.

"Yeah, let's go," agreed Bryan in an aggravated tone.

Moving quietly, they scampered down the steep bank zigzagging their way, using small oaks to hang on to.

"Look, she's on the other side of that pile of dirt," pointed Josh.

As they approached, dust was billowing up from her general direction. Suddenly she screamed. The boys quickly rounded the pile to find Tammy lying flat on her back against the edge of a pit.

"Tammy are you all right, what happened?" asked her cousin.

"I'm sick, how horrible!" she raved, holding her hands over her eyes.

"What's wrong?" demanded Bryan.

"Look down there and you'll see," she pointed.

Glancing down into the pit, there was something sticking out of the dirt. Bryan slid down to the bottom to investigate. It was a curved piece of rusted metal. Brushing the dirt away something white became visible.

"Ah!" was Bryan's only exclamation.

"What is it?" Josh demanded.

"A skull," Bryan finally replied turning away to climb back up. "He was buried with his helmet, a Spanish helmet."

"Wow! You know what this means?" realized Josh. "It means it all must be true, the camp, the map, the trail, and—"

"And the 'Canyon of Gold,' " finished Bryan.

"Tammy, are you going to be all right?" Josh asked.

"I think so," she replied. "That totally blew me away."

"Old Joe must have discovered the significance of this place years ago. And he has dug all these pits looking for gold, artifacts, or at least some clue that would lead to other mines," Bryan thought out loud. "But this is not right leaving these pits open like this."

"Shh! I heard something," warned Josh.

"Well, it's no wonder, you two are making enough noise to raise the dead," Tammy hoarsely whispered.

Bryan gave her a disapproving look as he got up. He then motioned for them to follow. Cautiously, crouching down they moved back toward the canyon wall. Suddenly the red goat appeared, between them and their escape route. The goat had its head down ready to charge.

"This way," motioned Bryan.

Following his direction, they backed toward the old mine. They approached to within twenty feet of the mine, when the goat finally decided to charge. Running to the mine entrance, the large wooden door was found to be secured with a heavy chain and lock. It wouldn't budge. Their backs were now against the door.

"Look, here's a loose board," discovered Tammy. The board swung to the side.

"Let's go, fast," ordered Bryan.

Josh slid through first, Tammy second, and finally Bryan. Once inside, the goat stopped its charge.

"That was close," sighed Bryan.

"Hey you guys it's dark in here, where's the flashlight?" asked Tammy whose voice echoed into the dark unknown.

"In my pack," replied Bryan turning so Josh could pull it out.

Josh switched on the light to reveal a cylindrical tunnel leading back into the mountain. Running along the crest of the tunnel was a one foot wide quartz vein.

"The echo in here is kind of spooky," said Bryan.

"Don't say that, the dampness in here is bad enough, like breathing in a paper bag," complained Tammy.

"Let's have a quick look around before Crazy Joe comes back," spoke up Josh flashing the light down the tunnel.

The echo of their footsteps boomed into the black unknown as they trudged forward.

"I don't know if I can go much farther, this dark tunnel is giving me the willies," whispered Tammy.

"You'll be fine, just stay close," encouraged Josh as he flashed the light on the ceiling to check its integrity. The old timbers glistened with jewels of moisture.

"Look, there's something down there reflecting the light," pointed out Bryan.

After another one hundred and fifty feet the tunnel suddenly ended.

"There on the wall," directed Josh with the flashlight.

"It looks like gold," guessed Tammy.

"No, it's not, it's fool's gold, iron pyrite," replied Bryan. "See the large cubic crystals, that's fools gold."

"They must have given up on this vein of quartz and stopped right here," figured Josh.

"My dad was right, this mine must have played out a very long time ago. There's no evidence of recent activity," added Bryan.

"Josh, shine your light over behind those rocks," asked Tammy.

"Why, did you hear something?" questioned Josh.

"No you ninny, it's just dark over there and we don't know what could be back there," she insisted.

"Okay, let's take a look," replied Josh.

Leading the way Josh stepped around the rocks, shining the light along the wall.

"Wait, shine the light back over here," directed Bryan. "Yeah, right there."

"There's an opening there," realized Tammy.

"Yes, you're right," agreed Josh.

The light revealed a four foot square opening in the wall. Sticking the flashlight into the opening of the wall, a room fifteen feet long by ten feet wide now became visible.

"It appears to be empty, wait there's something over in the corner. Let's go in and take a look," said Josh.

Ducking through the opening, they found themselves standing in the center of a hewn out chamber. There was the ominous sound of water dripping into a small pool in the back of the room. Josh ran the light around the perimeter along the floor to again stop in the corner.

"Tools! Old tools, the handles have pretty much rotted off, but look, the heads are hand forged, they must be very old," said Bryan.

"If they had any connection with this mine, that would put the age of this mine way back," replied Josh.

"Josh, turn your light down on the floor," asked Tammy. "Look, how the floor glistens, it sparkles."

"Wow, what's causing that?" wondered Josh.

"I think I might know," replied Bryan. "But in order to prove it, let's take a sample home with us."

Bryan slipped off his pack, emptied the contents out of a paper sack and scooped the sandy dirt into the bag.

"I'm getting very cold," said Tammy.

"We have to leave anyway, the batteries in the flashlight are dying quickly," answered Josh.

Bryan hurriedly put his pack back on while Josh held the light so he could get the straps on straight.

"Hey, Bryan, you project a mean shadow. Look how it curves up onto the ceiling, hanging over us like a vulture," pointed out Tammy, shivering from the cold.

"Yeah," agreed Bryan briefly glancing over at the wall and ceiling, ignoring any intended meaning. Suddenly Bryan stopped and glanced back at the wall. "Josh, give me that flashlight for a second," he asked.

Bryan shined the light directly on the wall in front of them.

"Look at this!" exclaimed Bryan as his heart began to pound.

"Oh my!" added Josh staring open mouthed.

There high on the wall chiseled into the rock was the symbol for the 'Door of the Sun.' It was about six feet wide and five feet tall.

"That was on the map," recalled Tammy.

"Right, it confirms that we are on the trail to the 'Canyon of Gold.' This is definitely the first site indicated on the map, the first X," replied Bryan.

The flashlight now began to grow dim.

"Let's go before we're stumbling around in the dark," urged Josh.

Bryan was frozen in awe.

"Bryan we have to go!" pleaded Josh.

"Yeah, let's go," finally replied Bryan.

Rumbling back down the tunnel, they were soon back at the entrance just as the flashlight gave out.

"Peek out the board, do you see anything?" asked Bryan.

"Ah-h, no, nothing that way, or that way, all clear, unless that goat is waiting in ambush," replied Josh.

"Okay, this is what we need to do, first proceed as quiet as we can out the door and along the bank to where we can climb back up to the trail. Even if the goat does return we'll have to run for it. Tammy, you stay between us. Josh you take the lead. I'll take the flank," directed Bryan.

"Yes, Captain!" returned Tammy.

Josh grinned at Tammy.

"What happened? This morning I was a general," teased Bryan trying to keep a straight face.

Josh crept out first and stood erect against the door. Next, Tammy did the same and Bryan followed. There was no sign of the goat as they edged their way along the bank. Ascending the bank the boys let Tammy go up first as they took the rear guard.

"Whew! I'm glad to be out of there," said Tammy as they regathered behind the rock outcropping.

"Investigating mysteries can be hazardous work, I wouldn't blame you if you didn't want to be involved in this anymore," hinted Bryan.

"But I do, this is cool, when can we go again?" she replied.

"Cool?" replied Bryan. "Are you crazy?"

"Girls are hard to figure," said Josh.

"Come on, who deciphered the Spanish word, found the grave, and helped discover the secret room," she argued.

"We can't deny your contribution, Tammy, but for goodness sake, please don't run off like you did again," raved Bryan.

The afternoon was well along as they marched down the trail, daydreaming of the things they had seen and the possibilities that laid ahead. The reality of the 'Legend' now loomed up before them. There was yet to be greater discoveries that would soon exceed their imagination.

8

NORTH FORK

A rriving home, Bryan found a letter from his mother in the day's mail. Fumbling he finally got it open. It was a short letter, expressing how she missed them. Ha! When did that start? he thought to himself. She was inviting him down to visit for a week at the ranch where she was residing. He thought about it as he folded the letter. His initial reaction was a resurfacing of the old pain, but down deep the desire to see her again was there.

Late in the afternoon, his father rumbled in driving their older GMC pickup loaded with bales of hay. After hearing the news, he told Bryan he was free to go if he wanted to.

"I don't kno-w, it's hard," he responded.

"Yes, it is hard, but it'll be good for you—and your mother, in more ways than one," said his father with an intended double meaning.

"Well, I guess I will go," Bryan finally replied.

"Very good, now let's get this hay unloaded," his dad requested.

That evening Bryan took the dirt from the mine, and proceeded to wash it in an old beat up gold pan that was stored on the back porch. Working with it over top of the laundry tub, he swirled the water around the pan while tilting it, causing the lighter fines to float out over the edge of the pan. Keeping the right amount of water in the pan was critical. Bryan now tapped the bottom to release some of the fines caught in between the larger pieces. Each succeeding wash gradually reduced the amount of material in the pan. Emptying most of the water, it was time to analyze the contents. After running his finger along the crease of the pan he held it up.

"Will you look at that," he remarked. The tip of his finger was glistening with flakes of gold. "Gold! There was gold in that room at one time," Bryan anounced to himself. "Another piece of the puzzle now becomes clear."

Picking out the small aggregate, he poured the flakes into a small vial to show later.

That night as Bryan struggled to sleep, his mind alternated between thoughts of his mother and the 'Legend.' One worried him; the other intrigued him.

Next morning, Josh and Tammy stopped by briefly on their way into town to run a few errands.

Bryan wasted no time in sharing his discovery. "Guess what was in that room in the mine?" questioned Bryan as he pulled the vial out of his pocket and handed it to Josh.

"Gold! Gold was stored in there at one time," excitedly concluded Josh.

"Remember those rocks piled up in the tunnel?" recalled Tammy. "I have an idea they were used to seal off that room."

"That's what I was thinking too," agreed Bryan.

"Hooray! You two agree on something," applauded Josh.

"What's the next step?" asked Tammy ignoring Josh's comment. Turning, she glimpsed Bryan's gaze darting away from her.

"We need to reexamine the map, list our next set of clues, and finally I guess, search the North Fork for those clues," replied Bryan.

"We'll be back later, probably in the afternoon after we finish a little job for my mom," informed Josh as he opened the Jeep door to get in.

"Josh, does Bryan have a girlfriend?" asked Tammy after they were well down the road.

"He hates girls."

"Oh, he does, does he," she stated in a matter of fact tone, sitting there with her arms folded.

"What's with you?" asked Josh.

"Nothing!" she replied. "Nothing!"

Josh smiled to himself.

After they returned later that afternoon, Bryan told them about his intended trip to visit his mother later that week.

"Good for you," responded Josh.

"I hope so," replied Bryan as they mounted the ladder to the loft. "Tammy, if you'll do the honors," he pointed.

Tammy went to the wall, pulled out the wooden shim, and extracted the map. Josh and Bryan pushed a bale of hay to the center of the loft to serve as a table, and a couple of others to sit on.

"So far we have found and verified the location of 'Metallic City,' " said Josh pointing to that location on the map.

"The map shows that the trail goes up to where the river forks, and keeps forking left, up to this designation, 'Where Eagles Fly,' " observed Tammy.

"I believe the North Fork is the correct route shown," commented Bryan.

"Like Tammy said, all we need to do is just keep branching left," reiterated Josh.

"Okay good, but far as the phrase, 'Where Eagles Fly,' there hasn't been any eagles up in these canyons for an awful long time, so this may be no clue at all," stated Bryan.

"When can we go?" questioned Tammy.

"I'm leaving on Friday, so it would have to be Wednesday or Thursday," said Bryan.

"Tomorrow should be good for us," replied Josh.

"The thing is, we'll have to leave extra early in order to have enough time to look around, once we get up there," added Bryan.

"How early is early?" questioned Tammy.

"Oh, about six a.m., should do it," replied Bryan. "But if that's too early for a city girl, stay at home, take the day off."

"When pigs fly! You're not dumping me buster. What do you mean—city girl? There's nothing wrong with living in the city. And another thing it wasn't my idea to come up here to Hicksville in the first place. Furthermore, it was my mother who forced me to come up here!"

"You know something, if you weren't a protected species. I'd—I don't know—you girls are all the same, you talk too much, you don't seem to have any sense of loyalty, and you're usually pampered to death."

"Oh, is that so! Let me tell you a few things about boys."

"Okay, okay, enough, it's settled," intervened Josh, "we'll come by about six and pick you up."

"Be sure to bring enough food, it's going to be a l-ong day," meaningfully glanced Bryan.

Tammy folded the map and pigeon holed it back into its hiding place. She was still miffed at Bryan.

As they drove away, Tammy asked, "What's his problem anyway?"

"Well, I think ever since his mother left a couple of years ago, he's had this grudge against females in general," answered Josh.

Though angered, deep down she somehow understood.

Next morning at gray dawn, there was a cold tingle to the air as the stars blinked out one by one—heralding another day of life and adventure.

Being a few minutes ahead of schedule, Bryan decided to wait for them beside the road. Sitting down he leaned against his pack and waited. Closing his drowsy eyes for a minute, the

Spanish explorer again appeared in his thoughts. He could visualize him marching up river. What things would he be looking for? What landmarks would he use or make?

Breaking his sojourn, the deep sound of a vehicle severely out of tune approached. Bryan waited until Josh had screeched to a full halt before getting up.

"You must have slept out here all night, look at your hair," pointed Josh.

"My hair?" he questioned.

"It's sticking straight up," laughed Tammy.

"Oh," responded Bryan feeling the top of his head.

Tammy continued laughing and finally managed to get a few more words out. "I knew there was a good reason for getting up so early. And you know, the experts were right when they said you could see all kinds of wildlife out at this time of the morning."

"Well it's good to see that you're in such a fine mood," chuckled Bryan. "Even if it is at my expense."

Secretly in her heart, Tammy had begun to warm to Bryan's personality, despite their many clashes.

Leaving the outskirts of town, Josh put the pedal to the metal, and before long they were parked and on the trail. The sun was just now hitting the trees high up on the far side of the canyon, while they were yet meandering in the shadows below. Light dew beaded the summer grass, quickly wetting their shoes. After another thirty minutes, Crazy Joe's place came into sight below them. This time there was smoke coming out of the stove pipe. Nothing else seemed different than before.

"Shh! No sound as we pass by," cautioned Bryan.

Quietly and in single file the threesome continued up the trail until they were around the corner and out of sight.

"We don't want to draw any attention," reiterated Bryan.

Descending the drainage soon brought them down to the river's edge. Red-orange Indian paintbrush dotted the gravelly banks with a splash of color. The roar of the river pervaded the air and sunlight streamed into the bottom of the canyon as they approached the Forks.

"This is great, the map comes alive right before our eyes," said Tammy as she came to a bank overlooking the Forks. As she looked up into the canyons she tried to mentally superimpose the map over what she was now seeing.

"Let's rest for a couple of minutes before we cross to the North Fork," suggested Josh.

"Once we start up the north tributary, we'll need to keep our eyes peeled for any signs of an old trail, rock markings or anything unusual," reminded Bryan finding a flat rock to sit on.

"There should be some kind of trail, even after all these years," commented Tammy sitting facing the river.

Bryan couldn't help notice how her hair shimmered in the sunlight as an early morning breeze gently brushed it back. How different girls were. He never concerned himself before, so why now? Changing thought, he pondered his grandfathers recurring words about "those who were watching" up in these mountains.

Josh commented to Tammy how changeable this country was. How landslides due to earthquakes or storms could transform an entire section of the canyon.

"I'm ready!" spoke up Tammy, anxious to get started.

"Okay, wagons ho!" signaled Josh.

Following the edge of the river past the junction, they safely crossed the South Fork on a log that had come to rest among the rocks. But hopping from rock to rock crossing the North Fork, Tammy slipped on a slime coated rock and one foot went into the water.

"You okay?" asked Josh.

"Yeah-h, just it's icky walking in a wet shoe," she answered, trying to compress the water out through the shoelace holes.

Looming in front of them was the mouth of a rocky steep canyon. Could this really be the gateway to the 'Canyon of Gold?'

"We might as well stay on this side of the stream, until we're forced to cross, or that it's apparent the trail is on the opposite side," concluded Bryan.

"This does seem to be the dominate side," agreed Josh.

"And watch for snakes," added Bryan.

"S-nakes!" exclaimed Tammy coming to an abrupt stop.

"Oh, don't get shook, they wouldn't be interested in a bowlegged girl anyway."

"What! I'm not bowlegged. You, you, country bumpkin!" she retorted, about to bop him one.

The course climbed rapidly over solid metamorphic rock scoured by centuries of erosion. The stream bed was spotted with water filled potholes, reflecting the surroundings like mirrors that were seemingly imbedded in the reddish banded rock.

"This sure is rough and tumble," commented Josh.

"It should level out further up," guessed Bryan.

"The steps in this bedrock reminds me of the steps in front of the courthouse back home—a long platform then several small steps, then a long platform again," observed Tammy pausing to catch her breath.

"Let's hope the judge isn't up here waiting for us," laughed Josh.

The ascent soon took its toll on them sapping their strength. Huffing and puffing they had to stop numerous times to rest. The hot summer sun beat down upon them unmercifully. After what seemed to be an eternity the canyon finally became more gentle and widened to allow trees to grow along its irregular slopes.

"Look at this, it appears to be a post that has been broken off," noticed Josh as he kicked at the side of it.

"Hmm. You must be right, this didn't grow like this," agreed Bryan.

The post was about six inches around, extending about two feet out of a hole in the rock.

"A post? Another good sign," realized Tammy.

"I wonder though, what it was used for?" questioned Josh.

"Come on, let's look for what else we can find," motioned Bryan.

In half an hour they had found eight more such posts, some broken off at the ground, others standing three or four feet high. It was impossible to ascertain how tall they were originally, or what they were used for.

"They seem to be spaced out about every three to four hundred feet," observed Bryan.

"Only thing we can do is follow them right to where they lead," stated Josh.

"Well, quit yakking and let's go," urged Tammy.

Continuing further up the North Fork, the explorers passed more posts as the canyon now opened up to include a narrow meadow strewn with large round boulders, some six to seven feet in diameter.

"A good name for this place would be the *Bowling Alley of the Giants*," commented Tammy.

"You certainly have an amazing command of a very predictable vocabulary," replied Bryan.

"Well, Bryan, you always seem to be planning things, but I doubt if they ever work," she returned.

"You know no such thing," he objected.

"Look, the stream forks again," pointed Josh.

"Yeah, but the posts are continuing up the meadow on the right fork," observed Bryan.

"They sure do," affirmed Josh. "That's perplexing."

The three now paused to rest, contemplating their next move as a chipmunk regarded them from a nearby rock.

"The thing is, everyone that's been up here probably has followed these posts to their end, evidently without success," reasoned Tammy.

"I hate to admit it, but you're probably right," agreed Bryan. "It would've been easy for anyone to find the 'Canyon of Gold' if this led right to it. We need to continue to follow the map and go left."

Josh now took the lead as they advanced along the meandering left fork which gradually worked its way toward the edge of the meadow.

"Tammy, if you got lost up here, how would you find your way home?" asked Bryan.

"I wouldn't get lost in the first place. I'd just follow the trail back down the hill," she taunted.

"But what if you lost the trail," quizzed Bryan, thinking he might razz her a bit.

"It's simple, just follow the drainages downhill, use the sun to keep a rough track of my bearings, and at night spot Polaris, the North Star," she answered.

"Woo, city girl, I'm impressed," replied Bryan.

"I hope that's a compliment—country boy," Tammy snapped back.

"Ha, listen to you two magpies," chuckled Josh.

It soon became apparent that the left fork was considerably more steep then its counterpart as they approached the upper limit of the meadow.

"Rock mound," announced Josh pointing ahead.

"Looks very recent," commented Tammy.

"Somebody has definitely been busy up here," agreed Bryan.

"Maybe we're too late, this could be referencing a mining claim," speculated Josh.

"Well-l, let's check it out," replied Bryan in a half-disappointed tone.

The terrain again turned wild, steep and rugged. After another half mile of exhaustive climbing, the creek again forked. Reaching this juncture they decided to rest and eat lunch. Without a word of explanation Tammy walked ahead a short distance. She came back declaring she had found another rock mound. And again it was marking the left fork.

"Then these rock mounds must be just trail markers, not part of a mineral claim," replied Bryan as he prepared his pack to go.

"Somebody must be following the same route we are, and they must have a map as well," concluded Josh.

"Could it be those two guys that Josh told me about, who ran the professor off the road and stole the original map?" questioned Tammy.

"That could be, but I can't help wonder about Crazy Joe, who has been prospecting in these mountains for many years. Yet these mounds are recent, I would tend to agree—it's probably someone new," replied Bryan.

"Crazy Joe, far as we know has no idea about the map. It was only recently discovered and only a few are aware that it even exists," spouted Josh—his mouth still half full of food. "Although, he's had thirty years to follow up on any other clues."

"Maybe we have waited too long; but how did they know where to look? Think how long it took us to figure it out?" pondered Bryan.

"It's water under the bridge now, someone is definitely ahead of us," stated Tammy.

"Let's think optimistically, that we're not too late, it's entirely possible they may hit a snag along the way," suggested Josh.

"Whatever the case, we need to be extra careful, they could be up here somewhere, right now," cautioned Bryan.

After a few more minutes, the trio began the trek up the second left fork. The course again became fairly steep. In a short time, Tammy began to fall behind, even when the boys purposely slowed their pace.

"Bryan, she won't admit it, but she's plum tuckered out, I don't think we're going to be able to go much further," whispered Josh.

"We'll stop ahead, up there, where it appears to level off," pointed Bryan.

Making it to the top of a steep grade, a whole new vista opened up. It was a large deep basin, resembling a giant crater with inaccessible sides. Snow still clung to the highest of the jagged peaks that ringed the perimeter of the basin. A talus field covered nearly all of the basin floor with aspen trees growing in scattered clumps around its edge.

"If I didn't know any better, I would say that we were on the moon," first responded Josh.

"It's like the end of the world up here," commented Bryan. "Listen! absolute silence, eerie, isn't it?"

Tammy finally approached moving slowly. "How much further do we have to go?" she complained.

"This is it, looks like the end of the trail," answered Josh.

"Good!" was her reply with a deep sigh of relief.

"Say, good ol' sunshine is putting some color in your face," pointed Bryan. Tammy stuck her tongue out at him, and he chuckled. "Josh, see that U shaped valley up there on the left about five hundred feet up?" pointed out Bryan.

"Up there? I see it," he replied.

"The words of the old man that my dad talked to, keeps coming back to me: 'It is above the heads of mortal man.' Could it possibly be in such a place, like a hanging valley?"

"Anything is possible, but there has been no indication of our other clues, 'Where Eagles Fly' or of the 'Wandering Sky,' " replied Josh.

"I know, but what else can we do, but check these things out as they come available. It's even possible that we may have unknowingly bypassed those clues," stated Bryan.

"I'm not going up there!" Tammy said. "You have to be a mountain goat to get up there."

"No, Tammy, you don't have to do any more climbing, just wait for us at the bottom of the slope," pointed Bryan. "Josh, I think we can go out around that red volcanic outcropping on the left, contour across the slope to the far side and angle back to catch the valley on its right side."

"Okay, let's give it a whirl. Tammy just a few more steps, then it's all back downhill," encouraged Josh.

"I would rather call a cab," she quipped. Near the outcropping Tammy found a comfortable place to lie back and rest in the shade.

Stirring up the dust, the boys plowed their way up the slope and across as they had planned. Tired but successful, they finally reached their goal. Stepping into the yawning valley they found it to be only about a mile long before it also ended in insurmountable cliffs and a rugged ridge line.

"Listen to the echo up here, it must have just the right acoustic shape or something," noticed Bryan.

"Echo Canyon," named Josh.

Meandering up through the boulders, dwarf pines, and white thorn, their search for evidence of any kind proved fruitless.

"We must have missed a turn somewhere, back down below," concluded Josh.

"I still wonder what those posts we saw earlier were used for, and who installed them?" questioned Bryan.

"Somebody went to a lot of hard work to install them in solid rock," commented Josh.

Reaching the brink of the valley, they stopped to study the grand view laid out in front of them, the basin, the mountains, and into the wild hazy ranges beyond.

"Somehow the route, that we've followed today just doesn't seem to be proportionate with the features or the map," thought Bryan.

"Depends on how accurately they drew it," replied Josh.

Dropping over the edge, they rambled down the slope.

"Woo! Did you hear that?" asked Bryan coming to an abrupt halt.

"What?" questioned Josh sliding to a stop. "Could be, Tammy," he realized after listening to the strange sound. "Let's go!"

Almost on a run they traversed the distance to the outcropping and back down to the basin floor.

"Tammy! Where are you?" called Josh.

"Tammy!" reechoed Bryan.

She was not where they had left her.

"Whose idea was it to bring her along anyway?" complained Bryan.

"Over here, quick," finally responded Tammy from a distance. Working their way around the boulders, Tammy finally came into view, bent over, looking at something on the ground.

"What's wrong?" questioned Josh.

"Wrong?" repeated Tammy looking up.

"Yeah, wasn't that you making that sound, a couple of minutes ago?" asked Josh.

"No. You heard something?" she asked.

"Yes, it was hard to tell, but we thought you may have been in trouble," answered Josh.

"No, it wasn't me," she confessed.

"If it wasn't you, what was it?" asked Josh.

Bryan turned to look back up at the gaping mouth of Echo Canyon.

"Josh, I wonder somehow if what we heard came out of the canyon above us, not from down here," theorized Bryan.

"The difficulty with the acoustics of echoes is that it's hard to distinguish where the initial sound came from," replied Josh.

"As I think about it, it does seem to to me that the sound we heard was quite distinct from the sliding noise that we were making during our descent," added Bryan.

"If the source of the sound wasn't me or you two, than what's left?" reasoned Tammy.

In silence they all glanced up at the yawning canyon.

"Oh, by the way, I found a footprint over here," announced Tammy.

"Footprint? Let me see," said Josh.

The footprint is located in a flat sandy area.

"It's about ten to eleven inches long and appears to be the right foot," she informed.

"The heel! The square pattern again, its the same print that we saw down by the river and near the road," realized Josh.

"By the blood," mumbled Bryan under his breath.

"What?" asked Tammy.

"Nothing. The ground is so dry it's hard to tell if this print is minutes old or days," continued Bryan.

"Hmm. There's another print over here," pointed Josh. "It's the same person; and I don't see any other prints."

"Than this person was probably alone. It may not be the same two guys that we overheard on the trail that day," speculated Bryan. "Unless they had split up."

"I think its time we make tracks," suggested Tammy.

"It's possible that someone is watching us right now," said Josh glancing back up toward Echo Canyon.

"Nothing more we can do here," agreed Bryan.

The trip out of the basin and down the creek was surprisingly quick. Soon they were back to the second fork and proceeding down to the 'Bowling Alley.' The sun was now well in the west, throwing shadows across the canyons.

Suddenly, Tammy stopped. "There's someone up on the ridge," she pointed grabbing Bryan by the arm.

"I don't see anything," he replied.

"He's gone. I got a glimpse of him for just a second, kind of bent down, sneaking along the ridge," she explained.

"That's good enough for me, I'm out of here," said Josh picking up the pace again.

"Oh, one more thing, he, that is I think it was a he, had long hair," added Tammy.

"That's interesting," replied Bryan.

The boys looked at each other in realization of the possible fulfillment of the story told by Bryan's grandfather about the Indian secret that would be guarded.

Had they come to a dead end in their search? There seemed to be no more clues. Did the presence of the man who followed them, indicate that they were close and had to be watched? Who was the person with the mystery footprint? There were many questions, but for now no answers.

9

EL CAMINO DE RANCHO

As the bus left *Columbia*, Bryan peered out of the window at the great wall called the Sierra Nevada. The 'Legend' taunted him. If the 'Canyon of Gold' was easy to find, others before him would have found it. The words: "the door is closed," kept echoing in his thoughts. Over a period of many years changes in terrain and vegetation can dramatically reshape the look of the land. And there was always the human element, which could lead to mistaken orientation and the inability to relocate the initial discovery.

What about those posts? His grandfather revealed that in 1876 or thereabouts, a telegraph line was run across the mountains to Bodie, but was abandoned some years later with the invention of the telephone. Ha, what did he say about the notion they had? That electricity couldn't go around corners very well, so wires were strung as straight as possible.

Coming down out of the rolling foothills the view soon switched to the valley below and the hazy Coast Range on the far horizon. Bryan's thoughts changed from what was behind to what lay ahead. How would he and his mother get along? Had she changed? What was so important to her there? These thoughts faded as he drifted off to sleep.

The bus lurched, awakening him. Looking around he saw large buildings, concrete overpasses, and car jammed freeways.

Evidently they had reached the outskirts of San Francisco. There was a kind of gray haze that hung over the city. In every direction there was concrete and pavement. Artificial surfaces everywhere. It only made sense that they would have an artificial atmosphere too, he sarcastically thought to himself. How can Tammy like it down here? Maybe it's all she knows.

Soon the bus left the City and was heading south on the Pacific Coast Highway. The white curling waves of the Pacific Ocean now came into view about a half mile to the west. Large jagged rocks spotted the coastline in places, the waves crashing against them, leaping skyward in one final attempt to breach the barrier, and then retreating amidst a banner of white foam. Was there a battle raging here? Assuredly there was, in more ways then one, so he thought in his own mind as he settled back into his seat. The mountains seemed to be in contrast, more peaceful and in balance.

After nearly an hour, Bryan caught sight of a sign that advertised Pt. Lobos. He knew he was near his destination. As the bus pulled up in front of the bus stop and came to a halt, a lump formed in his throat. Getting off the bus with bag in hand, he spotted several people standing around talking and greeting one another. A short man in a blue suit with matching cap approached.

"Are you, Bryan?" he asked.

"Yes I am," Bryan answered.

"I'm Charley, your mother sent me down to pick you up," he said shaking Bryan's hand.

"Nice to meet you," returned Bryan. "You must work for her at the ranch."

"Yes, I do," he replied as he opened the door of the black sedan parked in front of the bus.

Bryan slid in while Charley put his bag in the trunk. Driving south out of town, the route took them along a number of different back roads, passing various large sprawling ranches.

"How long have you worked for my mother?" Bryan asked trying to be conversational.

"Oh, about a year now," he answered.

"You've probably spent quite a bit of time at the ranch," assumed Charley.

"No, not really. It's been a very long time," replied Bryan.

"Hmm," was Charley's puzzled reply. "This is it, El Camino de Rancho to your right," he announced.

Up a slight slope away from the road, over the top of a white wooden fence, he could see brown buildings set far back. There was a vague recollection here. As they turned off the main road into the wide driveway, two horses looking over the fence greeted them. Several hundred yards up the driveway they passed under a high archway with *"El Camino de Rancho"* written across the arch. Immediately the Spanish theme of the ranch became apparent with its red tile roofs and archways.

Also catching his eye and clashing in all respects was an old dilapidated building looming up behind the house, apparently on an adjacent property.

Charley pulled up beside the main house. He got out and opened the trunk to retrieve the bag, while Bryan came around the car. Walking through the first archway, Bryan found himself on a veranda surfaced with red tile that ran all along the front of the building. Looking around as he walked, a woman wearing sunglasses appeared out of a doorway and approached. He felt a cold sweat coming on. Could this be his mother? he wondered. Drawing more closely he could see that it was. She was about five foot eight inches tall, had a fair complexion with black hair. She looked older than before.

"Bryan, you're here, I'm so glad," she said putting her arms around him and giving him a hug. It was like hugging a stranger.

"Let me look at you," putting him at arm's length. "You're taller, a bit on the thin side. You've been eating okay haven't you?"

"Yes Mom, I've been eating fine," replied Bryan, grinning a little.

"Come on in, there's so much I want to hear and to tell you," she said directing him into the house. "Charley, put his bag in the guest bedroom please," his mother ordered.

Bryan entered a large room with an open beam ceiling and large windows revealing a picturesque view to the south. The room was decorated in an El Rancho style with sombreros and lariats artistically displayed along two walls.

"You probably don't remember being here, it was many years ago. Yet it seems just like yesterday," his mother rattled on.

"Not really," said Bryan. Though a vague recollection did exist.

While his mother went to check on dinner, Bryan looked out the large windows at the expanse of the ranch, its rolling hills and pastures. He could hear the whinny of the horses in the corral located next to the barn. Immediately on the wall to his right were portraits, hand painted, some appeared to be very old. One picture particularly caught his eye. It was of a bearded man probably about thirty years old. His features, his eyes, so striking. Why was he drawn to him, who was he? It seemed that many years before he had gazed into those same eyes and wondered the same.

Leaving the front room, Bryan wandered into what appeared to be a large dining room with hanging chandeliers and a glazed red tile floor. A stocky middle-aged woman was busy clearing off a table in the back.

"Rosa, please don't forget the sauce this time," said Mrs. Anderson coming out of the kitchen from the right. "Bryan, come on into the study, let's talk."

He was ushered into a room lined with books. At the far end was a grouping of paintings on easels. Bryan paused to view them before sitting down.

"These paintings are beautiful. You must have painted them," realized Bryan.

"Yes, they are now my bread and butter so to speak," she answered.

"I'm impressed," he added.

"Wait till you see the rest of the ranch," was her reply. "Now, tell me, how's your father, and how are you doing in school?"

Bryan related about his Dad and the pack business, his school project, and even a little bit about the mystery trail up the river. After fifteen or twenty minutes, Rosa came in and announced that dinner was ready.

Later that evening, Bryan's mother invited him out to look at her prized show horses. While walking along the fence that curved on out to the corral, Bryan suddenly stopped.

"What's that old building back there?" he asked, pointing across the fence.

"That's the old fort, *Santa Domingo*, built in the late 1700's," she replied.

"Santa Domingo!" repeated Bryan, recalling its significance and possibly understanding now his father's reaction to that name.

"I think it's officially closed to visitors, because portions of it have become unsafe. Occasionally I see someone over there working on it," Mrs. Anderson added.

Walking up to the horse corral, Bryan remembered this was where the "map" was found. What a coincidence! he thought.

The horses snorted at him, but an experienced hand quickly relaxed them.

"Horse handling must be in our blood," his mother commented, smiling. "Tell me, how is your dad really doing?"

Pausing he thought for a moment. "Not that good, business has been poor. He doesn't let on though, but I can tell it's eating him up on the inside," disclosed Bryan now feeling more at ease with his mother.

"His stubborn pride still won't allow him to accept help. Nothing has changed, he still thinks he's it, machismo," she replied.

Bryan was somewhat surprised by her comment and was about to jump to his dad's defense, but decided to hold his tongue. His mother sensed his agitation from that remark and decided to change the subject. She called the horses to her.

"The big Peruvian here, I've had for about a year and the Appaloosa has been here for a long time, before your grandmother passed away."

"They are beauties, a far cry from Midas and Thunder and the rest of the pack horses," replied Bryan.

"Midas and Thunder, ha!" she laughed, elapsing into memories of the past. She broke these off realizing the effect that they were having on her. "We'll ride the ranch tomorrow, you'll enjoy it," she announced.

Walking back toward the house, his mother quizzed him on his plans for the future, especially after graduation.

The next day dawned warm, the fog had not drifted in during the night. On his way to the dining room, Bryan found his mother standing in front of a mirror fixing her hair, dressed in a tan riding outfit. It reminded him of their "good old days."

"Oh, Bryan, good, it's time for breakfast," she said finishing up. "They're getting the horses ready for us now."

A hearty breakfast was waiting for them in the next room. "Food like this could drive a man to eat," laughed Bryan.

She smiled back at him.

"Where are we going to ride to?" he asked.

"It's a surprise, just wait," was the reply.

He couldn't imagine what could be a surprise. Finishing breakfast, Mrs. Anderson excused herself to make a phone call, and announced she would meet him at the stable.

Their mounts were tied up in front of the corral ready to ride. Bryan's horse was a buckskin mare named "Pat." His mother rode a Black Tennessee Walker, her favorite around the ranch. He had to smile, seeing his mother coming toward him wearing a cowboy hat and a saddle bag over her shoulder.

"Mom, you look like a page right out of the history book," commented Bryan.

"Bryan! How old do you think I am?" she grinned.

"Mom, you know I didn't mean it that way," he defended.

"I know, son," she replied. "Gus!" she called.

After a few seconds an elderly man dressed in jeans and a blue shirt emerged from the stable.

"Yes Ma'am," he answered.

"Gus, we'll be back in the afternoon. We'll be over the hill," she said.

"Andrea! I wouldn't admit that to anyone," he laughed.

"Have your laugh, Gus, but this is a surprise for Bryan," she smiled.

Mounting his horse, Bryan thought about the fact that he hadn't heard his mother's first name used in a long time. It was as if she didn't have one. She was always "Mom."

"Have fun," said Gus waving them off and returning to work.

Riding south through the fields, the main house and the ranch buildings soon became small and insignificant. Climbing part way up the side of the sandy bluffs that curved around to the west side of the ranch, they looked back over the whole spread.

"What you see here is only part of the original El Camino de Rancho, a Spanish land grant given to your great-great-grandfather. There are only about three thousand acres left of the original grant. Your grandfather, my father, sold off a major part of it years ago," disclosed his mother.

"Why did he sell off so much of the land?" Bryan asked.

"Some kind of bad business debt," she replied. "Now for the best part, follow me."

A faint trail contoured along the slope and gradually climbed to the top of the hundred foot high bluffs. Mrs. Anderson glanced back at Bryan as they came up over the top.

"Oooh-weee! So this is the surprise," he remarked.

There below them was the blue Pacific Ocean, it's beautiful waves curling and crashing on a gently sloped beach, pristine, untouched. The ocean stretched far into the horizon, seemingly infinite, making him feel as if he were standing at the edge of the universe.

"This is our backyard, you like it?" she asked.

"Absolutely, it's a hidden paradise," he replied.

"What's unique about this place, is that north and south of here for a great distance there are rocky cliffs and jagged rocks, it's like a sanctuary. In the past it was a safe harbor for the sailing ships coming up the coast," she added.

"That's why the fort is located here and the reason that great-great-grandfather settled here as well," concluded Bryan.

"Very astute," replied Mrs. Anderson. "Come on, let's go on down."

Following a path along the top of the bluffs they reached a point just south of the old fort that dropped into a natural dip. A trail now became visible leading down the back side of the bluffs to the beach below. The windward side of the bluffs were draped in numerous locations by colorful ice plant and small shrubs. Bryan was cautioned about slippery sections along the trail where the horse's hooves would slide on the gritty steep slope that was notched into the marine bedrock. Crossing the beach to the water's edge they turned north to ride along the surf.

"What's the story on those pilings just offshore?" asked Bryan pointing ahead.

"That's what's left of the old Spanish loading dock," she replied. "Ships would come in and dock there, load and unload."

"Hmm," contemplated Bryan as he envisioned glorious Spanish galleons docking and men busily unloading supplies.

Dismounting, mother and son walked the beach talking, finding all kinds of colorful shells and shiny pebbles. Returning to the horses, they laid out a ground cloth and unpacked the bagged lunch prepared by Rosa. As time went by it seemed that they were gradually drawing closer.

Later that afternoon they made the ride back "over the hill" to the ranch.

"One evening we'll come up and watch the sunset, it's very beautiful," said Mrs. Anderson as they began the descent from the top of the bluffs.

Bryan then remembered the fiery sunsets in the mountains, the alpine-glow. How could he compare these places, what was he doing here? It seemed so foreign. But his mother is here. Somehow he had to sort out the facts and deal with his feelings.

That evening after dinner, Bryan strolled into the front room and gazed out at the lengthening twilight shadows. Turning around, his attention was drawn to the paintings on the back wall. Stepping in front of each one, he tried to figure out who each one was. Three were of men and two were of women.

One of these has to be Grandfather Julian, and his grandmother should be one of the ladies, Bryan thought to himself. But which one? Probably the one next to him.

"So, you found the family tree," exclaimed his mother coming around the corner.

"I was trying to figure out who was who," he replied.

"Well, here on the far left is your Grandfather Julian, and next to him is your Grandmother Isabella. In the middle here are your great grandparents, Frederick and Maria," she pointed out.

"But who's this? I feel as if I should know him," asked Bryan.

"This is *Captain Maximo Camino*, your great-great-grandfather who settled here more than two hundred years ago," she revealed.

"So that's where the name of the ranch came from," realized Bryan.

"That's correct," she affirmed.

"But what about his wife?" he further asked.

"There is really nothing known about her," was the vague explanation after an ominous pause.

"Huh," responded Bryan, surprised.

"Let's go out on the patio for a bit," his mother coaxed.

While this discussion was going on, Rosa was busy straightening up a few things around the front room and couldn't but help overhear their conversation. After Mrs. Anderson left the room, she approached.

"Señor Bryan, your mother is a good woman, but she not tell you the whole story, look in the basement, and you will see," she said in broken English.

He was about to ask her what she was talking about, but before he could get a word out she was gone.

This strange revelation kept haunting him the rest of that evening. Before retiring for the night, Bryan sat on the edge of the bed and contemplated how quiet it was here. He missed the whispering of the wind through the pines at night that would sing him asleep.

Next morning, Bryan heard hammering coming from the old fort next door. Investigating, he found the main gate open and a brown pickup truck with a roof rack parked near one of the buildings. Thinking that this might be the perfect opportunity to look around, Bryan walked up into the enclosure. The old adobe walls were severely cracked and weather stained. The grounds were overgrown with weeds. Drawing more closely, the hammering came from inside an open doorway.

Bryan stuck his head in the door and said "Hello."

A man of medium build with graying hair, turned to see Bryan standing in the doorway. He was dressed in blue jeans and a plain T-shirt.

"Hi, what can I help you with?" he asked, slipping his hammer back into his tool belt.

"I was wondering if it's possible to look around?" asked Bryan.

"Well, the fort has been closed for the last couple of months undergoing some repairs, but those are just about complete. It should be open again probably next week," he replied.

"I'm visiting my mom next door, I'll be gone next week," said Bryan.

"I'll tell you what, come over here and help me set this post and I'll give you a quick walk through," he offered.

"Sounds great," agreed Bryan.

"My name's, Bud," he said extending his hand.

"I'm Bryan."

"Just hold this post right up against the beam right there where I have the X marked in pencil," he pointed.

Bud went out and brought in a stepladder, and with a short-handled sledge hammer, mounted the ladder and beat the post into position. Grabbing a couple of nails out of his pouch, he toenailed them into the top of the post to secure it to the beam.

"That oughta hold it," said Bud, stepping down off the ladder. "Okay, Bryan, let's have a quick look around," he said removing his tool belt.

"I understand that this is where they found the old Spanish map and some other papers not too long ago," stated Bryan trying to get some kind of verification on that, as they stepped outside.

"Yeah, now that you mention it there were some papers of some kind found in one of the back rooms. They were given to the University to investigate as I recall. Say, your mother must have told you about that," replied Bud.

"No, it was from a *Professor Burke*, that I heard about it," explained Bryan.

"Oh yes, I think you're right, he must have been the one who took the papers. You know the Professor then?" he asked.

"I met him when he was up in *Columbia* looking around," answered Bryan.

"Oh yeah? Huh," commented Bud.

Through an old weathered door they entered a narrow room, empty except for a couple of old wooden beds.

"This is one of the bunk houses, as you probably can see," said Bud.

Their feet echoed on the worn hardwood floor as they headed for the open doorway at the other end. The next room contained a couple of old tables and a number of matching chairs. Pots and pans hung on the wall adjacent to a set of sagging shelves, and a small wood cook stove sat in the front part of the room, dull and grey.

"This is the mess hall where the men ate when not out on patrol, and the kitchen was there," he pointed.

Proceeding out of a doorway left of the kitchen area, they went back outside. The adjacent building was fronted by a plank sidewalk and a roof overhang.

"This is where the Commanding Officer stayed, his office and quarters," said Bud opening another door.

The small room contained a desk and a couple of wooden chairs. Its walls were covered with old yellowed maps and pictures, now covered by protective clear plastic sheets.

"Right through here, was his private quarters," continued Bud, stepping through a doorway into a back room that was completely empty.

Bryan tried to imagine the room as it would have been.

"In the next room is where they found the papers you asked about," his tour guide announced.

Opening another door at the far right end, they entered a very similar room with the exception that there were no other doors leading into the room. Bryan knew Josh would be bugging him with questions, so he realized that he would have to be very observant and take good mental notes. One arched window was centered in the room, looking east toward the El Rancho next door.

"The papers and a map were found right here," he pointed. "Just below the window in the wall."

"What led to the discovery?" questioned Bryan.

"The wall was weak in that area and needed repairs, and I guess, Cleve, who was in the process of breaking away some of the loose plaster made the discovery," answered Bud. "Matter of fact this whole room was a mess, even the floor was cut in places and had severe dry rot."

"Hmm," subconsciously answered Bryan still thinking about the wall.

Bryan ran his hand over the wall just above the window. "You didn't do any repair or patching above the window did you?" asked Bryan.

"No, not in recent time, but the way it looks someone may have given the whole room a plaster coat or white wash many years ago," he answered. "Say, I've got to turn the water off on some plants. Look around, I'll be right back."

"I'll be right here," replied Bryan.

There seemed to be depressions in the wall above the window filled in with plaster or some kind of filler. Picking out a small piece of the plaster with the edge of his fingernail there appeared to be a groove in the original wall.

The other vague depressions must also have the same groove, thought Bryan.

Backing up and moving to the right to catch the light, the significance of what he saw hit him. Almost breathless he backed against the wall.

"No way, it can only be a similarity," he told himself.

"Seen enough in here?" asked Bud booming back into the room.

"Yeah, I think so," slowly responded Bryan. He glanced one last time at the arched window before passing back into the next room. The rest of Bud's tour seemed to just blur by. His mind was still bogged down with puzzlement at what he had seen. There were other similarly arched windows scattered through out the various other buildings, but none had the same grooved pattern emanating from the arched opening.

After thanking Bud for his whirlwind tour, Bryan headed back to the ranch. Walking along the fence behind the main ranch house, he stopped across from the arched window in the east wall of the fort, to ponder what he had seen. The window was interestingly located directly opposite the ranch house.

It has to be true, that is where the map was found, he reasoned to himself. The *'Door of the Sun'* symbol has risen again! And the grooves in the wall are evidently the rays of the sun. Additionally, the map was found in the position of the unknown pointed object projecting below the base line of the semicircle, which in this case is the bottom of the arched window. Therefore the window itself is the sun, the source of light, looking eastwardly toward the sunrising. Wow! Whoever set up this ingenious scenario must have been a very intelligent person. Because the map was hidden in the Commanding Officer's extra room, did it mean that he was the one behind all of this, or at least a party to it? There had to be a degree of truth to this, he thought to himself. Research could reveal who the Commanding Officers were, but which one was involved? No way to tell.

Walking over to the horse barn, Gus was in the process of reshoeing a horse. This reminded him of his dad. How was he doing? What were Josh and Tammy up to? Was he beginning to get home sick? Maybe. The lives of his mother and father were so far apart, but yet in some ways alike.

"Rosa! Rosa!" called Mrs. Anderson from somewhere in the house.

She had been working all morning on a painting that had to be finished that day. Bryan stepped into the house to see what was happening.

"Oh, Bryan, I've got to go on a quick trip to the City on business, would you like to come?" she asked.

"To the City? No, I think I'll pass," he answered.

"Tell you what, to make up for my absence today, let's make that ride up on the bluffs this evening and watch the sunset," she suggested.

"Yes, I would like that," replied Bryan.

"Good," was her comment as she zipped up her purse.

After helping to load three paintings in the car, Bryan waved to her as she headed down the driveway.

Turning around he got a glimpse of Rosa in the window. A split second later she was gone. What is it that she knows anyway? She seems so mysterious, pondered Bryan. Walking back through the house, Rosa was nowhere to be found.

The basement, thought Bryan. Something in the basement she said. What could it be?

Since the metal exterior doors of the basement were rusted shut, he found the stairwell inside the house that led down into its dark environs. Clicking on the light, he descended into the shadowy world below. The first thing to come into view were old trunks lined up on the floor. Shelves along the walls contained fruit jars, wine bottles, and various other dust covered containers. Old tools were laid out on a table. It appeared that these rusty relics had not been used in forty years. Toward the back of the basement he found stored furniture. Hanging in the corner were empty ornate picture frames, and leaning against the back wall were old paintings.

It wasn't obvious what Rosa was talking about. Maybe there was something in the old trunks, thought Bryan, walking back to them. The old trunks were covered with cob webs and a thick layer of dust. Bryan slowly raised the lid on the first trunk. It was hard to see anything in the dim light, but he could distinguish clothing. Lifting them up into brighter light, he could see they were very formal of a time forgotten. Bryan could almost imagine the scene, Spanish music playing and dancers whirling about under soft lights. Those days are gone. What a shame, he thought, putting the clothing back and closing the lid. Checking the other trunks, similar items were found, but nothing that could tell a story.

The other possibility was the old paintings that had been leaned up against the back wall. Most of the paintings were fairly large. Turning them around one by one to face the light, Bryan found most of these to be scenic landscapes or seascapes. Before turning the last picture around, he noticed the frame appeared to be similar to the ones upstairs. Bringing it around to the light, the golden hand carved frame showed signs of being burned. The canvas was so badly coated with dust that it was too dark to see what was there. Bryan coughed after blowing the dust off. It was the face of a woman, a beautiful woman, her hair and dress indicated that she was an Indian. Who was she? The painting was old, very old. Why was the frame partially burnt? Could this be what Rosa alluded to? he pondered.

Placing the pictures back as he found them, he glanced around the room one last time before ascending the stairs. He made it a point in his own mind, that he would not open up this sensitive issue with his mother, until after further research.

Later that evening, up the trail they rode to the top of the coastal bluffs to wait for the sunset. A mild sea breeze accompanied the waves ashore. A ship as a mere dot could be seen far out on the glistening water. Finding a comfortable spot to sit as they waited for the show to start, Bryan's mother had waited for this opportune time to talk with her son.

"Bryan, I've been meaning to talk to you about something important," she began.

"About what?" he asked.

"About the future. After your grandmother passed away, the ranch became mine and I'm not going to be here forever either. Someday all this will be yours. What do you think about that?" she asked.

"I don't know what to say," he slowly responded. "This place has never been a part of my life."

"It can be, if you come down and live here," she added.

"I don't know if I could do that. I love the mountains and can't imagine being anywhere else," he answered back.

"You're like your great-great-grandfather. It's said he loved the mountains too, but that's what killed him in the end," she commented.

"What happened to him?" Bryan asked.

"Well, he apparently had a lot of irons in the fire. There was a lot of political intrigue at the time. He spent a lot of time in the mountains for what reason I don't know. It's all unclear now, but on one of trips up into the Sierra, he never returned," she revealed. "It's just, I don't want you to have the same fate. There are better things here for you."

"But what about dad, you married him and his whole life almost totally revolves around the mountains?" he pointed out.

"I guess that's the blind side of love," she answered. "But don't take me wrong, I like the mountains to a degree, but I only see futility bound up in their midst."

"I don't feel that way, they make me feel buoyant, I feel drawn to them like there's something waiting there for me. They're almost at times part of my heart and soul it seems."

"You definitely take after your grandfather on that account. But what's to become of the once mighty empire of the El Rancho de Camino? Apparently it will vanish into history," she sadly concluded.

"Mom, no. That is not the way it has to be. Please give us another chance, we can fill both shoes," said Bryan reaching deep down to express himself.

His mother wiped away a couple of tears and put her arm around him and gave him a hug.

"Look, the sun is dipping into the sea," she pointed.

The reflection of the orange ball glistened across the expanse of the ocean. Low clouds along the horizon began to change color. Soon rays issued up through them as the sunset deepened.

The scene now burst into full significance, because there before him the *'Door of the Sun'* again appeared. Could someone who stood in this very place centuries ago, seeing the same scene, have copied this glorious sight as a symbol of their bold endeavor? He explored this thought in his mind, and concluded that's what had probably happened. But was the sun setting or rising? Here it is setting, at the end of its journey through the sky. But what about the 'Door of the Sun,' could it be a sunrise, the beginning of a journey? It was an interesting thought to explore, he pondered.

As the sun slid below the horizon, colors in the sky and in a low band of clouds changed from a pink to a piercing red and finally to graduating shades of purple.

It was now four days later, and Bryan was on the bus headed back home. There was much to contemplate, such as his relationship with his mother. He now understood her feelings on many things including his father. And one thing was for sure, they definitely had become closer. But she still felt compelled to pursue what she believed to be her obligation. Though, he could sense down deep she wanted the family to be together.

More Than Legend

There was one thing that was still unsettling, who was the woman in the picture he had found in the basement and why was the frame burnt?

As the mountains drew closer, his thoughts refocused on the surprises he had to share with Josh and Tammy, but still there were no strong clues for them to follow up.

Maybe it was time to forget the 'mystery' and enjoy the rest of the summer. As the bus turned, the mountains loomed upward and Bryan reasoned to himself that the mountains and the 'mystery' would be there an eternity, why hurry the pursuit?

10

REVERSE IMAGE

W alking home from the bus stop in town, everything seemed so quiet. Only Graffiti was there to greet him. It was already late in the evening. The sun had descended behind the mountains and the light of day had begun to grow dim. Finding the door locked, he dug the key out of his bag and unlocked it.

His father knew he would be back that day. A note should be waiting for him on the table and sure enough, there it was. It was dated that very day. As usual his dad was of little words. He left that morning on an unscheduled pack trip taking a team of scientists to Iceberg Lake. It would be a six-day round trip. Iceberg Lake was an unusual destination, it was one of the highest lakes above the timber line. Finally the note mentioned, chores and then a hearty, "Welcome home."

"Six days! My goodness," exclaimed Bryan.

After unpacking, Bryan heard the call of hunger coming on strong.

"Guess I'll be baching it for a few days," he said peering into the refrigerator. "Ground beef and a salad, sounds good to me," he added reaching for the meat.

Unrolling the butcher paper, he removed a good helping of meat and returned the remainder to the refrigerator. Taking a head of lettuce, he set it in a large wooden bowl just as a loud knock at the front door resounded. A little startled from his preoccupation by the sudden knock, he opened the front door.

"Hi Buddy! Welcome home," boomed Josh.

Tammy who was standing behind him also said "Hi," with a little wiggle of her hand.

"Josh, Tammy, how did you sneak in here without me hearing you? Generally I can hear you coming three counties away," questioned Bryan glimpsing the Jeep in the yard.

"I finally got around to adjusting the timing and did a bit of tuning," answered Josh as they stepped inside.

"I was about to fire up the stove to fix something to eat, are you two hungry?" Bryan asked.

"Thanks for the offer, but we ate a little while ago," answered Josh. "We were going to meet you at the bus stop, but we couldn't get away in time."

"I have some things to tell you," announced Bryan placing the meat in the frying pan and turning the gas on, "but I'm having trouble in believing it myself."

"There was some excitement here too, while you were gone," replied Josh finding a chair to sit in.

"Yeah, there was a shooting up in the canyon," jumped in Tammy.

"Shooting?" questioned Bryan.

"Yes, and it was up on the North Fork to boot," answered Josh.

"Who was it? Anyone hurt?" followed up Bryan.

"Well, that's the strange thing, the word around town is that the man who was shot refused to give his name. He evidently just had a flesh wound, and abruptly disappeared," said Josh.

"I guess, he even refused to say whether or not he'd seen the culprit; evidently he acted really strange," added Tammy.

"Hmm. It appears that the North Fork has become a busy place," Bryan commented as he switched on a couple of lights around the room. He recalled to mind, the shooting that he had heard, and the blood he had seen on the roadway some three weeks before.

"It appears that the same clues that we followed have ultimately led others up there too," concluded Tammy.

"Seems that way doesn't it. Ah!" yelled Bryan as the meat started cooking too fast, spitting grease out of the pan.

"Here, give me that spatula. Some cook you are," said Tammy grabbing it out of his hand.

"Okay! Okay! Guess I'm not cut out to be a cook," chuckled Bryan. "Now, listen to this," he said turning a chair around backwards and sitting on it.

Bryan began relating about his tour through the old fort. And then concerning the location in the back room where the Spanish map had been discovered, and the grooves above the arched window. Josh and Tammy were both stunned as he revealed what appeared to him to be the real significance of the window and its associated markings.

But as he started to relate about the sunset, Tammy jumped back from the stove with a scream, as a flame leaped up from the burner. Bryan ducked low and reached over and clicked off the gas, and then grabbing a pot holder, slid the frying pan off the burner. Everyone was coughing as smoke filled the room. The fire quickly went out. Waving the smoke away Bryan looked in the pan.

"Oh no, my dinner! I guess it was never meant to be," complained Bryan.

"Ha ha ha," laughed Josh.

Bryan gave Tammy a sharp look.

"Don't look at me, it's that stupid stove," coughed Tammy.

"Oh-h-h yeah," commented Bryan as he shoved the pan to the back of the stove.

Suddenly, Graffiti started barking wildly, somewhere back by the barn. The three froze and listened.

"Stay put, somebody is lurking around," said Bryan as he slipped out through the screen door and silently disappeared into the darkness. After what seemed to be an eternity, they heard Graffiti running and barking around the back of the house and into the woods beyond. In a short time he was back, apparently not finding anyone. Bryan finally came back in with a concerned look on his face.

"Somebody was definitely out there, but they're gone now," he announced.

"I wonder if they over heard anything you may have said about the Fort and the 'Door of the Sun?' " questioned Josh.

"I don't know, Graffiti didn't let them get very close, but with the door wide open, our voices could have carried pretty far," Bryan replied.

"Something that's been kind of bothering me, is the place where we've been hiding our only map. What if someone sees us up there, it could be a tip off," spoke up Tammy.

"With someone nosing around, it makes me a little leery too," added Josh.

"You're both right," agreed Bryan. "Let's go retrieve the map, and make two more copies tonight."

Everyone agreed with that motion.

"Josh, I'll grab a flashlight, and if I can twist your arm I would like you to come out and help," requested Bryan.

"Isn't there a light out there?" asked Tammy.

"No there isn't, this is out in the wild boonies remember?" replied Bryan as he tried the flashlight to see if it worked.

"We'll be right back," Josh told Tammy.

"You better be," she said peeking out the door after them.

Graffiti approached the boys as they crossed the yard, probably wondering what they were up to. It wasn't long before they had accomplished their mission and returned.

"I tell you what, I'll find a couple pieces of paper and you two can begin tracing the map. Frankly, I'm starved. I'm going to try one more time to cook something here," announced Bryan following Josh back into the house.

"I hope you have the phone number for the fire department handy," teased Josh easing the tense atmosphere a bit.

Bryan noticed Tammy looking intently at the pictures on the walls and then at some of the books in the bookcase.

"Find anything interesting?" asked Bryan.

"Well, so to speak I guess. They say you can tell a lot about a person or persons by their possessions. It's an interesting comparison with me and my mom who live together also."

"Your dad is not living with you, I take it."

"No, not anymore," she affirmed.

While Josh laid out the map on the table, Bryan located a couple of sheets of paper, and Tammy found the switch for the light over the table. It fell suddenly quiet as the map tracing began, and Bryan went about fixing a salad and attempting to cook another piece of meat.

"My dad is on a trip up to Iceberg Lake, and he won't be back for another five days," informed Bryan plunking down in a chair next to the table, waiting as the food cooked.

"Sounds like a very cold place," commented Tammy without looking up.

"It is, the snow barely melts off even in August. It's up above eleven thousand feet and very remote," answered Bryan.

"I'm still amazed how you went to visit your mother, and right next door waiting for you was the Fort," stated Josh.

"It must be just coincidence," answered Bryan. "Nevertheless, the added information might not help us at this end to find the illusive 'Door of the Sun' anyway." Bryan jumped back up to check the meat and set the table. "Finally it's done," he proclaimed sitting down to eat.

After a couple of minutes Tammy declared that the first copy was done as she held it up. Bryan had a mouth full of food, when suddenly he dropped his fork onto the plate with a loud clang. Josh and Tammy looked at Bryan to see what had happened.

"What's wrong?" asked Tammy. "You choking?"

Bryan couldn't talk with his mouth full but he pointed at the map. Josh and Tammy looked at each other. Finally he swallowed the food and could answer. "The map! Look! Hold it up again, Tammy," spurted out Bryan. "The mountains fall into place," he said pointing through the back of the map.

"You mean the map is reversed?" guessed Josh.

"It must be, come around here and look. Here, let me hold it, your arms must be getting tired, Tammy. Better yet, let's do this," excitedly spoke Bryan. He stepped over to a tall lamp and set it on the floor and placed the map upside down across the top of the shade. "Okay, now look, before the paper gets too hot," directed Bryan.

"Eagle Peaks, here," said Josh moving his finger across the paper. "And this could be the Three Chimneys toward the east."

Bryan took the map and waved it in the air to cool it and put it back on the lamp. "Yes, and northeasterly a short distance is East Flange Rock. It would seem that we have a match," concluded Bryan.

"You know what this means?" asked Josh.

"Yeah, we've been barking up the wrong tree," answered Tammy.

"That's right, the South Fork is where we should have been looking all along," declared Josh.

Putting the map back on the table, they reseated themselves in silence for a few seconds, as it all sank in.

"The original map that the Professor had, was sewn onto a leather backing, so there was no way for a person holding it to see through the back. So only those who knew the secret could properly decipher the map," concluded Bryan.

"The Spanish phrases, the writing, was written in forward hand or correctly, but the map portion must have been cleverly drawn in reverse," also realized Tammy.

"Ha!" exclaimed Josh. "The others are all at each others throat, searching the North Fork, while it's actually at the other extreme. How clever this reversal."

"Maybe not clever enough, the 'Legend' indicates something happened to them or their operations," commented Bryan as he picked up the map again.

"While everyone is busy searching the North Fork, that should leave the coast clear for us to pursue the search on the South Fork," said Tammy.

"There is still an element of danger. The recent shooting points to the fact that these men are desperate and they have run out of clues. My guess is they'll be watching," pointed out Josh.

"Imagine, about an hour ago, we didn't have any clues. Personally, I was going to shelve the whole idea and go swimming or something," recalled Bryan.

"I thought you were starved, Bryan, you didn't finish your dinner that you've been yowling about," Tammy jokingly pointed out.

"I am, but this discovery temporarily disconnected my stomach so to speak," chuckled Bryan while he continued looking at the map.

"Josh, remember this peak right here in the center of the map, the one that everything seems to be tied to?" he asked.

"Yeah," responded Josh after getting up to peer over Bryan's shoulder.

"Now that we have pretty well figured out what area this map covers, I figure this must be the *Obelisk*," announced Bryan.

"The Obelisk? Isn't that the same peak that we saw from just below the Forks?" Tammy asked.

"Yes, we certainly did," confirmed Josh.

"From what I remember, the shape of the Obelisk is not quite the same as it's shown here," argued Tammy.

Bryan just shook his head as he thought about it. "That's true, but the shape of the Obelisk does change depending on your angle of view," he contemplated.

"No matter what peak it is, we still have the main clues, the primary route and the other clues further up the trail," stated Josh.

"True enough," agreed Bryan, still staring at the map.

"Josh, we better get home, it's getting late," reminded Tammy.

"Yeah, time flies when you're having fun," acknowledged Josh. "Oh that's right, you're going to be here all by yourself tonight."

"Hey, don't fret, I'm used to it," Bryan replied laying the map down.

Tammy knew what it was like to be alone, and wanted to say something, but the words would not come out. It was hard for her to reveal her softer side.

Josh with a smirk on his face, stopped, and turned before reaching the door. "What is it with you? The moment you get home, all heck breaks loose."

Tammy smiled at Bryan in silent comment to her cousin's statement.

"We'll see you tomorrow and make plans then," said Josh as they headed out the door and said their goodbyes.

That night, Bryan tried to sleep, but his mind kept working. It wasn't until late that he finally slid off into dream land. He awoke the next morning with the realization that there was something he was supposed to remember. What was it? After getting dressed he went into the kitchen to see about breakfast. Finally, it came back to him in flashes. He had imagined again, the Spanish explorer venturing up the canyon, stopping and extending his right arm to the mountains.

"Riverhawk! That's it!" spurted out Bryan. What was it that grandfather's Indian friend told him? "Do not let your right hand lead you into the mountains," he recited to himself. It's obviously a warning, but in this case it's a reinforcing clue. But wait, let's think about this. The right-handed side would correspond with the South Fork when facing east. But would that also mean that as the stream continued to branch that the right side would be followed each and every time? It must, he concluded.

Again the fire of the pursuit was in him. He had to gather supplies and formulate a plan. But again, the thought of hidden eyes watching and trailing them tempered that exuberance into a realization that they would have to conduct themselves primarily in secret operations.

Since Josh and Tammy probably wouldn't be over until later, he had a chance to do a few things. Pouring a bowl of cereal, he sat down to run through the list of chores on the back of his dad's note. One of those was a reminder to check on his grandfather a couple of times during the week. This was a good time to quiz him further on anything that this Riverhawk may have told him. After finishing the outside chores, he thought he would go into town and do just that, and stop at the library on the way back.

After feeding Graffiti, he was off to town by himself. There was very little traffic in town, only two pickups were parked in front of the hardware store. Even Placer St. was unusually quiet. So it was, life on a typical day in a sleepy gold rush town.

Banging on his grandfather's door, it finally opened, but Mr. Anderson hesitated in recognizing him. "It's me, Bryan."

"Bryan?" he questioned. "Oh, yeah," he finally responded.

"I came by to see how you were doing, Grandpa," said Bryan following him into the front room.

"Same as always," he answered sitting down.

Bryan proceeded to relate a little bit about his trip to visit his mother.

"That's one thing that riles me good, a woman should know exactly where her place is, and if she doesn't she should be shown," grumbled Mr. Anderson.

Glancing off that striking comment Bryan detoured to a question.

"Oh, three or four weeks ago, you were telling us about an Indian friend of yours, named Riverhawk," began Bryan.

"Riverhawk! Who's that? I never knew anyone by that name," he fired back.

"Are you sure? He was the one that told you 'not to let your right hand lead you into the mountains,' remember?"

"No, I don't remember any such foolishness," his grandfather finalized.

"Huh," replied Bryan.

His grandfather was having one of his memory jogs. Some days his stories were so vivid that you could just about step right into the scene, and other times he couldn't remember anything about it. After a pause, his grandfather glanced over at the picture sitting on the mantle.

"Where was that fishing picture taken?" Bryan asked.

"It was taken on the South Fork, many many years ago. Both Bob Miles and Charley Connley are dead now. It's a heck of a note, when you want to see your friends, you have to visit the cemetery," his grandfather stated.

Bryan got up to look more closely at the grainy picture, particularly the peaks in the background. It appeared to him that one of them was the Obelisk, turned slightly, tending toward the shape shown on the map.

"Do you have any chores to be done or groceries to pick up today?" inquired Bryan bringing him back out of the past.

"There's a list on the table, and the garbage can needs taken out front. If there's one thing in life you learn, you can't escape garbage," he said in a matter of fact tone.

"Yeah, I guess so," laughed Bryan.

Leaving his grandfather's, he continued on to the library. It was a contemporary building, painted light brown with lap siding and numerous windows. Coming in, the glass door rattled as he opened it. The interior was small but neatly arranged. In the back, a couple of elderly men sat quietly reading the daily newspaper. Mrs. Stone, the librarian, busily typing, glanced up to say hello as her fingers flew across the keys. She asked about his mother, having heard that he went down for a visit. Leaning on the counter he quietly related the desired news.

Afterwards, he searched the bookshelves and found three books that covered archeology and the historic past. Sitting at a vacant table he leafed through the books, but couldn't find anything that even remotely looked like the 'Door of the Sun.' He knew somewhere he had seen it before, but it remained an illusive recollection.

Closing the last book, Bryan couldn't help but wonder what his grandfather was thinking when he glanced over at the photograph on the mantle. Was there something faint and distant that reminded him of that trip to the South Fork, many years before? Maybe, but it may have been too long ago for him to recall.

Putting the books back, he headed down the street toward the grocery store to pick up the items on his grandfather's list. His footsteps echoed on the plank sidewalk as he neared the store. Suddenly, a man wearing a cowboy hat came out of the store and stopped. It was Mr. Krasnik, dressed in jeans and a white long sleeved shirt. He looked in his direction.

"Mr. Krasnik!" called Bryan waving his arm.

Just as suddenly as he appeared, he disappeared around the opposite corner of the brick structure. Reaching the same corner, Bryan glanced down the side street, but he was nowhere to be seen.

"Huh," responded Bryan. "What was that all about?" he thought to himself.

As he pushed open the door, it struck him that he exhibited the same strange behavior at school. Ever since that day, he had been trying to avoid him. Why? A flash of memory of Mr. Krasnik standing there talking to him about his school project, recalled to mind the bandage on his forehead.

As the door jingled and closed behind him, he lost his train of thought as he was now confronted with the task of finding the items on the grocery list. Grabbing a hand basket, he zigzagged through the short but densely packed isles and soon returned to the front counter.

"Say, Mr. Ferguson what happened to the old fishing map?" asked Bryan, pointing over along the wall.

"Map? It's gone! If that doesn't beat all. It was there this morning. I'm almost sure it was. It's been there for so long, I guess I haven't paid much attention to it. That's strange, who would want that old map anyway?" rambled on Mr. Ferguson.

"That was almost an antique."

"It sure was, I put it up there when I opened up for business back in forty-four. How strange."

Heading out the door, Bryan pretty well knew why someone would be interested in that old map, but it would be more than what Mr. Ferguson could swallow.

Crossing the street on a diagonal, he headed back to his grandfather's house, but in doing so he had a funny feeling that he was being watched. Out of the corner of his eye there appeared for a split second a dark figure. Who could it be? Rounding the corner, he spotted the narrow alley between the old firehouse and Mr. Motley's garage.

Yes! he thought, perfect.

Hurrying, he ducked into the alley and backed down into its dark domain and waited. Who would it be? He could feel his heartbeating. In absolute silence a tall figure of a man passed by. Bryan knew all too well who it was, with his long black hair and long overcoat. It was Dark Shadow, ever present, ever watching. But why was he on his tail? Down deep he knew. His resolve was fired up to follow this thing out. It was even stronger now, this urge that kept calling him.

Dropping off the groceries, he hurried home. There was daylight a burnin'.

11

SHADOW ON THE TRAIL

Their next move dictated a different tact and some new strategy. One thing was for sure, they had to act before his father returned with the pack train. Things would be really hopping around there once he arrived.

"Oh no, that's right," Bryan remembered as he walked up the driveway. "The ditch! That pain-in-the-neck ditch." It was on his dad's list. Located behind the house, it ran along the base of the hill for several hundred feet. Years in the past, heavy thunderstorms would cause flooding all along the north side of the house. Every year it was now a scheduled maintenance assignment.

Since Josh wasn't there yet, he thought it would be good if he at least got started on the job. After unhooking Graffiti and letting him run free, Bryan headed for the barn to find a pick and shovel. Toting the tools over his shoulder, he circled around behind the barn to walk to the far end of the ditch. He heard the drone of bees buzzing in the old apple orchard as he passed by. Tossing the tools down at the end of the ditch, he removed his shirt, as it was already getting fairly warm. Grabbing the shovel, he began scooping out the earth and rock that had rolled down into the ditch. Pausing to rest after about ten minutes, Bryan noticed what appeared to be a footprint in the soft dirt on a slight rise beside the ditch. Peering closer, it proved to be true. It was a good sized print, shaped in such a way that the person must have been wearing a soft soled shoe. Bryan immediately thought of the prowler from the other night.

"Bryan! Where are you?" called a voice from near the house. It was Josh.

"Over here!" Bryan yelled back waving his arm. "Josh, it's about time. I thought banker's hours were appalling," he complained, straightening up.

"Well, this banker has been cashed out," Josh fired back.

"Cashed out?"

"Somebody did a number to the tires on my Jeep last night, they were slashed."

Bryan's face clouded as he heard this. "Things are getting serious. It must be a warning." He next related to Josh the strange events that had transpired in town that morning, and to think this all had to do with the quest for the 'Canyon of Gold.'

"Well, one thing is for sure, we can't use my Jeep anymore for transportation."

"We can use my dad's pickup, if we have to."

"Are you sure?"

"No, but we can't stop now, this thing has got me all fired up."

"Wait till I catch up with that slasher, whoever it is owes me four tires, and compensation for a whole bunch of misery."

"Say, where's Tammy?"

"She and my mom went down into the valley on a shopping spree and are going to stay overnight with my Aunt Millie."

"Shopping, that's disgusting."

"Hey, don't knock it, it got them out of the house for a couple of days."

"Oh, by the way Josh, I just noticed a strange looking footprint over here," pointed Bryan.

"Huh, no distinct pattern," commented Josh bending over to get a good look.

"I don't think we better waste anymore time. My dad is gone for a few days, and your mom and cousin won't be home for another day. That gives us a perfect opportunity to do something a little different."

"Different?"

Before answering, Bryan glanced around. "Yeah, because there are so many eyes watching everything that moves, I suggest that we slip out during the night and access the trail when no one should be able to detect our movement."

"Hmm. The moon hasn't been coming up till real late at night, so if we did leave early enough, I guess that could work. But there's one glaring problem. Really no matter what time we drive up to the trail head we'll be noticed. During the quiet of the night they'll hear a vehicle and see the headlights heading up that way."

"That's true," realized Bryan sitting down on the edge of the ditch. "I know, we can have someone drop us off and go from there."

"But who?"

"Well, Jack owes me a favor, maybe he can do it."

"Okay, if you're serious about this, I guess I better run on home and gather a few things."

"If you find a flashlight bring that too. We'll sack out tonight till its time."

"I'll be back later this afternoon," said Josh turning toward the road to head home.

"Hey, some adventure, huh?" Bryan called after him.

Josh smiled. "If we live to tell about it."

After Josh left, Bryan settled back to the task at hand. Why did the ditch all of a sudden look so much longer? Frustrated anticipation must be it, he thought. Fiercely attacking the ditch, Bryan quickly realized that this wasn't going to work, he had to pace himself. Just the same, perseverance yielded some painful blisters. Hurting but victorious, Bryan finally reached the upper end of the ditch. Returning the tools to the barn, he was ready for a shower and a late lunch. Graffiti, standing by the back porch wagged his tail, but due to the pain in his hands Bryan refrained from petting him.

After cleaning up and taking care of necessities, Bryan made a couple of phone calls. Jack Carter he found out was out of town for a couple of days. Who else could he call?

"I know, Ben Murphy."

Ben worked down at the Miner's Shack, a hole-in-the-wall cafe in town. It so happened that he lived on the back road leading to Twain Harte.

"Perfect," responded Bryan after putting the receiver down. Ben would pick them up after work, between ten thirty and eleven that night.

His thoughts now turned to organizing his pack and finishing a few loose ends.

Glancing out the kitchen window, large white cumulus clouds, "castles in the sky," loomed up over the Sierras, their billowing masses forming into large anvils. Thunderheads were a firefighter's worst nightmare. But called by others, "the god of overtime," that is by those that were looking to pick up a little extra money on the fire line. A change of weather definitely appeared to be in the works.

The house seemed oddly quiet, somewhat ominous. Maybe just the knowledge that his dad would be gone for a few days made it even more obvious. How long did it take for him to get over the absence of his mother? Awhile, that was for sure.

Turning to pick up the trash can, Bryan noticed a torn letter or something in the bottom. Whatever it was his dad must have thrown it in there before he left. Unfolding and holding the halves together, the letter head jumped at him. It was from White Pines Timber & Mining Co., and addressed to his father. Reading down the page it was apparent that they were offering him a sum of money for the property. The letter was written quite direct, making the point that if he failed to sell it to the timber company before it was sold off for back taxes, his dad would get nothing. It was their intention to acquire that property one way or another. He had thirty days to respond and that was final.

Bryan sighed as he threw the letter back in the trash. How could they save their place? What could he do? A job wouldn't pull in enough money to pay the hundreds of dollars they were behind. Maybe his mom could help. He knew his dad wouldn't ask for help. Something had to be done and soon.

"I have to find this, 'Canyon of Gold,' it has to be real," he exclaimed to an empty house.

Later that afternoon, Josh finally came back, carrying his pack and a few other items.

"Why the long face?" inquired Josh.

"I found a letter in the trash from White Pines, they're threatening again. Truth is, we may lose the place no matter what."

"Not if we hit the big one," encouraged Josh.

Suddenly a strong wind filled the trees. "Strong afternoon breeze," commented Bryan glancing outside.

"Did you notice those thunder boomers building up?"

"Yeah, they should diminish this evening."

"On the way over here I was mulling over our plan for this evening, and there is one thing that sticks in my craw."

"What's that?"

"The part about a night drop seems like a good strategy, but if we hike the river trail there's a good chance we could still be easily spotted."

"That's a good point, I haven't checked the maps to see if there are any other alternate routes in that direction."

"Oh, not to change the subject, but did you get hold of Jack?"

"No, Jack is not available, but I did get hold of Ben, down at the Miner's Shack. He'll pick us up after he gets off work between ten thirty and eleven," said Bryan pulling a map out of the bookcase. "This old Forest Service map is fairly good, it shows a lot of the terrain."

Laying the map out on the table, their eyes followed up the Stanislaus River and along the South Fork into the rugged maze of peaks and valleys.

"Huh, Skull Creek, it's the first fork to the right. I've seen it on maps before, but never thought about the significance of its name."

"You wouldn't want to lose your head up there," joked Josh.

"Remember the bones that had been found? I wonder if there is any obvious connection?" recalled Bryan.

"Just think, the 'Canyon of Gold' is in one of these canyons right before our eyes," pointed out Josh.

"It would take twenty years to search this whole maze, but maybe with a few clues we can cut it way down," thought Bryan. Look here, notice how the road to American Camp parallels the South Fork for a distance, then veers away. And there's this drainage that drops off the ridge and swings on down to the South Fork, not far from the road."

"A short cut for sure," blurted out Josh.

"Well maybe, but look at the elevation change, a drop of about eight hundred feet."

"That's true, easy in, but a real puffer on the way back out. Nevertheless it still cuts off a lot of trail."

"I guess, the real beauty, Josh, as you pointed out earlier, it would be less visible to roving eyes. We'll completely bypass the Forks, where they will be watching."

"Really the best of both worlds."

"The only adjustment we need to make, is to have Ben drop us off another three miles further up the road," stated Bryan.

"Oh, by the way, I did find a flashlight."

"Good, because we're really going to need them both now."

"Besides being dark, we will have to feel our way down an unknown drainage," agreed Josh

"By gray dawn we should be well on our way up the South Fork."

"Sounds exciting, but it's going to be a long night."

The boys spent the rest of the afternoon making final preparations, and that evening they lounged around playing checkers and listening to the radio.

"Josh, I wish you would stop that infernal gum chewing."

"Hey, it's good stuff," he rebuffed.

Both of them kept watching the clock, but it moved ever so slowly. They were too anxious to relax.

Finally at about ten minutes to eleven, there was the sound of a vehicle and headlights on the road. An older pickup truck rumbled into the yard.

"It's about time!" spoke up Josh.

Securing the door, they grabbed their packs that were waiting for them on the front porch.

"Hi Ben, we really appreciate the lift," called out Bryan.

"No problem," Ben replied through the open window on the passenger side.

Ben Murphy was two or three years older than the two boys, had a beefy build, rounded features, and wavy black hair. Following in his father's footsteps, who was a Fire Captain on the Summit Ranger District, he was pursuing a degree in natural resources and fire suppression.

Throwing their gear in the bed of the truck, they stepped up to slide onto the front seat next to Ben.

"Oh, by the way Ben, instead of dropping us off at the bend, drop us off up on the ridge about two miles in, if that's not a problem," asked Bryan.

"What's up there? That's out in the middle of nowhere. Besides, it's pitch black out tonight. Okay, what are you guys up to?" questioned Ben while turning the pickup around.

Bryan looked at Josh.

"Ah, we're doing a study on owls. The darkness will help us to sneak into our observation post," barked out Josh.

"Owls? That's a hoot," laughed Ben.

"Their nocturnal habits may yield some beneficial data," added Bryan joining in with the charade.

"You couldn't get me to go running around the woods at night for some owls," he said pulling out into the roadway.

As Ben shifted the old '49 Ford up through the gears, the engine made a clicking sound as it revved up between shifts. The old pickup with its three speed column shift was the classic of its day. A faint musty smell was discernible from inside the cab of the old truck.

"It's best if you keep this under your hat, Ben. We don't want anybody to disturb our observation area, while the study is still on," requested Josh.

"Ha! I doubt if I could pay anybody to go looking for your owls. But one thing is for sure and I don't know why, there sure has been a lot of extra traffic running up and down this road the last couple of weeks. It's almost like there's another gold rush on or something."

Again the boys glanced at each other, but said nothing.

Passing the "bend," the ancient truck rattled across a cattle guard and climbed the switchback up to the top of the ridge. Flickering between the scattered pines, Bryan could see the lights of town below. How quiet and serene it all looked now, but yet he could sense the current that flowed hidden. Was this insanity? Were they really doing this?

Following along the ridge for a few minutes, the road soon took a subtle dip.

"This is it, Ben, anywhere along here," spoke up Bryan.

He brought the pickup to a screeching halt. "Are you sure?" asked Ben still a little mystified.

"Yep! this is it."

"Okay!"

Grabbing their packs out of the back, they thanked Ben again, after which he drove on leaving them alone in the dark with the stars twinkling above.

"Well, here we are, for better or for worse," announced Josh.

"Let me find my flashlight. Save yours for later."

"It's about ten minutes after eleven," said Josh after finding and clicking on his flashlight for a split second.

After slipping his pack on, Bryan flashed his light into the trees on the east side of the road. "Let's follow this depression down over the ridge and watch for a trail of some kind."

"You got the flashlight, you lead the way Captain."

"Yes sir! Ow! My hands still hurt," Bryan replied.

Meandering among the trees and bushes, the depression soon deepened into a drainage swale. Shadows of branches and leaves now took on fearsome aspects in the darkness.

"I hope we don't run into some of our furry friends out here tonight," voiced Josh in a loud whisper.

"Shh! Try not to crunch down so much brush, it's a dead giveaway."

"I'm trying not to, but I can barely make anything out. Hold the light a little further back if you can."

"Look, a deer path over to the right," pointed out Bryan, flashing the light around between the trees. A faint narrow trail could be made out, wandering out of the trees from a southwesterly direction and then paralleling the drainage swale.

"Hope it goes all the way down, so we don't have to do much more of this brush crashing."

"Time will tell."

Once on the faint path, the course was smoother except for an occasional cedar or fir limb that they had to dodge around. The rich scent of bear clover perfumed the air as they entered its forest domain. The deer trail soon met others that veered off into the woods, and would on occasion jog for no apparent reason, but would always return to the drainage swale. Further on, the descent became steeper and rockier.

"Let's stop and rest for a few minutes," suggested Bryan stopping to take a deep breath.

"It's after midnight," commented Josh as they sat down against a large fir.

After Bryan switched off the light, the darkness seemed to close in on them. The serenade of crickets seemed to add to the effect.

"Good gravy, is it ever dark out here. I can't even see my hand in front of my face," said Josh.

"Imagine yourself an Indian hunter, years ago, stalking around in this sheer blackness. They didn't have flashlights or any such thing, just a keen eye and a sensitive ear."

"Stories I have read, showed how they could walk in absolute silence as they approached their prey."

"Yeah, what a contrast. Here we come crashing down through the woods, crunching brush and flashing a light around."

"How far do you think we have come?" asked Josh.

"Oh, probably about a mile and a half, which should be about half way."

Suddenly, the two froze. There was a crash in the brush some distance away toward the southwest, downhill of their position. After a pause of silence, there was another explosion of noise echoing though the woods. They didn't move a muscle, the impenetrable darkness was claustrophobic, smothering them in suspense. Crack! The sound of dead branches and brush breaking, again echoed. After a few seconds it was apparent that the direction of the disturbance was moving northeasterly and not toward them.

About the time they began to relax, another sound quite different filled the air. Womp, womp, womp! It headed right for them. There was a flutter of wings and whatever it was landed in or by a tree about a hundred feet away.

"Wait a second," whispered Bryan.

A distant echo told them the disturbance was definitely moving away.

"Let's have a look," said Bryan.

Stepping out from under the tree in the general direction of the second noise, Bryan clicked on the light and flashed it on the trees while moving slowly to his right. Josh was right on his heels. A faint reflection caught their eye. Jerking the light back, it stopped on a singular figure perched on a large oak branch. Its head turned.

"It's an owl!" exclaimed Josh.

"Ha, ha, you got your owl study after all," laughed Bryan.

"But who or what did we hear roaming down below?"

"Good question. It could have been one of your furry friends, or something worse."

"It wasn't worried about making a lot of noise, that's for sure," commented Josh.

"We're not supposed to be here, nobody is supposed to be up here at this late hour to hear these things."

"The sound was moving in a southwest to a northeast direction. If a line was projected backwards where would it intersect?"

"Well, if I have my bearings right, it probably would come out somewhere around Crazy Joe's or maybe a little south of there," thought Bryan.

"Hmm, and going northeast would lead up into the high country, into the head waters."

"Whoever or whatever it was is gone now. We'd better be on our way, we have an appointment to keep."

"Yeah, but with whom and what?" rhetorically asked Josh.

"Let's try to walk as silent as we can this time," suggested Bryan adjusting his pack.

Picking up the trail again, the course wound its way among a series of large metamorphic dikes, which resembled giant spearheads. From there they dropped down a rugged hillside, and in the darkness, unable to see below, it felt as if they were journeying into a bottomless pit. After picking their way down the rocky slope and dropping about a hundred feet, the terrain again leveled out to a moderate incline covered with a thick carpet of scented bear clover. Other drainages now began to join the main swale, increasing the size of the small stream. The carpet of bear clover soon gave way to a small stand of densely growing pine and cedar trees.

"Must have been a fire come through here, look at all the seedlings—there all the same height," pointed out Josh.

"Wait!" exclaimed Bryan coming to an abrupt stop and aiming the flashlight to one side of the trail, then across to the other side.

"Broken branches!" realized Josh.

"That's what caught my eye first. But look, on the ground, beside the trees. Whata ya see?"

"The pine needles have been disturbed."

"Plain as day, isn't it? No prints though, but—nothing," said Bryan swinging the light from one side to the other side very slowly. "Maybe we're not dealing with an animal here."

"Possible clues we can look for are small remnants of fur caught in the broken branches."

"Good idea, but my flashlight has just about had it," said Bryan as the beam diminished to a yellow glow.

Josh pulled his light out and clicked it on but nothing happened.

"Shake it," suggested Bryan.

Finally the light flickered to life.

"Whew, we would have been up a creek without a flashlight," joked Josh.

"I don't think we better waste anymore time here. Let's get down the hill, before our one and only light goes out."

"Agreed, let's go."

From there the path wandered through the thicket of young trees for a thousand feet or more. Beyond, a mixed forest returned, carpeted with bear clover and spotted with oak and pine. The descent continued. Unseen gurgling springs issuing from a nearby rock strata, added even more volume to the small creek. Green plants lined the edge of the stream, and up along the banks were small spindly yellow flowers, that seemed almost colorless in the dim light. The relief of the land now began to fold, and the faint path soon descended into a small canyon, with the flow of gurgling water leading the way.

"I figure we only have about thirty minutes of light left. How much further do we still have to go?" asked Josh turning back to Bryan who was right behind him.

"I don't know, probably another mile and a quarter."

"We better pick up the pace."

"No telling when the moon will come up. You're right, we better go for it, noise or no noise."

It was easy to fall into a trot on the down hill slope, however sudden turns and gravelly sections at times caused them to slide.

Though unseen they could sense as they descended, the height of the canyon walls soaring above them. The glistening stars were bounded by a black invisible horizon. Their movement was so busy, it almost seemed that they were vying for a position in the eternal expanse. The rushing water had grown into a roar as the stream gradient increased. In spots there was barely room for the narrow path along the steep bank. Birds roosting for the night among the foliage were periodically flushed out. Down, down the small canyon plunged, until after some distance it finally became gentle.

A glow on the south horizon toward the southeast now became apparent.

"We must be getting close, the canyon is beginning to open up," spoke Bryan.

"None too soon, my flashlight is going fast."

After another five minutes, they had traversed the rocky, eroded drop off into the South Fork Canyon. That subtle glow over the ridge had now materialized into a nearly full rising moon. Seeing their breath in the pale light they now realized how much the temperature had dropped off.

Resting a short time by the edge of the river, they gloated on their success and paused to watch the shimmering moonlight reflecting off the water.

"The moonlight will now show us the way till gray dawn gets here in about three hours, but we have to watch our step wandering in and out of the dark shadows. About what time do you have, Josh?"

"Let me turn this watch around and see if I can read it. It looks to be about 2:10."

Feeling rested, they threw their packs back on and began slowly marching upstream along the South Fork, which skirted along the base of sheer volcanic cliffs that towered hundreds of feet above. The right side of the river canyon was mainly in dark shadow. Glancing ahead it appeared that the river canyon split. The course as it had been planned would be to take the right branch, Skull Creek.

Rounding the bluff, the moon again burst over the high intervening ridge, showering light onto the floor of the intersecting canyons. The large moon rested just above the volcanic ridge, like a clock sitting on a high mantle. The crude trail again dodged the light by veering into a niche in the wall.

Suddenly, Bryan stopped cold and extended his arm to stop Josh. There ahead of them, across the trail was a shadow. It appeared to be the distorted shape of a man, and it moved. Someone was walking above them.

"Over here," motioned Bryan as he ducked in behind a large rock. "This is no red goat this time," he whispered.

The shadow now moved beyond their immediate sight.

"Look!" pointed Josh after tapping Bryan on the shoulder.

Moving along the ridge, silhouetted against the full moon was the dark figure of a man carrying a rifle. His gait seemed to be a little unsteady.

"Whoever it is, looks like he has long hair," whispered Bryan.

The lone figure soon passed out of the light and stopped in front of a rocky dome that loomed up behind.

"He must have stopped in the shadow of the ridge," figured Josh.

"Looks like it. He hasn't come out on the other side yet."

After two minutes, there was no change.

"He definitely must be sitting up there watching," said Josh.

"How can we get by? There's no way to get around this bluff without being seen. It would be like stepping out onto a stage under a spotlight."

"I guess we'll have to wait. Let me take the first watch—you get some shut-eye."

"Okay, but don't hesitate to wake me if you see something," agreed Bryan snuggling in, using his pack as a pillow.

After a while Bryan jerked awake and looked around. It had already begun to get light. Josh was curled against the rock asleep.

"Josh, Josh!" called Bryan in a hushed tone.

"Huh?"

"How long have you been asleep?"

"I don't know. I was awake for about an hour and then I must have nodded off."

"Well, where is our mystery man now?"

"Hard to tell."

"Look! up on the ridge," pointed Bryan.

In the early morning sun, a slim figure could be seen standing, stretching, and then looking around.

"This guard is not going to let anybody pass. He has quite an observation post up there. Looks like we're stumped."

"Hmm, it appears so. Dang! Always something."

"I guess all we can do is retreat and regroup," said Josh looking back downstream.

"Yeah, let's go," agreed Bryan in a frustrated tone. "Keep against the wall in the shadows."

Ducking down, they skirted along the edge of the canyon wall, dodging behind large boulders that afforded them cover. In a short time they had made their way back to the small creek, from which they had descended earlier.

"The mystery deepens. Who is this person anyway? Is there more than one? And what do they know of the whole affair?" questioned Josh.

"Somebody must know something, or they wouldn't be keeping vigil around the clock over the South Fork."

"What if they have found the 'Canyon' and have been in the process of extracting the gold in secrecy all this time?" further theorized Josh.

"That has the ring of possibility, but to mobilize such an operation would take horses, mules and equipment. You would think that something like that would be noticed, even to a small degree."

"This is beginning to get tricky. We have two sets of eyes to evade now. One we successfully bypassed by coming down this drainage. But now, how do we get by this new obstacle?"

"Back to the drawing board as they say."

Climbing up into the trees, they found a level spot by the creek to stop, eat, and take a catnap before making the return trip. Scattered around the small sandy clearing were numerous ferns and tall spindly grasses that bowed from the weight of the morning dew.

"Far as I know this creek doesn't have a name," said Bryan looking in its direction.

"What shall we call it? How about Bypass Creek? No."

"That's not bad, but what about Midnight Creek?"

"Hmm. I like that, it has meaning," commented Josh.

"Midnight Creek," repeated Bryan.

"Being a pioneer could prove to be an interesting experience—exploring and naming."

"In our case it's kind of a reverse process. We have two hundred years to unravel."

12

THE GOLDEN MEDALLION

I t was about noon before they finally stumbled back into town, tired, but not deterred from their overnight trek. Josh went directly home to check on things, before his mother and Tammy returned from their shopping trip. Before he disappeared out of sight, Bryan yelled that he might drop by that evening. Josh waved in recognition, already well down the road.

Again that day, cumulus formations were building in the mountains and a gentle breeze filled the pines on its way to the lofty summits.

After making sure the animals had plenty of food and water, Bryan swept the pine needles off the front porch. Tiring quickly, he climbed back onto the front porch and dropped onto the wooden bench and laid back looking up into the pines, deep in thought.

For days he had been pondering where he had seen the "Door of the Sun" symbol. The memory of this was very vague, but it seemed to him by way of a mental picture that this symbol was at one time familiar to him. But where? Something he or someone else had? There were a few things stored up in the attic, could there still be something around? His curiosity was rekindled. What was up there anyway?

In the short hallway in front of the back bedroom, he pulled on the cord that brought down the fold-down ladder out of the ceiling. Climbing up through the ceiling, Bryan reached up and caught the string that turned on the light. Most of the boxes and items were at the far end of the attic, lined along the floor and on high shelves against the wall. The boxes along the floor contained old picture albums, books, and some old seventy-eight phonograph records. A cardboard box on the top shelf next caught his eye. Sliding it down, he found it was full of papers, receipts, and tax records. Standing on his tiptoes, he slid the box back up onto the shelf, but it wouldn't go back all the way.

"What in the world?" wondered Bryan as he tried shoving it back again. "Okay, what's going on here?"

Grabbing something to stand on, he peered over the shelf to see a small box jammed against the wall. Retrieving the small box, he found it to be made of a dark wood. It appeared to be handmade and very old. Inside were a couple items of jewelry, including a necklace made out of teeth and shells.

"Wow, where did these come from?"

But wait, there was still something else underneath. A cloth pouch contained something flat and hard. Shaking it out of the pouch, it fell into his hand. It was a gold odd-shaped disk. Could this be what he remembered? Turning it over, he gasped. There on the other side was the symbol he sought. He stared at it for the longest time in near disbelief that it was real, that he was actually holding it. Finding this in his own house made him tremble. What were the implications? Where did this come from? It was a half circle, the appropriate shape for a rising or setting sun. On the corners and in the center of the straight section were flared notches, indicating that there must be another half that could interlock, and form a complete circle.

"This must be the top half, but where is the other half?"

Slipping the golden medallion back into the pouch and returning the other items to the wooden box, he placed the box back on the shelf and quickly descended back downstairs. Examining the disk in the bright sunlight that poured in through the window at the far end of the house, the shiny disk glowed in his hand. The symbol was identical to the one on the map and on the mine wall, including the minor detail of the pointed object at the bottom.

What would be his next step? Who would know more about this? Because of the jewelry, chances are the box belonged to his mother, and was left forgotten up there all these years. Should he call her? He had to find out fast. Time was of the essence. His dad would be back in about two or three days. Another attempt must be made before he got back. Thoughts raced through his head. What should I say? The disk burned in his hand. I'll just ask about the necklace and the disk, and go from there.

The clock showed it to be about three o'clock as he reached for the phone index and fingered through it to find his mother's number.

"Well, here goes."

After dialing the number, he could feel his heart beating. The phone was ringing at the other end. Click, "El Rancho de Camino, may I help," was the response by an accented voice, probably Rosa's.

"Hello, this is Bryan, can I speak to my mother please?"

"Bryan? Oh, one momento please."

There was a twenty-second pause.

"Hello, Bryan?"

"Yes, Mom it's me."

"What a pleasant surprise. After you left, the house seems so empty. I miss you."

"It was nice to be with you again too. I especially enjoyed our sunset ride. Say, Mom I was just up in the attic and ran across a wooden box with a necklace and a gold medallion in it. I was wondering if you could tell me where the items came from. Is it yours? They look very old."

"Oh, I totally forgot about those. Well, I guess we should've had this discussion years ago. Did you talk to your father about this?"

"No, he's out on a trip."

"What I'm about to tell you has pretty much gone undocumented. First of all, the necklace you found belonged to your great-great-grandmother, she was the daughter of an Indian Chief. I hate to admit it, but the Spanish side of our family has been prejudiced against the Indians, and I guess I've fallen into that somewhat myself."

"Prejudiced, why?"

"Because from what I understand they killed Captain Camino!"

"What? I thought he just disappeared?"

"No, it was more involved than that. I was just side stepping the issue without dredging up the past."

"What about the golden medallion?"

"That belonged to your great-great-grandfather, Captain Camino. The story as I heard it was, that it was meant to lead someone back to his secret hiding place in the mountains. But no one ever understood the inscription. And the Indians, that is the few who may have known of its location have all died—at least a century ago with their mouths sealed."

"Mom! You know what this means?"

"No, what?"

"That Captain Camino, was the one behind the two hundred year old legend up here concerning the greatest gold strike ever made."

"Your father and grandfather occasionally talked about that, but I never made that connection."

"The proof is on the golden medallion, the sunburst. I have seen this same symbol on the map found in the old Fort, as well as on the wall above the window where they had found it. And in a third location up on the Stanislaus River."

"Really? I'm surprised, I wasn't aware of these things, or that you were involved in looking. Sounds like you're close to figuring it out."

"Just about, I think I have it narrowed down," Bryan firmly replied.

"If the legend is true, it's only appropriate that you should be the one to find the Captain's mine."

"Remember the sunset as we saw it up on the hill that evening? I believe that Captain Camino must have stood in the same place and saw the same scene, and it must have impressed him so, that he adopted the radiant sunset as the symbol of his endeavors."

"Hmm. Bryan, that's genius."

"I don't know about that, but I sometimes feel that I'm on some kind of an irreversible mission. Every time I think I've arrived at a dead end, a new clue surfaces. It almost seems that the mountains are calling me at times."

"Have you talked to your father about any of this?"

"No, I've held back till I could prove something. Oh, by the way, dad probably doesn't want me to say anything about this, but he received another threatening letter from White Pines the other day. Basically, they were making the point that he would lose the property with no compensation if he didn't sell it to them. And that they would get it anyway for failure to pay taxes."

"I wish I could help, but even if I could I doubt whether your father would let me."

"Click." There was a distinct sound of a receiver being put down.

"Who was that? I don't think it was at this end," questioned Bryan.

"I have an idea who it was."

"You mean Rosa?"

"I think so-o," she replied lowering her voice. "She's been a good worker, but for the last month to month and a half, she's been up to some strange things."

133

"I noticed that too, when I was there, she was acting kind of mysterious. How long has she been with you?"

"She worked for grandma, so its been a very long time now. I'm told her family has worked here at the ranch as far back as the Captain's time. Matter of fact they claim to be descendants of a sister-in-law of the Captain's and have been left out of any inheritance which they claim is due them."

"Hmm, that could explain a lot," as he thought of the burnt painting.

Before hanging up, his mother had him promise that he would call her back in a couple of days.

"Mom said Rosa has been acting strangely for the last month to month and a half," Bryan muttered to himself. "That goes back to about the time when the map was discovered. On the other hand, it could have been anybody listening in." Perhaps the phones are bugged, he further pondered. Either way someone undoubtedly over heard their discussion. It seemed probable that somebody would soon be after him, or at least be tailing him. He had to leave.

Bryan grabbed his pack and started repacking it. He would go to Josh's and see if he could stay there for a while. After securing the house, he made sure Graffiti and the animals had a couple of days worth of food. Bryan got in his dad's pickup that was parked in the back, and fired it up. It had been quite a while since he drove the truck. He felt a little guilty not getting his father's permission, but it had to be done.

Accelerating up the road, his thoughts wandered to the one major problem yet ahead. How were they going to get past the lookout perched above the South Fork? The events of the last few days had come fast and furious. Discovery of the medallion had brought this whole thing into a personal connection, bringing a sharp focus on him. The ball was now in his court.

Turning onto Marble Quarry Road, it was a short jaunt to Josh's house. His mother must have returned, for their '62 Rambler was parked in the driveway. He parked on the north side of the dirt and gravel driveway. There under the old oak tree was Josh's Jeep, all four of the tires were flat.

"Bryan, you're early," came Josh's voice from the doorway.

Walking toward the house, Bryan's attention was transfixed on the Jeep.

"Quite a sight isn't it?"

"Depressing, I feel bad that I've involved you in this," replied Bryan.

"Hey, it was my decision too. Don't worry, easy come, easy go."

"I have some news that weighs heavy on me," said Bryan stepping inside the small well-ordered house.

"Hello, Bryan," greeted Josh's mother from the other side of the room.

"Hi, Mrs. Knight. Did you shop till you dropped?"

"Ha, no, but it was good to get away for a couple of days."

Bryan could hear Tammy's voice from the other room saying something about, "country boy." Josh led the way out to the screened porch located at the back of the house. Out of a partially opened bedroom window, music from a radio subtly played as they sat down. Tammy soon followed them out, standing with her arms folded across her chest. She seemed to have something on her mind. Her eyebrows arched.

"I heard that you two took off without telling me," she said appearing to be annoyed about being left out.

"We didn't decide till you were already gone. Besides, it was hard enough for us to make that midnight run," defended Bryan.

"Now, what possibly could have happened since I saw you last?" Josh wondered.

"Remember how I was thinking that I had seen the 'Door of the Sun' symbol before?"

"Yeah."

"I found it!"

"Wow, I'm dying to hear, out with it!" coaxed Josh.

Bryan began by relating the events that led up to the discovery in the attic and what he had found. "And here it is," he said pulling the medallion out of his pocket and handing it to Josh.

" Ooh, that's real gold!" spoke up Tammy looking over her cousin's shoulder.

" 'The Door of the Sun,' " breathed Josh bending over to get a closer look. "It's bigger than life."

"What does this mean?" questioned Tammy.

"That's what I wondered too. So I called my mother to see if she knew anything about it. And bingo! I hit pay dirt."

"Well, tell us!" begged Tammy waving her arms.

First of all, there was a necklace in that box that belonged to my great-great-grandmother. Apparently she was the daughter of an Indian chief."

Tammy briefly searched Bryan's face for the characteristic high cheek bones, but detected none in his features.

"But the medallion was from my great-great-grandfather, Captain Camino."

At that instant, Josh understood the connection between the map, the Fort, and Bryan's great-great-grandfather. "It's almost too much to believe," he stated, still half dazed. "In the beginning this little adventure seemed initially interesting, an innocent diversion. But looking back, it's all been fitting a pattern, something bigger than all outdoors it seems."

"But despite all this, we may be too late. Someone else may already have found it, and may be guarding it, as we observed last night," stated Bryan.

"Perhaps the only way we'll ever know is to sneek in there and take a look," commented Tammy.

"Yes, but how do we get past the lookout they have posted?" posed Josh.

"Obviously there is no way to get by during the day, when everything is so plainly visible. And at night there is the moon lighting things up. If it is a moonless night, then a flashlight becomes a necessity, and that's a dead give away," stated Bryan.

"What about this idea? Stay up on the ridge above the South Fork, and then we can drop down into the river somewhere beyond this so-called lookout point," proposed Josh.

"Lookout Point," repeated Bryan. "That's a good name; but as we saw this morning it's basically a sheer cliff from that point on."

A short period of silence ensued as they contemplated the problem. The music on the radio had stopped, and at the top of the hour a newscaster came on with the latest news. After a few minutes he paused to give the weather and then went back to playing music.

"Did you hear that?" questioned Tammy.

"What?" asked Josh.

"The weather report! He said there's a weather watch posted for the mountains for the next couple of days. Thunderstorms are likely. That's not going to help us though," she realized trailing off.

"Not necessarily, this could be exactly the diversion we need. Think about it. During a thunderstorm, the guard will no doubt seek shelter, especially standing up there on that point. When that happens we could conceivably slip by," suggested Bryan, straightening up.

"Hmm, that has the ring of possibility. Additionally, we could also wear dark clothing, that would help us to blend with the rocky landscape," added Josh.

"We have a plan!" announced Tammy. "Thanks to my keen ear."

"Yes, Tammy," grinned Bryan.

The day had waned. Bryan was invited to join them for dinner and to stay the night, since his dad wouldn't be home. Secretly he had no intention of returning home that evening anyway. Nor did he reveal the possibility that someone may be following him.

It was beginning to get dark when the two boys stepped outside. Pink feathery remnants of large clouds still clung to the lofty peaks. Deepening colors ran their course down into the foothills.

"Josh! Where are you? Come here!" his mother called from inside the house.

"Uh oh, what did I do now?"

"Why didn't you tell me we had some mail? I just found a letter from your Uncle Albert laying on the piano."

"Ah, sorry Mom. I forgot all about it," replied Josh sticking his head through the doorway.

His mother lapsed into silence as she began reading the letter. "Oh no, he's went and done it again. Guess I'll have to run over there in the morning," she sighed.

Tammy entered the room, stopping to listen.

"What has your uncle done?" asked Bryan whispering to Josh.

"He probably got drunk and was thrown into the slammer again."

"Oh no."

"Well, it's not the first time," Josh whispered back.

"It's best you kids stay here. I don't know what to expect this time. I'll probably have to stay the night, but let's hope not," concluded Josh's mother.

Turning away from the door, the boys found a large rock nearby to sit and ponder their next move.

"It looks like the way things are working out, tomorrow may be our best opportunity to make the ascent up the South Fork," stated Bryan.

"Let's say we do get by this 'Lookout Point,' what things are we to look for?" questioned Josh, probing for the practicality of pushing ahead.

"Basically, just what's shown on the map," he replied throwing his hands up. "And observe if anyone is actively working up in the headwaters."

"Okay, first was 'Where Eagles fly.' But who knows even if there are any eagles up there, as you once pointed out. And if there is, they may have changed nesting areas," recounted Josh.

"And then there is 'Wandering Sky' and the 'Door of the Sun,' " added Bryan.

"But what was it that the man from the Reservation told your dad?" questioned Josh.

"He said, it is "above the heads of mortal man" and that "the door is closed" or something similar," recalled Bryan. "I know the trail of clues does look weak, but I have a feeling we will find them."

Tammy came out of the house and approached them.

"Tammy, don't tell mom, but we're planning to hike up into the South Fork tomorrow," informed Josh. "But I don't recommend you coming this time."

"What? If you don't let me come, I'll tell your mom," she threatened.

The boys had the look of frustration in their eyes.

"Tammy!" pleaded Josh.

"Looks like its no use," said Bryan. "I think we're stuck."

"Stuck! Oooh! I've solved clues just as good as you guys and maybe better."

"It's just that this time we don't know what kind of danger we'll face," explained Bryan. "There's a man up there with a rifle, watching everything that moves."

"All or nothing," bargained Tammy standing with her arms folded.

The boys shook their heads.

"All right, all right, but you must stick very close," said Josh.

"That's better," she said turning away.

"Why is it that women always seem to get their way?" remarked Bryan as Tammy disappeared around the corner.

"I heard that country boy!" came the call from around the corner.

"Ha, ha," laughed Josh.

13
THUNDERSTORM

Clouds had already begun to form over the higher peaks as the three intrepid explorers made their way down "Midnight Creek." Leaving as soon as practical after Josh's mother had left for Placerville, they drove up to the ridge and hid the pickup. Soon after they began their descent a gentle breeze scurried through the trees gently lifting the boughs.

"What a contrast to when we came stumbling down through here during the middle of the night," remembered Bryan.

"It was like walking in a tunnel. We couldn't see jack," recalled Josh.

"How about Jill?" laughed Tammy.

"Her neither."

Again the group grew silent as they clomped down the trail. After passing the metamorphic "spear heads," the course wound its way down to the babbling springs. Crossing the flat, Bryan stopped.

"I think this was the place. Let's look around for a minute."

"What place?" asked Tammy.

"Right through here is where we heard something go crashing through the brush the other night. We heard it from further up on the mountain," informed Josh.

"Ooh, monsters. You he-men aren't afraid of the big bad wolf are you?" teased Tammy.

"We weren't," defended Josh, "its just we didn't know what it was," defended Josh.

"Here are the broken branches we were looking at," pointed Bryan.

Dropping their packs, they scattered to look for clues.

"Look for bits of fur or anything snagged in the branches," Josh explained to Tammy as they worked their way off the trail to the left. Bryan headed off in the opposite direction.

After about five hundred feet, Josh gave up and turned back toward the trail and met Bryan coming back from the other way.

"See anything?" asked Josh.

"No. Where's your cousin?"

"Ah, she still must be looking."

"Tammy!" called Bryan. "Tammy!"

"Don't have a cow, I'm coming," she finally responded. "I found something. Look."

"Hmm, a white thread," observed Josh.

"Just like you said, there it was dangling on a broken branch," Tammy disclosed.

"It's not an animal that had this, it wore clothing," concluded Bryan examining it up close.

"Somebody was sure on the move the other night and they didn't care if they made a lot of noise either," remembered Josh.

"I believe what we heard here the other night was never meant to be observed. But on the other hand because of the increased activity up in these hills, what we observed could be a way to scare people away," Bryan thought out loud. "But what breed of man would walk in such a fashion through these woods and mountains at night?" The essence of the 'Legend' and Indian stories pervaded his thoughts as he contemplated how this might fit in.

"Which way from here is this place you guys call 'Lookout Point'?" asked Tammy.

Both boys pointed roughly in line with the direction that the midnight stalker had taken. Then the realization hit them.

"This person then must be associated with those who are watching over the South Fork,"concluded Tammy.

"Makes sense to me. Let's hit the dusty trail," replied Bryan.

"Wait, this reminds me of the story your grandfather was telling us that day, about those that would be watching," recalled Josh.

"There are definitely some strong similarities."

"What story is that?" questioned Tammy as they again took to the trail.

Josh glanced at Bryan.

"We might as well tell her, she's fully involved now," said Bryan.

As they descended Josh and Bryan related the story as they had heard it.

"The fact is, because most of this wilderness up here is unexplored and quite a few people have vanished, a certain foreboding has materialized itself into legends and stories. I hope that doesn't cause you to shake in your boots," mentioned Bryan.

"Me? No-o! Actually I'm intrigued if anything."

"Ooh-wee!" exclaimed Josh.

Above the soaring forest that surrounded them, the cloud masses continued to boil up with a slight hint of darkness in their recesses. The glorified deer path ventured on leading them down into the deepening canyon. The creek gurgled on its cheerful way to meet its brothers below. They hesitated as a mule deer bounded up a side gully to finally stop and peer down upon them in curiosity, its ears and tail twitching.

Dropping in elevation, the landscape gave way to more and more chaparral, Mountain mahogany, and manzanita.

"What was the name of the brush with the red smooth bark again?" asked Tammy.

"Manzanita," replied Josh. "Indians used to take the berries and make cider out of them."

"Speaking of manzanita," related Bryan. "A ranger from Sequoia told me about an old Indian woman who lived down near Three Rivers. She told him that there were eleven varieties of manzanita in the area. At first he scoffed at the claim, but after a number of years of observation he found she was right, there were exactly, eleven varieties," related Bryan.

"The Indians must have known this land like the back of their hand," commented Tammy.

"Indeed they did," affirmed Bryan whose thoughts again wandered to those days of long ago.

Sliding and tripping, they made their way down the steepest and rockiest part of the descent. A gusty breeze blew by them on its way up canyon. The roar of the river heralded their approach to the South Fork. It was about noon when they finally reached the sandy flat, where the two of them had rested before.

"Let's stop here and use this as a staging area. We'll rest and wait for the opportunity to go on up," said Bryan pulling off his pack.

"If it ever does," doubtfully replied Tammy.

"It looks like it more and more," he optimistically commented while glancing up at the billowing clouds above.

Tammy walked over to the edge of the embankment and looked down into the wild river. "Look at the purple flowers," she pointed.

"Lupines," informed Josh.

While Tammy admired the flowers, Bryan pulled Josh back under the trees to talk. Finding a comfortable spot, they sat down facing each other.

"I'm worried that we may have erred in allowing your cousin to come along," confided Bryan in a hushed tone.

"I know, but as you recall we didn't have any choice. We would've had to wait until she goes home in about two weeks."

"That's the whole pivotal point isn't it? This opportunity today may be a one shot deal. I hope nothing goes wrong," Bryan added. "Oh, by the way I brought my eight-inch gold pan along on a hunch."

"A hunch?"

"Yeah, tell me if I'm crazy."

"You're crazy!" fired back Josh.

"No, now listen. Assuming that we get past Lookout Point, there will no doubt be other forks and side creeks that we may have to decide between."

"Remember the warning about 'never let your right hand guide you into the mountains?' " recalled Josh.

"But do we trust that though? We could encounter a change in the channel alignment that could throw us off. That's why panning at creek outlets may give us a positive or negative indication of what may lay above."

"Bryan, you're a regular Sherlock Holmes, you know that?"

"Ha, you make me laugh," said Bryan.

"Seriously, I think it is a great idea. We should start right here and set a base line of sorts. So that we can reference back to it as we go."

"Good thinking Mr. Watson, let's give it a whirl."

"There you guys are," suddenly spoke Tammy. "I thought for a minute you guys had sneaked off without me."

"No, that could only be wishful thinking," sighed Bryan.

Tammy didn't say anything but the look in her eyes said, "I'll get you later."

"Grab something to eat, we'll be right back," Josh told her.

"Where are you going now?"

"Gold panning," he replied back.

"Really, I've never seen it done before."

"Well, come on down and take a gander," invited her cousin.

Plumes of dust raced with wind as they slid down the rocky bank to the gravelly river bed.

"This annoying wind is picking up again," complained Tammy as she pulled the collar up over her neck.

"No wonder look!" said Bryan pointing off to the south.

"Woo! It appears we're in for a serious blow," agreed Josh.

Large black cloud masses were now raising their ugly heads above the distant ranges.

"We don't have long, let's wash a quick pan," said Bryan bending down to the edge of the river.

Thunderstorm

While Bryan went through the routine of panning and explaining the different moves, Tammy watched.

Meanwhile, Josh walked a short distance upstream. Around the bend out of sight was 'Lookout Point.' He wondered what really had transpired here two hundred years before? In his imagination it was almost possible to hear the crack of hoofs on the river rock as an imaginary pack train headed upstream.

"Josh, come here and look," beckoned Tammy.

"Have we hit the big one?"

"No, but we do have a few flakes," answered Bryan.

"As an old prospector would have said: 'There is gold in them 'thar' hills,' " voiced Josh.

"Tammy, do you have any idea where gold even comes from?" asked Bryan.

"Now wait a minute, I'm not stupid. Just like Josh said, it washed down from somewhere up in these hills and mountains."

"I didn't say you were stupid."

"But I'm a girl, right, isn't that what you were going to say?"

"No! Why do females always have to fly off the handle anyway?"

"Oh, am I upsetting your superior male ego?"

"All right already! Come on, the point is these gold flakes came from a vein of parent rock somewhere up in this drainage system. Our job is to find the lost mother lode," said Josh annoyed at both of them.

Everyone fell silent for a moment.

"Here, take the gold," offered Bryan extending the pan to her.

"I don't want any of your ol' gold. Besides, I don't have anything to put it in. Wait, I have an idea."

Reaching in her pocket, she pulled out a gum wrapper and unfolded it exposing a wad of previously chewed gum. Flattening it, she took the tip of her finger and pressed down on the flakes. Adhering to her finger, she was able to deposit them on the gum. Once the flakes were transferred, Tammy folded the gum over them and rewrapped it.

"Huh, when you thought you've seen it all. I don't think you could find that in the very best miner's encyclopedia," commented Josh.

Suddenly there was a crack of thunder off to the south that jolted them to the reality of the advancing storm.

"It's just over the ridge, we better run for it and get our rain ponchos on before it hits," warned Bryan.

A flash lit up the sky. Crack! Boom! Came another volley as they raced up the bank. The wind gusted in erratic bursts.

"Reverse your slickers, so the dark side is out," yelled Bryan over the intensifying storm.

Nestling under an overhanging rock, they decided to munch down a few morsels of food. An ominous stillness was suddenly broken by the roar of pelting rain.

"Looks, like we're in for it," said Josh.

"Maybe it wasn't such a good idea coming along after all," muttered Tammy, her dark eyes peeking out from under her hood.

"No turning back now," said Bryan in a matter of fact tone. He wasn't going to allow anything to interfere with this unique opportunity.

After about three or four minutes, the rain began to drip through cracks in the rock, plunking down all around them.

"I think it's time. Let's make our move upstream now. By the time we get there the storm should be raging, and hopefully it will have done its work, allowing us to slip through unobserved," decided Bryan.

Strapping on their packs and adjusting their rain jackets, they were off into the rain and into a part of their lives they would never forget. Tammy's facial expression seemed to ask: "Are you sure about this?" As quick as the shower started it tapered off. Dark clouds raced over the tops of the canyon ridges. Following along the river, the rocky course had grown slippery due to the rain. Staying up on the occasional sand bank helped their progress. Already the river gorge began its turn toward 'Lookout Point.' Black and white clouds clung to the looming peaks far above, while others quickly ventured north.

"It won't be long," said Bryan eyeing the rapidly changing weather.

Darkness again fell over them as vicious black thunder clouds rolled in overhead. Portions of the clouds shaped like arms began to descend toward the rocky ridge crests along the canyon, like a giant creature reaching down to scoop up victims.

" 'Lookout Point' will be coming visible most any time, we'd better hug the wall," warned Josh.

A deafening peal of thunder crashed and echoed. Almost instantaneously the wind gusted and a heavy shower set in. Lightning struck far above with an explosion. A fluttering noise grew louder. Chunks of bark, branches, and sections of a tree trunk started falling all around them.

"Watch your head," warned Josh.

Pieces of the exploded tree fluttered and rained down on them for another half minute.

"That was close," Bryan sighed.

Their path was now strewn with chunks of bark and limbs amongst the boulders as they held to the vertical canyon wall. Large falling drops of rain splattered on the rocks making it even more miserable.

"Stay low, we'll probably be visible from the 'point' any time now," said Bryan glancing back at them through the driving rain.

Splashing and sloshing their way through shallow pools of accumulated water, they curved along the canyon wall until they reached the furthest point to where they would remain hidden. Streams of water now began to pour down the walls. Lightning stabbed down nearby with such a terrible blast and flash of light that it almost knocked them backwards.

"Woo!" they all exclaimed.

"We were almost toast," realized Josh.

"I don't know if I can do this. How long is this crazy storm going to last?" whined Tammy.

"Sometimes they can last two or three hours," replied Bryan.

"Oh, that's all that I wanted to hear."

"Josh, grab the field glasses out of my pack if you would please," asked Bryan.

"Stay here," suggested Josh. "We're going to creep up to the edge of the cliff."

With glasses in hand they crept up and stooped low at the base of the protruding cliff.

"What do you see?" begged Josh.

A couple more flashes of lightning struck the ridge above.

"Ohh! My eyes. Talk about burn out," exclaimed Bryan. "The first flash lit up the whole top of the ridge, and there was no one up there."

"Here, let me look." After about twenty seconds, Josh lowered the glasses. "You're right, the coast is clear."

They excitedly scrambled back to where Tammy was waiting.

"In this storm only a fool would be out," laughed Josh.

She wholeheartedly agreed, giving them both a dirty look. Another burst of thunder broke overhead.

"Okay Tammy, there's no guard in the guard house, let's get going before the storm breaks and he returns," excitedly informed Bryan.

"It wouldn't be none too soon," she replied with her head bowed to keep the water out of her face. Literally and figuratively she looked to be totally under the weather.

"Don't worry, you won't melt," encouraged Josh.

"I'm soaked, I feel horrible," she fumed. "I wanna go home!"

"You're the one who insisted on coming," reminded Bryan.

The storm kept up its rampage as they rounded the corner and approached the junction of the two rushing streams. The wind out in the open was even stronger, making it hard to navigate.

"Hey!" spoke up Josh.

"What?" asked Bryan.

"Nothing, I'll tell you later," he yelled back.

Angling to the right, Skull Creek began its climb into a narrow, boulder strewn canyon. Despite the fierce rain, Bryan managed to glance up at the towering ridge far above that hid Lookout Point. How did they get up there anyway? he wondered staggering forward.

For a moment the storm seemed to abate.

"Finally!" stated Tammy.

"Feels like the air is getting colder," observed Josh.

"The wind does feel a bit icier," agreed Bryan.

"Don't tell me it's going to snow!" she mocked.

"No, I don't think that's possible but it—" Before Bryan could finish, hail began to fall.

"Ah! What next?" she squealed.

"Is this what you were going to say?" motioned Josh.

"Yep, it certainly was."

The hail storm sputtered and seemed to shift gears.

"Jimminy Crickets!" yelled Josh as the hail started coming down harder, almost the size of quarters.

"Take your packs off and hold them over your heads," shouted Bryan over the roar of the hail hitting the river rock. The sound was like ricocheting ball bearings.

Without hesitation they stopped and wrestled off their packs.

"How bad can it get?" flashed Tammy, her long hair plastered against her face.

The boys did not answer her. They knew it could get bad.

"Well, we can't just stand here, let's head up and find shelter," suggested Josh.

After hiking only about a thousand feet, the hail covered the ground and turned the creek into flowing slush. They soon lost track of time, had it been five minutes or twenty minutes? The canyon narrowed and in the short distance that was visible, it looked like a winter wonderland. Lightning illuminated the clouds above, followed by thunder reverberating up and down the gorge. After a few minutes the sky began to lighten up and the thunderstorm subsided.

"Look at the creek!" pointed Tammy.

"It's rising," realized Bryan.

"And fast," added Josh.

"Up against the bank," barked Bryan. "We have to find high ground."

The churning creek flowed with slush, as it crept like a snake out of its bed toward them. Thunder rumbled off to the north.

"E-E-E! This is getting as bad as one of those fantasy-adventure novels," squealed Tammy. "This can't be real. Josh! Wait till your mother hears about this! You're supposed to be watching out for me, remember?" she rambled on as the water approached their feet.

"Quiet! Keep up with us. There's got to be a safer place up ahead," coaxed Josh.

Trudging upstream the swollen creek was nearly wall to wall.

"I don't see any break in these walls, their solid nearly all the way up," observed Bryan.

"What are we going to do?" questioned Tammy frantically.

"Keep going!" was the reply.

The creek now surged over their feet and sloshed against the bank.

"Oooh-wee! That's cold," howled Josh.

Filtered light began to illuminate the rugged crest line ahead. The water continued to rise in surges, reaching to just below their knees.

"It's hard to say how high this stream could go before it crests," commented Bryan.

"I can hardly feel my legs to move them," confided Tammy.

"Here take my hand," offered Bryan.

"No, I don't want to hold your ol' hand," she protested drawing her hand back behind her. Suddenly she slipped and Bryan caught her. Somewhat annoyed, he put her hand in his and pulled her along. She could feel the strength in his arm and somehow it felt good.

They were now wading up to their knees in the icy water.

"My legs can't move," said Tammy finally.

"If it's any consolation my legs are getting numb too," replied Josh.

"There's a cleft in the wall," pointed Bryan. "Maybe we can boost Tammy up into it."

Sloshing through the rushing current, they looked up at a V shaped fissure, which was just above their heads.

"Okay, Tammy here goes," said Josh as they pushed her up into the notch. "Whew! now what?"

"Maybe we'd better go look for high ground too. Wait! Look up there, is that what I think it is?" spoke up Bryan in a concerned voice.

"What? Where?"

"Up there to the left, just above Tammy's head, it looks like a scour line."

Josh's eyes grew big. "You mean the water could go up that high?"

"It has in the past, so it appears."

"Woo!"

"Stay here, Josh. I'm going to go look around. I'll be right back. If the water comes up high, pull yourself up to where Tammy is. There's probably room enough for both of you in a squeeze."

"We probably should stick together," protested Josh yelling after him.

"Don't worry, I'll be right back."

Josh watched Bryan wade upstream and out of sight.

"You all right?" asked Josh looking up at her.

"Just froze to the bone," she answered, shivering.

A few minutes passed and the creek surged to above his hips.

"Josh, I don't see Bryan, you better get up here, the current will probably carry you away if it gets much higher."

More Than Legend

"Bryan! Bryan!" loudly called out Josh.

But there was no answer. Only the roar of the swirling stream.

"I'm coming up. Stand to one side."

Josh strained and pulled himself up into the notch. Turning he put his back against one side of the cleft with his legs folded in front of him.

"Fancy meeting you here, Cousin," said Josh tipping his cap.

"Ha ha. I wonder if Bryan is all right? I don't think he can get back now. How do you put up with him, he's so bull headed," she sighed with conflicting emotions.

"You should talk," commented Josh. "I told him not to go," he added.

The emerald green creek had turned to a chocolate brown. It lashed at the bank just below them, churning and boiling. A crack of thunder diverted their attention away from the creek.

"This isn't exactly summer in the city," commented Josh.

"Wait till I get through with you two, you'll think summer in the city!"

"At least you still have your fire. We'll need it to get us through this one," he said reflecting on her statement.

"The water has come up another foot, it must be over five feet deep now. Will it ever stop?" Tammy fretted.

"Wish I knew. We can shimmy another two or three feet further up into this fissure, but that's about it."

Floating debris, mostly tree limbs and a few logs began to appear in the churning torrent. After ten minutes the thunder finally ceased and the stream level also seemed to abate.

"E-ha! The creek must have crested, it's going down," announced Josh.

"The sun is trying to peak out again too. Kind of ironic, like nothing ever happened," commented Tammy.

The creek continued to drop quickly and then seemed to slow as it approached about two feet in depth.

"Hey! Is anybody home?" called Bryan as he suddenly waded into view.

"Where have you been anyway? You abandoned us," scolded Tammy.

"I found a trail that takes off over the ridge, about a quarter mile ahead. The water is receding but it's still backed up to here. Some storm, huh?" declared Bryan as he sloshed his way toward them, smiling.

"That was close," stated Josh.

"And by the way, who ran off this time?" taunted Tammy.

"You two are mighty fine, sitting up there like a pair of vultures ready to pounce. Come on down, time to leave your cozy nest. Let's get up to the high ground and dry out."

Slowly they responded and turned to slide back down into the creek.

"The water must be much deeper, further down stream. Being dammed up by all the debris that collected behind the large boulders that we came by earlier," theorized Bryan as he looked down the canyon.

"Oh, by the way, I was going to tell you—just before we turned into this canyon, right at the base of 'Lookout Point,' I could have sworn I seen some movement behind us," recalled Josh as he let go and landed in the creek with a big splash. "I happened to glance back down the river and saw what I thought was somebody following us, way back at the curve of the South Fork."

"I'm not surprised," replied Bryan. "But one thing is in our favor. They are below the flooded area and we are above. It may be another day before they can get through."

"Yeah, but if that's true, we can't get back either," realized Tammy. "Watch where you put your hand," she warned as the boys eased her down

"That's true, there's no returning tonight," confirmed Bryan. "Come on let's make tracks." Suddenly he stopped and turned to face her. "Oh, by the way. If you hadn't noticed there was only room for the two of you up there. I took the gamble so that— you, would be safe."

Tammy was speechless. Momentarily she was lost in his scolding eyes.

Wading through the muddy brown water, they rounded a slight bend in the gorge to see a gravel bar along the right side ascending out of the stream. From that point on they were able to take to the gravelly shore. The clouds had moved away and the advanced afternoon sun shone upon them.

"What an amazing day," said Josh glancing at the sun.

"Let's stop and warm ourselves on these rocks and dry out," begged Tammy. "I'm so cold-d."

"That's probably a good idea, we may lose the sun completely as we drop into the canyons beyond," sympathized Bryan.

"Oh my hair, my clothes, what a mess I am," she moaned.

"Where is this trail, you mentioned?" questioned Josh as he made himself comfortable on a bench of rock.

"Just ahead the creek makes a sharp turn to the left into a deep channel, but the trail, if I'm correct veers off to the right and runs up and over a rocky ridge. Could be a short cut."

"Short cut?" questioned Josh.

14

"WHERE EAGLES FLY"

After a satisfactory drying out period, the mountain trek was again resumed. The water coming downstream was still cloudy and gritty, but not as dark as it had been during the height of the storm. As Bryan described, the creek turned left and narrowed into a deep channel through solid rock.

"Your trail must wander up that rock slope over there," pointed Josh.

"It's only logical, isn't it" confirmed Bryan.

Leaving the creek bed, grayish brown metaphoric slabs stair-stepped their way up the rugged slope.

"Hey! Look at these scratches on the rock, what do you think made these marks?" questioned Tammy.

"Hmm, old hoof marks probably," guessed Josh bending down to take a closer look.

"Good, you guys are figuring it out," said Bryan.

"The scratches seem to be extremely weathered," noted Josh.

"I think this confirms we're on the right track," concluded Bryan.

"Come on! Let's find this place!" said Tammy getting all fired up.

"That's the spunk," smiled Bryan. Josh grinned.

In climbing the metamorphic staircase they noticed that sections of the rock slope contained dark red streaks and squiggles running through its surface. Almost as if someone had taken a pen and dabbed it in an ink well, and let it run all over. Reaching the top of the ridge, a narrow band of fir and Jeffery pine greeted them.

From this vantage point they could see the tops of numerous canyons curving and meandering into the distance, and the dark edges of shadows now forming on the west walls. Bryan caught sight of the *Obelisk* peaking over the summit of the intervening crest. It was again changing shape as the angle of view changed. Could it be the peak in the center of the Spanish map? Time would tell.

Dropping over the ridge, the trail traversed across a bare slope peppered with volcanic extrusions and basalt. Spindly plants flourished along the edge of these outcroppings, waving to and fro in the gentle breeze. It was now apparent that this trail over the ridge had cut off quite a distance from the canyon route, which looped off to the northeast and rejoined the trail just ahead. Josh suggested calling the trail over the hump, Bloody Ridge. But Tammy didn't like the sound of that and came up with, Abstract Ridge instead.

A gradual descent over half of a mile brought them back down to the creek. Shadows from the westerly wall now enveloped them.

"We better pick up the pace to make up for some of the time we lost during the storm," encouraged Bryan.

After half an hour the creek again split. A large log laid askew at the junction of the two streams.

"Time for our secret weapon," Josh suggested as they plunked down on the end of the log.

"What-t secret weapon?" questioned Tammy with an air of doubt.

"This," said Bryan pulling out his gold pan. "Here Josh, you do the left side at least four hundred feet upstream and I'll do the right side."

"Tammy, come on, you can pan a little if you want," offered Josh.

While the two crossed the creek and headed upstream to pan, Bryan peered into the rippling water as he contemplated their next move. There was one thing that they hadn't been doing he realized. Jumping off the log, he headed up to where they were panning.

"How's it looking?" he asked.

"Give us another minute and we should have some results," answered Josh as they watched Tammy handle the pan.

"From here on out we should begin hiding our tracks and setting a false trail," recommended Bryan.

"Wha-a-a-t?" questioned Tammy glancing up from the pan.

"Depending on which stream pans out, we'll make a false trail up the opposite creek. Then carefully hop on the rocks back downstream and do the same for a distance up the creek that we'll be ascending."

"Say, why not just run the false trail into the creek. Then they would run all over the place trying to figure out where we came out," further suggested Josh.

"That's a marvelous idea," said Tammy.

"Yeah, that's using the old noodle," agreed Bryan.

"Let's see what you have there, Tammy," said Josh stooping down. "Only a couple specks, looks like nothing significant on this side."

"Okay, let's walk the rocks back; and then I'll pan the other stream," said Bryan. After five or six minutes, the second pan was completed. "Jumpin' jack rabbits! Look at this, a pinch of gold," showed off Bryan.

"Again the right-handed rule is proven correct," pointed out Josh.

"That's true, but I still don't trust it fully," expressed Bryan.

"What's this right-handed rule?" asked Tammy.

"Let's make tracks, while we talk," suggested Bryan.

They laid in the false trail and doubled back. Josh explained the warning that had been given to Bryan's grandfather many years before.

"Now, let's carefully step our way up this right-handed creek—staying on the rocks. After this we need to pick up our pace and get as far as we can before dark," added Bryan.

"Dark, oh no! that's right. We're stuck out here in the boonies, with all kinds of wild animals roaming about," Tammy realized looking around .

"Don't worry, both of us have slept out in these mountains many times and we've never been bothered yet," encouraged her cousin.

In a few minutes they had entered a wild, rugged gorge. Boulders the size of houses rested helter-skelter along the creek. The decision was made to hike the left side, it being somewhat less obstructed. Large pines, some straight and others leaning shot up between the enormous rocks. And out of the cracks grew gnarled dwarf pines. A red-tailed hawk soared in the air currents far above. The creek pounded against many of these behemoths that had fallen from the heights above. Direct sunlight reached only the highest peaks now. Straggling clouds clinging to the loftiest pinnacles began to show a tint of color. A coolness in the air set in.

"Aren't you guys getting hungry?" inquired Tammy.

"Yeah, but we better not stop now. We can make another mile before dark," Josh replied. "Here, chew on a stick of gum, that'll help."

"Not that glow in the dark stuff you call gum," she replied.

Bryan chuckled. "This is a bit too rugged to comfortably camp in. Hopefully we can find someplace better up ahead. And above all keep a watch for anything that has to do with our next clue, 'Where Eagles Fly,' " he added.

"Wish I could fly out of here," commented Tammy.

"Where Eagles Fly"

A miniature forest huddled itself along the left side of the canyon and from that point on the gorge twisted and turned toward the south.

Looking all around, Bryan, wondered if Captain Camino, had traveled this same stream and gazed upon the same sights. He could almost imagine in even greater detail than before, the Spanish explorer in his distinctive garb, riding a fiery steed and leading a pack train. But this time he had the face of his great-great-grandfather, Captain Camino. Those piercing eyes, that were captured in his portrait, seemed to be emblazoned in his memory. He never returned, he could still be up here somewhere. But where? There was the compulsion to shout out: Captain! Where are you? Give us another clue! But alas no one was listening. We just have to follow the leads to find his secret hiding place, the 'Oro de Cañon,' by ourselves.

"Look at the waterfall up ahead," spotted Tammy, snapping Bryan out of his mental sojourn.

"Drop it into low gear, looks like we're going to do some climbing," observed Josh.

"Hey! I'm not a truck," Tammy shot back.

"No, you're more like a sports car," replied Bryan.

Tammy smiled to herself.

Eroded bedrock that formed the floor of the canyon heaved upward and disappeared around the bend out of sight. The creek roared down the rocky descent, fanning out to form a waterfall about thirty feet wide to finally drop twenty feet into an emerald pool. Above was a series of smaller falls cascading along a singular line of descent. Spray from the falls drifted toward them, as they neared its edge.

"If this was in the heat of the day it would be refreshing, not so tingly cold," spoke up Tammy as they passed up through the spray.

To mount the steep rock formation, they zigzagged back and forth with difficulty as they tried to keep up their pace. Taking longer than expected they finally reached the top of the falls. They stopped to catch their breath while studying the polished rock slope ahead and the stream that raced toward them and then veered away.

"We better find that campsite soon or we'll be stuck out here in the rocks tonight," said Josh.

"Not me! Let's go!" replied Tammy racing off ahead of them.

"Say, how many miles do you think we've hiked today?" asked Josh.

"Oh, probably about six from 'Lookout Point.' It always seems longer because of all the weaving and climbing we had to do," commented Bryan.

"I see more trees up ahead," announced Tammy as the tops of numerous conifers now appeared above the horizon.

A gray light filtered down over the precipices, as the threesome topped the last section of the polished bedrock to enter the mouth of a wide picturesque U shaped valley. It was carpeted with green meadow and flanked with tall fir and cedar on its far right side.

"This is much nicer," commented Tammy.

At the edge of the meadow was a fascinating pool of clear water. So clear was the water that every pebble could be easily counted. It appeared that the thunderstorm had bypassed this valley as the ground appeared dry.

"The forest just ahead seems so isolated and aloof," commented Josh.

"How about we make camp in the lost forest tonight," suggested Bryan.

"Ooh! Sounds mysterious," commented Tammy. "Sounds like the title of a book."

"What sinister plot would this book have?" asked Josh.

"Nothing sinister, it would a place where people who are hopelessly lost are redirected to find a better life," she imagined.

"I like your positive spin on that," commented Bryan.

The valley made a sudden left turn heading back toward the east. Crossing the small creek, they headed for the dark forest across the grassy meadow.

"Our first order of work is to round up some firewood before it gets any darker," stated Josh.

"We better keep the fire small, it's not a good idea to advertise our whereabouts," added Bryan.

Entering among the trees, they located an ideal place to camp. Leaving their packs in a small clearing, they scattered to gather firewood. The chirping of birds echoed through the lonely woods as they foraged for dead limbs in the dimming light.

Having his arms full, Bryan was almost ready to turn back when he heard the gentle gurgle of a stream. Stepping in that direction, he found a small stream that meandered its way through the trees. "Hmm, another branch," said Bryan to himself, stooping down to peer along its course into the gray unknown. It must connect with the main creek further up the valley he thought.

After making a couple more trips, Josh and Bryan hustled to start a fire.

"I'm beyond starved," confessed Tammy.

"This outdoor life agrees with your appetite," said Bryan.

"Ha, that's about all," was her reply.

The fire popped and sizzled to life as they added small branches to coax it.

"Okay, good, now we can settle in," said Josh pulling things out of his pack.

A hush fell over the group as they began to eat. Their surroundings now disappeared in the darkness, except for a dull glow that lit up the ridge crests high above. Night birds became more active, their calls and screeches echoing far back into the woods.

"Say, I found a small creek back in the woods, over there," pointed Bryan, breaking the silence.

"You're not the only one who can find things, look here," said Josh reaching for and holding up a rusted, curved piece of metal in the flickering light.

"A horseshoe," identified Tammy.

"Little on the small side, could even be a muleshoe," thought Bryan.

"You're right, see the nail holes," said Josh handing it around.

"It must be very old. And being way out here too, I bet it could tell quite a story," said Tammy.

"Quite possibly the missing years of my great-great-grandfather's life," replied Bryan. "It's possible he may have even camped here, maybe many times."

"Wow! You think so?"

"This is older than any shoe type I've ever seen. But really until we find 'Where Eagles Fly' or 'Wandering Sky' we won't know for sure if we're on the right trail," he continued.

"What is known about your great-great-grandfather?" asked Tammy.

While the group gazed into the fire, Bryan related what he had come to learn. In the meantime a partial moon began to rise from the head of the valley and a lone coyote howl could be heard, effortlessly drifting through the mountain airways. Tammy's sleepy eyes suddenly widened.

"The animals are coming," she breathed.

"No, they're a long way off, they shouldn't bother us," said Josh opening a new pack of gum.

Suddenly, there was the sound of crackling branches a short distance away. Tammy grabbed Josh's arm.

"Bryan! This is one of your tricks, isn't it?" asked Josh.

"Ah-h, no, not this time," he replied with a sober face.

Another noise sounded off, this time closer.

"Grab your flashlight," ordered Bryan.

Josh threw on several pieces of wood and the fire flared up. Over the crackle of the fire they strained to hear the slightest noise. How eerie it seemed. Firelight and shadow danced upon the trees, or was it the forest that was moving? Two or three tense minutes passed by without nothing being seen or heard.

"Josh, I know we're tired, but we better keep watch tonight. I'll take the first shift, you guys get some sleep," said Bryan breaking the silence.

It took a while for them to fall asleep, but finally their eyelids dropped like lead weights. The fire burned down to a dull glow. Looking up through the tops of the trees, it seemed that their quest, their location was as remote and unattainable as the stars that glimmered in the great expanse. He threw on a couple more pieces of wood to keep the fire going. A few sparks flared up. Far away another coyote call broke the night's stillness.

Sometime later Bryan jerked awake. He must have nodded off asleep. It had grown colder and dew had begun to form. Seeing the fire had reduced to coals he threw on a couple more chunks of wood. As the fire flared up he woke Josh.

Josh woke with a lurch. "Uh!"

"Your turn Buddy."

"Oh-h, I must have been dreaming," realized Josh rolling over.

"I'm going to get a couple of winks," said Bryan laying down.

The first direct morning sun hit along the ridge tops as it ascended out of the northeast. Bryan's eyes popped open realizing he may have over slept. He was cold and stiff. Tammy was still out like a light and Josh was nowhere to be seen. The fire had pretty much gone out, only a wisp of smoke lingered. Going out beyond the clearing, Bryan called Josh's name. It echoed through the woods but all was silent.

"Well, if that doesn't beat all!" exclaimed Bryan turning back to the campsite.

"What's wrong?" asked Tammy who evidently was just waking up.

"Josh is gone, he's nowhere to be found."

"That's strange, his pack is still sitting where he was sleeping last night."

"Well sugar! I guess the only thing we can do is look for footprints."

"I hope he's all right," worried Tammy.

"This is not like Josh. Which way did he go to collect wood last night?"

"Up through there, along the edge of the meadow," she pointed.

"He had a flat bottomed boot," Bryan recollected. "Anyway, let's circle around the edge of the clearing and look for any tracks that seem out of place or at least strange. But first of all, to help us distinguish our prints from his, let's take note that you have a small foot and mine have these wavy lines on the bottom."

"Okay," Tammy acknowledged.

With heads down they slowly covered the ground just inside the clearing.

"Here are our tracks when we first arrived, and back over here are the ones where we went to gather wood," pointed out Tammy.

"Okay, I'll buy that. Now over here is the direction I went, and I don't see any other prints except mine."

Continuing around the clearing, they found nothing along the southerly side.

"Ah ha! Look, a faint footprint," discovered Tammy.

"It must be Josh's all right. No distinguishable pattern and the size seems right. But where was he going?"

"Over here are more, but look the prints are turning and skidding," she pointed out.

Bryan squatted down. "Hmm, there are no other distinguishable prints here, but there are marks, that could have been made by a soft-soled type of shoe or moccasin."

"What are you saying?"

"He may have been abducted."

"What? How can that be, we didn't hear a thing?"

"I know, but it looks to me as if there was a brief struggle."

"What are we going to do?"

"We're going to follow them, let's break camp."

After smothering the campfire and packing up, they strapped on their packs and were ready to leave. Bryan grabbed Josh's pack by its straps as they left the campsite.

"Josh might have heard something early this morning, and went to investigate and somebody may have grabbed him from the edge of the clearing. Maybe that's why we didn't hear a thing," Bryan theorized.

"But that would mean someone else has found a way around the flooded creek, or they had already been up here," commented Tammy.

"Probably the latter. Whoever posts a watch at 'Lookout Point' must know trails that can take them almost anywhere, especially from off the top of all these ridges."

Suddenly, piercing sounds rang out, echoing from down canyon many miles away.

"Someone's shooting a gun!" exclaimed Tammy.

"Josh said he thought he had seen someone following us down on the South Fork. That someone, may be at 'Lookout Point' right now trying to come on through. The plot thickens."

"What have we gotten ourselves into here?" she asked in distress. "Where is Josh?"

Bryan could tell she was coming apart at the seams. Facing her he put his hands on her shoulders at arms length. Even though her hair which rested on her shoulders was a mess, it felt smooth and soft to his touch. "Don't worry, one thing at a time, we'll find Josh," he reassured her looking her straight in the eyes. She searched his eyes and a strange warmth came over her. She realized that she had to be strong as he was.

At first the trailing was easy, but once the course headed uphill over scattered granite outcroppings, the signs became scarce. The course angled back to a southeasterly direction climbing among sparse fir and cedar. Soon they were overlooking the miniature forest below and the green meadow that stretched about a mile beyond.

"There's a creek coming down the hill just ahead," pointed Tammy.

"That must be the one I saw last night down by the camp," replied Bryan stopping to look up in the direction she was indicating.

As she looked at him the same feeling again swept over her that she experienced when their eyes had met earlier. What was happening to her?

Working their way over to the creek, they soon discovered that it flowed toward them through a V shaped notch in a low granite ridge.

"We won't be able to follow a trail over this rock, but we can possibly pick it up again on the other side," figured Bryan.

A very narrow ledge trail, twelve to eighteen inches wide was the only apparent way to pass through. Tammy seemed to be a bit nervous about trying it. Just one mis-step could send them down into the raging torrent.

"Take my hand. As we go—lean to your right," instructed Bryan. This time she willingly extended her hand. "Don't look down, just straight ahead."

Her reply was a reluctant, "Okay."

Bryan noticed on the way large crystals of orthoclase forming a vertical seam in the pegmatite dike that rose up through the granite wall. Without stopping or changing gait they soon reached the other side.

"The *Obelisk* arises," pointed Bryan. To the southeast over the serrated granite crest jumped up the dark *Obelisk*, towering over them.

They now stood in a small basin decorated with scattered Jeffery pine and large round boulders.

"This is the closest I've ever been to the *Obelisk*," commented Bryan.

"At this angle the pinnacle is sharper at the summit," noted Tammy.

"If my hunch is right, the shape of the *Obelisk* will continue to evolve to that of the shape shown on the map."

"What if it does, then what?"

"We should be near our goal or in line with it. It's like lining up through a gun sight. But we better hustle and find Josh first. That is cautiously, we don't want to be caught either."

Half a mile across the walled in basin there were as of yet no signs to trail, but logic drove them on to the opposite side. As they drew close, it became apparent that the stream split and became two separate drainages that emptied into the basin. The creek on the left was by far the larger of the two. Along the stained north wall was evidence of a third stream, that had flowed there in the ancient past. It was apparent to Bryan that the streams in this area had shifted at some point in time.

"Decisions, decisions," proclaimed Tammy as they approached the junction of the two active streams.

"Just like life."

"Right or left, is the question."

"So far we've went right, three times. I'm apprehensive to just take a wild guess. Let's do a quick look around on both sides of the split for a short ways."

"Three rights don't make a wrong, does it?" she said trying to make a joke.

"Okay, Miss Right, you take this side, I'll cross over and take the left. Look for broken plants, anything that looks disturbed. And keep watching over your shoulder for anyone that might be following."

Bryan hopped across the rocks to the opposite side and began searching for signs. After almost ten minutes, both had advanced about five hundred feet upstream.

"Josh, you're ingenious! Tammy over here fast!"

"What? What?" she demanded jumping across both creeks to get over to Bryan's side.

"Right there, on the rock, see it?"

"Where?"

"There, are you blind?" he pointed.

"It appears to be green gum. Its Josh's gum!" she realized.

"He left us a sign to follow, or he just plain got fed up with that stinkin' gum," said Bryan.

Tammy laughed, but stopped short realizing how inappropriate it was.

"Come on let's go," urged Bryan, already charging up the slope.

"I hope he's not hurt."

"I suppose I've been selfish in involving you guys in this mystery without fully weighing the dangers."

"Actually, I think we were fascinated to the point that you couldn't keep us away," she replied.

"Keep your eyes peeled, there could be danger lurking around every corner."

"Let me catch up."

An increasing breeze buffeted the scattered pines that lined the channel.

"Could be another thunderstorm today," considered Bryan, scanning the horizon.

"No way! I'm not going through that again."

"Don't get shook. We may not even get a drop on us."

Tammy stopped in her tracks. "Did you hear that?"

Bryan stopped to listen.

"There, again."

"How is it a city girl can have such good hearing?"

"Stop calling me, city girl," she warned.

Further along, the sound became louder but indistinguishable. Rounding a corner, a concave canyon opened up before them.

"Sounds like a muffled voice," finally realized Bryan.

Rushing ahead to investigate, they neared the source of the sounds. Stopping behind a large granite outcropping, Bryan creeped out to its edge and peeked around. He gave Tammy a glance and edged back.

"It's Josh, bound and gagged. I don't see anyone else."

"Be careful it could be a trap to draw us in."

"Where Eagles Fly"

"Stay here, I'll slip over the top of this rock and see if anyone is lurking in the wings."

Leaving the two packs behind, he crawled up the eroded, gritty surface and paused near the top to scan the area behind and the ramparts above to see if anyone was watching. But no one seemed to be in sight. However, something of a different nature did catch his eye. Scrambling over the top, he paused again to check out the area on the opposite side. Again everything seemed clear. There was another muffled call for help from below. His heart was up into his throat as he slid down the other side, expecting someone to jump out at him any second. But nothing happened as he dropped to the ground. Swinging around, all was clear. Silently stepping over to Josh, he found him tied fast to a cedar tree that grew out of a rock bench. Bryan glanced around one final time.

"Josh, it's me, Bryan."

"Mmm ... mmmm."

"Let me get this gag and blindfold off."

"Whew! Boy, am I glad to see you. I figured if anyone could find me, you could. Kit Carson couldn't have done better and you didn't disappoint me."

"Tammy! Come on it's safe! Thanks for the confidence but are you all right?"

"Yeah, fine. How did you find me?"

"If it wasn't for that disgusting green gum you chew we wouldn't be standing here right now."

"Really, you found it. Ha!"

"Josh, you okay?" excitedly questioned Tammy rushing up.

"Fine, my feet are a little sore from stumbling around on the rocks but outside of that, hey, I'm in good shape."

"Who was it? How did it happen?" she begged.

"Wait—before you answer—where are they? Should make a run for it?" hurriedly asked Bryan.

"I don't know, there was the faint sound of gun shots way off somewhere and whoever it was took off in a hurry. We're probably fine for a little while.

More Than Legend

Now to answer your questions. This morning I was about to nod off when I decided to—well, take a leak. After that somebody grabbed me, gagged, and bound me. After awhile the gag loosened up, and I was able to drop the gum. Whoever it was, led me here and tied me up after hearing the shots."

"Did you see or hear who it was?" asked Bryan.

"No I didn't, but I believe there was only one person."

"We were so worried. I'm glad you're safe," said Tammy.

"Josh, Tammy, I spotted something quite unusual when I came over the rock. It's right up there on the cliff," pointed Bryan.

"Okay, show us," they responded.

Climbing up the talus slope to the base of the vertical-faced cliff they could now get a clear view.

"Marks of some kind," was Josh's first take.

"Huh, looks like birds with large wing spans," was Tammy's impression.

"Their scattered all over the face of this cliff," noted Josh.

"Well blow me to smithereens. Josh, you led us right to it," said Bryan in realization of what this was.

"Yeah, this is it, isn't it?" Josh also realized.

"You mean, this is what we've been looking for, '*Where Eagles Fly*'? I was thinking it had to be a place where eagles actually flew," stammered Tammy.

"I think that's what all of us had in the back of our minds," Bryan replied.

"Apparently, Eagles or some other large birds must have indeed been in this area at one time," deduced Josh.

"You know what this is? It's one of those Indian petroglyphs, actually paintings or carvings," identified Bryan.

"This means we're definitely on the right trail," Tammy realized.

A gust of wind raced up canyon as a fleeting cloud sent its shadow racing across the landscape.

"We better get moving, before someone returns," suggested Josh looking around nervously.

Returning for their packs, they quickly reorganized themselves, and were on their way to face the unknown dangers ahead and flee those from behind.

15

"WANDERING SKY"

Towering white clouds were already forming over the lofty summits of the Sierra, foreboding of more fireworks. Summer in the mountains was an ever changing experience. If you desired change, there was always the option to travel a couple of miles or wait a couple of hours. Beauty was everywhere, in the sky, in the rocks, in the rivers, in the forest, and even amongst the micro-flowers of the meadows—ever changing. There was no end of things to explore and examine.

The three decided there was no turning back now, even though they might be overdue that night. Having come so far, and with danger lurking behind they decided to continue at least through the day.

Gleaming granite now transformed to dark shale and basaltic flows. The *Obelisk* had disappeared again behind the ridges in its continuing game of hide and seek. Mirror-like pools of water were retained in the shallow depressions of the bedrock above the creek line, indicating that heavy thundershowers must have recently visited the area.

"Wandering Sky"

"I think it's time to stop, pull out the map, and evaluate our situation, before we go much further," recommended Bryan after they had hiked almost an hour.

"I need to rest and get something to eat before I perish," expressed Tammy.

"I second that," agreed Josh.

They stopped next to a twisted juniper tree that grew out of a large crack in the bedrock. Finding themselves a flat place to sit, they rummaged in their packs for something to eat.

"Finding the 'Eagles' has given me confidence that the 'Canyon of Gold,' can be found," stated Josh.

"At least we've put a little more space between us and the bad guys," commented Tammy.

"It would almost appear there are two sets of bad guys, and as long as they are in contention with one another, it's giving us a better chance to complete our mission," said Bryan as he watched the cumulus clouds gliding over the peaks. "Here's the map, let's look it over."

"There's where the 'Eagles Fly,' and we must be up here somewhere," pointed Tammy.

"Right, we must be close to the 'Wandering Sky,' " surmised Bryan.

"We're further along than I thought," realized Josh.

"What could this 'Wandering Sky' possibly be?" Bryan threw open for discussion.

"It may be like 'Where Eagles Fly,' we won't recognize it till we see it," thought Tammy.

"Hmm. And then what about the final clue, the 'Door of the Sun,' how do we find this 'Door?' " questioned Josh.

"I think Tammy's right, we have to watch and just take this one step at a time. We could guess till the moon turned blue. The answers lie ahead. I have confidence, that we will find them," concluded Bryan.

"That is if we're not intercepted first," commented Josh looking back downstream, perhaps thinking about his experience that morning.

Resting a few more minutes, the explorers resumed their course. Rumbling issued out of the back country.

"The boomers are back," announced Josh.

Tammy made a face at Bryan.

"Don't blame me, I can't control the weather," he defended.

"There's the *Three Chimneys* coming into view now," spotted Josh.

"Appropriately named so it appears," agreed Tammy.

Flashes loomed over the horizon. Thunder came in rolling waves crashing against the canyon walls and echoing down its corridors. Abruptly the canyon walls closed in, leaving a vertical channel about one hundred feet across.

"What's this?" first questioned Bryan.

No one spoke a word as they approached what appeared to be shafts or poles sticking up out of piles of rocks on the high ground above the creek.

"I think they're Indian markers, if I'm not mistaken," suggested Josh.

Examining them more closely they could see notches near the top in the decaying wood.

"They sure are severely cracked and disintegrating. They must be very old," concluded Tammy.

"Notice how these appear to have been crossed," added Bryan.

"Crossed like lances, this must be a warning not to pass," figured Tammy.

"Must be," her cousin agreed.

Bryan could hear his mother's voice again, as she related how the Indians were the ones who had killed Captain Camino. Then he remembered the painting in the basement that Rosa had tipped him off about. The Indian woman was undoubtedly his great-great-grandmother. What a seeming paradox.

The wind gusted through the channel, being drawn by the cloud masses building to the east.

"Wandering Sky"

"One thing is for sure, this is testimony to the fact that not many people have been here. These lances appear to be completely untouched," scrutinized Bryan.

"It's possible too, that no one has been allowed to venture this far before," added Josh.

"Just like the warning given to Bryan's grandfather," recalled Tammy. "What was his name, Fishhawk? Well, anyway the warning about those who'd be watching, and wouldn't allow those venturing to far to return, right?"

"The name was Riverhawk, but you are essentially right. It was an Indian warning, and all the stories seem to substantiate its reality. Just like what we see before us now," agreed Bryan.

"Like the ones at 'Lookout Point' or the guy who grabbed me." concluded Josh.

"I'm not sure how they fit into this. But my grandfather felt that the Indians in his day, didn't know what they were really guarding. Maybe they presumed it was a sacred burial ground or something. The Indians must have handed down from generation to generation whatever secret or obligation they thought was to be protected. Its true meaning for some reason was allowed to be lost over time," reasoned Bryan.

"Maybe this is a last chance warning to turn back," whispered Tammy.

"That may be, but I think what happened to me shows that we're well past that point," replied Josh.

"We know too much," added Bryan.

"Well, so much for that quiet, lazy summer away from the city," sighed Tammy putting her hands on her hips.

Chain lightning arced and sizzled overhead. Their scalps prickled as the air filled with static. The passageway ahead was dark and foreboding. They looked at each other.

Bryan stepped across the symbolic line and turned. "Whose still with me?" he asked.

Josh paused and stepped across.

175

"Well, what choice do I have?" protested Tammy. "Women have had to follow men everywhere, that's the reality of world history." Hesitating, she finally followed suit and sighed.

"Very good, let's continue, but cautiously," said Bryan with finality.

"Stay close," Josh again reminded Tammy.

Entering the vertical channel the reverberation of the thunder was deafening, it was like being in an echo chamber. Tammy held her ears and mouthed, "Too loud." The light was dim, but their eyes quickly adjusted. The storm eased just as rapidly as it had reached full intensity, and moved off to the northwest.

"Look's like we're not going to get dowsed today," announced Josh.

"I'd scream if we had to go through that again. My hair, my clothes, I'm such a mess," she complained.

Come on Tammy, get real. I know your kind, always running to the beauty salon every week and getting your nails done up. You don't need all that. The wilderness has a way of bringing out a person's natural beauty," criticized Bryan.

"I'm not being fanatical. I do take a little pride in my appearance though, not like some people I know," she snapped back.

"This channel has been swept super clean, probably by yesterday's gully-washer," observed Josh, not paying attention to their debate. "Just a few rocks and limbs left here and there."

The gorge gradually turned toward the north. Sunlight breaking through the clouds caught the upper rim of the vertical walls, highlighting its reddish cast. Shafts of light struck the ground near an area where a number of significant boulders were scattered about.

Unnoticed by the boys who kept more to the center of the channel, Tammy seemed to be attracted toward one of the shafts of light and meandered off among the boulders. Suddenly she screamed and fell from view behind one of the large rocks, calling for help.

"What now?" asked Bryan looking back over his shoulder.

"Help me! You idiots! Get me out of here!" she yelled.

Realizing this was for real, they ran over to her location not knowing what to expect. Coming around the large rock, they found her clinging to the side of an irregular shaped pit.

"Hang on!" yelled Josh.

"You grab one arm, I'll grab the other," barked Bryan.

"I've got her," grunted Josh.

"Pull then."

"I'm sliding, I can't hang on." Tammy screamed as Josh lost his grip and she started swinging.

"Josh!" growled Bryan straining to hang on.

"I can't reach her!" exclaimed Josh.

"Bryan! Don't you dare let me go!"

"I won't if you'll keep quiet! Hang on, I'll try to pull you up so Josh can grab your hand."

Bryan strained with all his might, dragging his arm across the bear rock. Josh managed to finally get a hold of her hand and with a combined effort they were able to pull her up the rest of the way.

"Tammy, how could you not have seen this big hole?" demanded Josh gasping for breath.

"I don't know. I was just readjusting the strap on my pack as I came around this boulder, and then all of a sudden the ground disappeared right out from under my feet," she recalled, breathing heavily.

"Did you get hurt?" asked Josh noticing Bryan holding his right forearm.

"Nothing that time won't heal."

"You're bleeding!" realized Tammy biting her lip. "Let me see."

"Don't you think you've done enough?"

"This is a bad cut. Here let me fix it." After pulling a T-shirt from her pack, she tore it in two, and proceeded to soak one piece in the creek and to clean his wound. She could feel his eyes upon her and had the urge to meet his gaze, but felt a little ashamed for causing all of this. Tying the rest of the T-shirt around his arm, she declared it done.

"Say, what is this up here?" pointed Josh grunting to get up.

"Probably just a piece of wood," said Bryan squinting his eyes.

"No, it's a bone. Here's another one, and another one. What the heck, there all over the place," discovered Josh.

Bryan staggered to his feet to investigate. "There are all kinds of bones scattered over here. Why are there so many?" Then the realization hit. He met Josh's gaze but they said nothing.

"One thing I see, is that they seem to be all downstream of this pit," noticed Tammy.

"Yeah, I see that. So, what do we have here, a well of bones?" Bryan replied as he walked over to the edge hoping to see down into the bottom. "Hold my legs," asked Bryan getting into position to slide over the edge.

"I bet this is just from animals being caught in this canyon during a cloud burst, like some foolish people I know," commented Tammy with an air of sarcasm.

"Pull me back," called Bryan.

"Well?" they asked.

Bryan's face was a little flushed probably from the blood rushing to his head. He hesitated to speak, then replied, "Let's get out of here, I really don't see anything of any significance. This pit must be a catch-all for all sorts of things." Putting his pack back on he continued, "I guess if you get enough water barreling down through here, anything is possible."

"Indeed so," agreed Tammy.

Josh knew Bryan well enough to sense that he was holding back on something. It wasn't like him to abruptly jump up and leave something half investigated.

"It seems kind of strange that these boulders are located just around this site," pondered Tammy having an inkling that perhaps more than natural forces had been at work here.

Strolling back toward the center of the channel, Bryan turned, and took in the whole scene one more time before continuing on.

"Tammy, I want you to stay a lot closer," he warned in a threatening way.

"I didn't know you cared," she replied.

"Ugh!" was his reply still a little miffed at her.

Josh edged up to Bryan. "Is there something back there you're not telling us?" whispered Josh.

Bryan looked at him out of the corner of his eye. "There is more than animal bones down there. We'll have to be alone to discuss it," he whispered back.

"Hey you two, no secrets," called out Tammy.

Glancing at Josh, Bryan returned to a normal voice and changed the subject. "You know, ever since we've been contemplating who we are up against, I keep going back to the same troubling thought. I have an idea that our Mr. Krasnik is mixed up in this somehow. But I don't know, maybe I'm off on this. It could just be circumstantial."

"Ever since the time we had to hide off the trail near Crazy Joe's, I've wondered myself if that familiar voice was his, but I'm not absolutely sure either," commented Josh.

"He has been acting very suspiciously. It all started after I turned in my school project. I caught him, when he thought no one was watching, jotting down some notes off of my display. And then what does he do, after praising my project? He goes and gives me a poor grade and refuses to talk to me. Just like that day at the store. I know he saw me, but he turned the corner and disappeared. You know, now that I think about it, that was the same morning when the old fishing map on the store wall disappeared," realized Bryan.

"Really? That just can't be coincidence, can it? No-o, I don't think so," replied Josh answering his own question.

"What about Crazy Joe?" asked Tammy. "Could he be the one behind a lot of this?"

"That's always a possibility," answered Josh. "And there is Dark Shadow constantly lurking around also."

"Lurking is right," seconded Bryan recalling the incident in town. "But the main thing now is to find the 'Canyon of Gold' before anyone else does or can prevent us from finding it."

"I can't help but think that if it wasn't for the discovery of the Spanish map, the quest for this legendary gold strike probably wouldn't be any further along than the 'Forks,'" reflected Josh.

"I suppose so. It was inevitable that someday the map would be found, but the timing of this revelation is quite compelling," commented Bryan.

Again a cool breeze sprang to life blowing up canyon. Overhead a group of ragged clouds drifted across the top of the gorge.

"That's odd, there's water coming out of the bank up ahead. There on the right-hand side," pointed ahead Josh.

"Must be a natural spring," thought Tammy.

As they approached, a small stream became visible issuing out of the canyon wall. The outlet was surrounded by a large jumble of boulders. A significant amount of water flowed out of its dark recesses.

"Hey, you guys, do you see what I see?" asked Bryan looking up .

"What do you see?" asked Tammy.

"Notice the walls near the top, straight up from the spring," he directed.

"Hey! It looks like this stream comes from a canyon further back," exclaimed Josh.

"If that's true, all of this area across here must be a giant rock slide that plugged off the mouth of this canyon," stated Tammy.

"It's so well camouflaged. The mosses, the trees growing out of the rocks, it blends in so well that the canyon could be easily missed," said Bryan.

"Then the spring is not a spring but a small creek," realized Tammy.

"You know for a city girl, you're not half bad at figuring things out," replied Bryan.

"Well thank you, Country Boy," she curtsied.

Bryan shook his head. "Anyway, the question now is, which way is the correct route, up through the hidden canyon or is it this way, continuing up the main creek?" he pointed.

"If it was up the hidden canyon, how do we get there, it's sealed off," challenged Josh.

Bryan set his pack down and spread the map out.

"I suppose, panning won't help us this time," considered Tammy.

"Probably not," answered Josh.

"We should be somewhere in here," pointed Bryan. "As you can see there is only one branch to the creek shown here on the map and it makes a sharp bend right here toward the northeast. Josh, which way would you say the *Obelisk* bears from here?" asked Bryan.

"Oh-h, probably just about in line with this stream and the hidden canyon," he figured.

"Okay, then this has to be the fork of the stream that heads right for the *Obelisk*. This slide could have been here for centuries but looking at the present vegetation and trees, I would place its age at about eighty to one hundred years," guessed Bryan.

"Another fork to the right," Josh uttered under his breath.

"Oh! No! You've got to be kidding," responded Tammy. "This rock slide is too difficult to climb up, just how do you plan on getting through that?"

"Well, that's one thing that can stop us cold, nature totally shutting us out," Bryan conceded. Getting up he surveyed in detail the obstacle that lay between them and their goal.

"We can't climb this, it's to dangerous," observed Josh.

More Than Legend

Finding his flashlight, Bryan grabbed up his pack and marched over to the subterranean stream and shined the light back into the dark passageway.

"There's good clearance above the water as far I can see. I should be able to wade in and breathe," considered Bryan.

"That's very risky, you have no idea how far it goes or what danger lurks hidden below or above," discouraged Josh.

"We're so close!" exclaimed Bryan. "Give me your rope Josh, I'll tie both of ours together and put one end around my waist. If there's a problem I'll tug on the line twice, then you can pull me out. If you get to the end of the rope, you tug twice, okay?" schemed Bryan.

"Don't do it," urged Tammy.

"Hey! your not my mother," he replied.

For some reason that comment hurt. It shouldn't have, but it did. What was wrong with her?

"I'll wade in slowly and check the stability as I go," he further resolved.

"It's still pretty risky, but it's your neck," Josh finally said.

"Don't worry, I may not get very far anyway," downplayed Bryan.

Footing was rocky and uneven as he went in. The ceiling arched about two feet overhead. Water was up to his waist and was painfully cold.

The rope glided through Josh's hand at first quickly, then slower by the time he reached the second half of the rope. After a minute, Josh held the end of the rope and tugged it twice to signal Bryan. The rope remained taut for a moment and suddenly went limp. Josh pulled on the rope but there was no resistance. Soon the other end of the rope floated out, untied.

"Oh! No!" panicked Tammy.

"Bryan! Bryan!" called Josh. He took his light and looked in as far as he could, but could see nothing. "I told him it was foolish, didn't I?" Josh said in an agitated tone.

Suddenly there was a splash and a booming echo. In a few seconds Bryan floated out.

"E-E-ha! I found a way through," he exclaimed visibly soaked from head to toe.

"We thought you were a goner after the rope floated back," said Josh visibly upset.

"When I reached the end of the rope, I could see daylight above, but I couldn't reach the opening. Just past it, the tunnel takes a dive underwater. I figured I had a fifty-fifty chance of coming up on the other side. So I untied myself, ducked under and then popped up into a pool of water on the other side of the slide," he excitedly related.

Tammy felt drained and wanted to call him a fool but held her tongue.

"Wait till you see the other side, it's clear sailing," encouraged Bryan.

"I'm not going swimming in that dark cavern," she said firmly.

"There's another way. The hole in the ceiling is about three feet above our reach. So this is what I'll do: I can go back up into the pool with the rope tied around my waist and pull the rope all the way out. Then I'll proceed to where the hole daylights and feed it back down to you guys. When you wade up to the hole, I'll pull you up through the opening. Sound doable?" Bryan asked.

"Okay, sounds safe enough, let's try it, Tammy," coaxed Josh. Tammy took a deep breath and put her arms up.

Bryan proceeded with the plan. Soon the rope reappeared and the two waded in pulling themselves along.

"There you are," said Bryan looking down upon them. "Give Tammy a boost, I'll pull her up first."

Tammy held on to the rope as Bryan pulled and Josh pushed.

"Tammy, let go of the rope and grab my wrists one at a time," ordered Bryan.

He then pulled her up out of the hole. For Josh, they both had to pull on the rope and then reach down to lift him up. Both Bryan and Tammy plopped down in exhaustion.

"Hey, I'm not that heavy," protested Josh.

"You want to make a bet?" replied Tammy.

"In your case Josh, they didn't stack it wide they stacked it tall," laughed Bryan.

Josh stuck his tongue out at him. "One thing about this, not many will be able to find their way through here and follow us," stated Josh changing the subject.

"Don't count on it, remember there could be other trails and this could mean nothing to them," Bryan responded.

"Oh, that's encouraging," he replied sarcastically.

"Look, how narrow this canyon is," noticed Tammy.

"I wonder how long it is?" questioned Josh.

"I don't know, but our goal is probably just ahead, let's see if we can find it before dark," challenged Bryan.

Ahead of them loomed a narrow slot, cut through the rock by centuries of water erosion, being only about 50 feet wide and towering to over four hundred feet above. On and off gusty winds whistled and moaned through the narrow passageway. The channel bottom proved to be very sandy. Numerous plants grew along the edges of the channel and others were pigeon-holed in the walls. Alternating bands differentiated themselves in the rock strata. An abrupt turn in the rocky corridor disclosed a change in geology and aspect. No longer were the walls vertical. They curved back and forth and narrowed to about eight feet apart. Only a narrow ribbon of light shone above them.

"We've found it, this is it," suddenly announced Tammy coming to an abrupt stop.

"What did we find?" asked Josh not having a clue.

"Are you guys blind? Look up!"

"Yes! Of course, it must be," realized Bryan, " 'Wandering Sky!' "

"It does wander around a bit, doesn't it," agreed Josh.

"Clever name," added Tammy.

"This has given us an additional view into the thinking of my great-great-grandfather," remarked Bryan. "What could he be thinking of next?"

16

"DOOR OF THE SUN"

With renewed confidence, the young but tired adventurers forged on in the declining light of the afternoon. A cool gusty breeze continued to blow at their backs.

Each one, daydreamed of the possibilities that laid ahead in the 'Canyon of Gold.' Bryan thought of his great-great-grandfather. Could this legendary 'Canyon' be his last resting place, or was he ambushed in some other place? In a momentary blur he thought of the "well of bones."

"A fully loaded pack train could barely get through some of these tight places," observed Josh breaking the silence after a few minutes.

"As they say: a miss is as good as a mile," commented Bryan.

"I hate to be a drag, but I'm getting mighty hungry here," Tammy announced.

"It goes with the gender," dryly replied Bryan.

"What?" half-laughed Tammy.

"Hang in there, we shouldn't have far to go," encouraged Josh. How true Josh's statement was, for around the corner two hundred years of legend awaited.

"Hey! Look! A natural arch," first spotted Tammy.

"How interesting, there must have been a core of softer rock that eroded away first," concluded Josh.

The gorge was approximately seventy-five feet wide in the area of the fiery colored arch. Bryan's eye caught sight of what appeared to be markings chiseled into the center of the arch.

"Those marks up there are manmade, I believe," pointed Bryan.

"The right side has broken away, but the other side—is a portion of the 'Door of the Sun' symbol, if I'm thinking right," recognized Josh.

"Yes! Yes!" agreed Bryan getting all fired up. "This is it! This must be the gateway into the *'Canyon of Gold.'* "

"Well, what are we waiting for?" asked Tammy catching the excitement.

"Who knows what we'll find," Bryan answered glancing meaningfully at them and then stepping through the arch.

Beyond, the narrow gorge began to open up into a rugged canyon with sloped walls of igneous rock, dashed in places by an occasional quartz vein, and above, castle-like vertical faced ramparts. To the northeast over the ridge crest, the tip of the *Obelisk* could be seen. Its outline now closely resembling the shape depicted on the map. Reaching the heart of the canyon, they scrutinized the harsh terrain all around them, looking for some hint of the mine or mines that should have been there. But there was no evidence of any mining.

"After a couple of centuries, nature can transform and hide things quite well," spoke up Josh.

"The mine had probably been hidden anyway," added Bryan. "Grab something to eat if you need to, I'm going to look around for a spell."

While Bryan walked up the canyon, Josh and Tammy nibbled on what little food they had left and speculated on what they would find.

"One thing is for sure, if the Captain's mine is here somewhere, Bryan will find it," said Josh.

"Yes, with our help. Why take a backseat to him, we can find it too," replied Tammy. "Matter of fact, let's find it first," she schemed.

"Door of the Sun"

Finishing up they scattered to begin their own search among the pockets of trees and undergrowth. Within the folds of the canyon walls old weather-beaten junipers wound their way into the cracks and crevices; but yielded no secrets.

After about half an hour, Bryan walked back from the upper end of the canyon and found Josh on one of the side slopes.

"This must be the correct place all right. Further up, where the canyon narrows back down is another 'Door of the Sun' symbol facing this way," informed Bryan, gesturing with his hands.

"So it's definitely in this vicinity," Josh replied.

"Dang, we're losing our daylight," Bryan complained. "Im going to check out the other side."

The search continued on both sides of the canyon. Finally without success they all wandered back to where they had left their packs.

"Are you sure we have the right place?" questioned Tammy.

"This has to be it, all the clues, the map, the symbols at both ends of this valley, it all seems to fit," responded Bryan.

"Maybe the whole thing is a hoax, in order to lead everyone away from the real mines," proposed Josh.

"It just can't be," refuted Bryan sitting down. Hunched over he held his head between his hands as he looked at the ground. Suddenly, he jumped back up.

"What is it?" questioned Josh.

"I'm not sure," he replied, kicking away some of the rocks next to where he was sitting.

"Bryan, have you gone nuts?" asked Tammy.

"Maybe, maybe not."

"It's smoothed off like a step," noticed Josh looking on.

"A step, you're right. Then there has to be more," Bryan surmised.

With that realization, their eyes followed up the slope.

"And where do they lead?" Tammy wondered.

More Than Legend

Josh and Bryan jumped up the slope kicking rocks left and right exposing more steps. Each exclaiming, "Here's another one!"

"This one up here is already uncovered," said Tammy.

After exposing all the steps, their discoveries suddenly ended about seventy-five feet above the valley floor. They looked up at the sheer cliff that was just above them, wondering what was the purpose of the steps that went nowhere.

"Wow, what does it mean?" questioned Josh scratching his head.

"Maybe they abandoned their idea, whatever it was," ventured Tammy.

Josh and Tammy stood above the top step watching Bryan move more of the loose rock away.

"Josh, give me a hand, I think this is more than a step," requested Bryan.

In a few minutes with Tammy joining in, they had cleared an area the shape of a crescent moon. An area that had been notched into the rocky slope.

"There's a pattern chiseled into this surface," noticed Josh bending down blowing the dust out of the grooves. "Matter of fact, this looks like part of the arch on the 'Door of the Sun.'"

More grooves were uncovered and cleaned out. It was now apparent that Josh was right. They were standing on a semicircular platform with the 'Door of the Sun' symbol inscribed across it.

"What's it directing us to?" asked Tammy dusting herself off.

"There's no more steps above here, why did they stop here? This spot must have some significance," Bryan pondered.

Lengthening shadows from the far ridge now engulfed them as the sun slipped over the horizon.

"I don't know if it means anything, but the 'Door' is facing across the canyon," noted Tammy.

"Perhaps the mine is located directly across the canyon in line with the setting sun," speculated Josh.

"That's a smart idea, Josh," commended Bryan. "I can't think of anything better to try; let's go take a look. I've asked myself that question before, about the 'Sun' symbol. Is it setting or is it rising?"

Sighting on a protruding knob they made their way back down. Fanning out they proceeded up into the shaded slope in search of the hidden mine. Despite falling temperatures the rock surfaces were still emanating a degree of warmth collected from the sun. Ranging around the outcroppings, the ravines, and through the trees, they again came up with nothing.

"I don't think anybody is going to find this first," Josh whispered in Tammy's ear.

"I don't know," said Bryan throwing his arms up. "This must be some kind of a joke."

"It's starting to get dark, we'd better make camp here tonight. There's no way we'll be able to get down the hill now," pointed out Josh.

"Yeah, we need time to think," acknowledged Bryan in pure frustration.

After gathering wood, They settled down to appease their appetites. A certain quiet set in over the small canyon as darkness set in. It was hard to imagine that this was the place of legend and they were there.

"The arch we passed through, wasn't that the 'Door of the Sun?'" questioned Tammy.

"I kind of jumped at that idea. It has the right shape and inscriptions and so-forth," Bryan answered. Pausing for a moment, he continued. "Although, the old man told my father that the door is closed, and it's above the heads of mortal man."

"Well, if that were true in a literal sense, you would think the 'Door,' if it was closed off, would have some residual evidence of boulders or debris. But it's clean as a whistle down through there," commented Josh as he kindled the fire.

"Maybe the Indian man meant the giant land slide that blocked the canyon further down," suggested Tammy.

"No, it couldn't be, that is if we still believe the map, and it's been truthful so far," replied Bryan.

Unfolding the map, he pointed to 'Wandering Sky' as the light danced and flickered across the sheet.

"The 'Door' is on the upper side of 'Wandering Sky' not on the downstream side," he pointed out.

"Looks like were stumped," concluded Josh.

"The map gave us four clues, right?" reviewed Tammy. "The first one was 'Metallic City,' perhaps named sarcastically after the iron pyrite found in the mine, or simply just due to their use of metal, which may have been a novelty to them. But anyway, second, was 'Where Eagles Fly.' It was an Indian painting, not a real place where eagles could be found."

"And then, 'Wandering Sky' was where only a narrow ribbon of sky was visible," added Josh falling in line with Tammy's rendition.

"The last two were based on some kind of natural but real phenomena," pondered Bryan trying to classify them.

"Taken literally the 'Door' should be a real entrance of some kind, leading into this so-called 'Canyon of Gold,' " said Tammy extending Bryan's logic to the next step.

"It's the sun part, that's mysterious," commented Josh.

"It could be by association, if it was named for the beautiful golden sunsets that Captain Camino may have seen on the ocean, or maybe the sun does actually shine through it," speculated Bryan.

"Not during sunset, so it appears," stated Josh.

"What about sunrise? Could that be it?" Tammy ventured.

"If it has a literal meaning, I would say sunrise would be the logical time while the sun is low," agreed Bryan.

"Good idea, we can scatter to different locations. One person can be down by the archway, another at the top of the steps, and then another position up the valley somewhere, poised as the sun rises," proposed Josh.

"Let's give it one more try, but the real 'Door' may still be blocked and hidden," said Bryan. "And there is another part of the 'Door of the Sun' we haven't considered yet. It's the pointed object at its base. What possibly could it be or mean?"

Everyone shook their head, for there was no way to know.

A cool wind began to blow again. The flames sputtered. "That's odd, a breeze starting up this time of night," noticed Josh glancing around the starry sky.

As Bryan stared and was drawn into the flames, his life unfolded in front of him, his youth, the pack trips, his mother, her departure, school, the 'Legend,' and how the mountains seemed to call him. What awaited him here? Would his mother ever return, or would she insist on going her own way, pulling him with her? What was to happen to his dad, the failing business, the house and their property? It seemed the future was one eternal path of struggle.

"Well, by now everyone is wondering where we are," said Tammy breaking the silence.

"Including the bad guys, they may not be far away," reminded Bryan.

"Yes, them too," replied Tammy.

"If the Indians are supposed to be guarding this secret, why aren't they here?" wondered Josh aloud.

"Because maybe this isn't the place," dryly answered Tammy.

"Perhaps it's what my grandfather alluded to. That in later generations—details were held back from them," contemplated Bryan.

"So what you're saying, it's possible that they may not know where this place is," responded Josh.

"They are probably aware of the crossed lances, but beyond that, who knows, it might be just like a forbidden zone to—them," trailed off Tammy. "What's that noise?"

"Sounds like a plane," recognized Josh.

"Plane!" jumped up Bryan. "Fast! smother the fire! They'll see it. Dang! It may be too late already," he exclaimed.

The resonating drone of an airplane engine neared as they frantically tried to stamp out the fire by scattering it and covering it in dirt. Suddenly the plane burst over the ridge flying low, almost overhead. After it passed over their position, it veered off to the southeast and circled back to cross again about a quarter mile south. A strong beam of light was switched on from the plane, illuminating the rugged terrain as it flew.

"They must have spotted our fire before we could get it out," concluded Josh.

"With that light it appears they are following the canyon out to its junction with the main branch," observed Bryan.

Though out of sight, they could still hear the plane buzzing around, probably near the big landslide, trying to spot the best way to get around it.

"They could even be communicating with someone on the ground, directing them on which way to go," said Tammy.

"Those dirty dogs! That's cheating, using a plane," fumed Bryan kicking a couple of rocks. "I didn't even think of the fire, my mind was off in left field."

Soon the hum of the plane had gone.

"Come first light, they'll be searching for a way around or through the rock slide just as we did," figured Josh sitting back down to a dark campsite.

"Who are these people anyway?" complained Tammy.

"We think we know who a couple of them might be, but there must be someone else involved either separately or together," answered Josh.

"You mean like your teacher?" she asked.

"He's a strong suspect for sure," Josh affirmed. "But somebody has to be behind the scenes pulling the strings."

"Any of you smell smoke?" questioned Bryan.

"Just from the smoldering campfire," Tammy replied.

"I mean outside of that. Standing over here away from it, I keep getting whiffs of smoke from somewhere else," he explained.

"I smell it now too," said Josh. "It's not impossible there's a slumbering lightning strike that's starting to take off."

"Door of the Sun"

"Between the bad guys and a possible forest fire, there won't be much sleep tonight," remarked Tammy.

"We will have to keep one eye open, but we do have to get some rest. Morning will come early. At gray dawn, we'll get up and go to our positions to watch. It's our last chance to find this illusive 'Door,' " stated Bryan.

"Smokey the Bear will be unhappy with us, if we don't finish putting this fire out," reminded Josh.

Finishing camp chores, and scraping together pine and juniper boughs and needles to bed down on, they soon drifted off asleep despite the perplexities that chased through their minds.

To Bryan it seemed like only minutes since he had fallen asleep, but the east sky showed the hint of a new day. Bryan rolled over and thought about the challenge that loomed in front of them. It would be easy to fold up and fade away, but this was his great-great-grandfather's mine, it was rightfully his to find. What more success could others have? Their backs were against the wall. Without success that morning, they would be forced to give up and back out. If that was the case, he would have to allow for an escape route.

"Hey, you loafers, time to rise and shine," he finally decided to call out.

Nobody moved. Finally Josh groaned and tried to roll over but flopped back.

"Come on, I can smell gold dust from here," grunted Bryan trying to rouse them, while struggling to his own feet.

"Woo! I'm not smelling gold, I'm smelling smoke," realized Tammy.

"Smoke!" acknowledged Josh, his eyes popping open. "There must be a fire brewin' over the hill."

"Your right! Look!" pointed Bryan.

Dark purple clouds of smoke loomed over the horizon to the north.

"I'm beginning to feel like we're at ground zero," commented Josh.

It was well into gray dawn as they spread out to wait for the sun at their appointed positions.

"Don't fall asleep," called Bryan before they were out of sight.

While Josh walked to the archway, Tammy climbed the steps to the inscribed platform, and Bryan slowly strolled toward the head of the canyon. After about half an hour the sun finally hit the top of the ridge with a reddish tinge, probably due to the smoke. Bryan sat on a ledge and anxiously watched the light and shadow changing across the face of the cliff. Everything was extremely quiet, only an occasional bird call could be heard.

Tammy was nodding off, when something caused her to jerk awake. Looking around, she couldn't see anything. But across the canyon in a recessed notch two small spots of light had now appeared. She watched them for a couple of minutes. They seemed to grow bigger, in a downward direction. Now convinced this was important she called the boys to her location.

"Look! back in there, almost like two eyes," she pointed.

"That's odd," remarked Josh.

"Let's see what it does," said Bryan taking a seat.

As the minutes ticked by the spots slowly changed into large triangles. Gradually the two triangles merged and the outer edges became more rounded forming a rough horizontal half circle. However, a triangular section in the center did remained in shadow.

"Did any of you check back in that notch, yesterday?" asked Bryan.

"I remember walking by there, but all I could see was solid rock and some brush," recalled Tammy.

"You realize that only from this vantage point can you get a clear view back in there?" observed Bryan studying the canyon relief.

After a few more minutes the center shadow had melted down to a slender point and the entire figure glowed red.

"I don't believe it," breathed Tammy.

"That's it!" exclaimed Bryan. "The 'Door of the Sun!'"

"Door of the Sun"

"That must be the spot," agreed Josh.

Running across the canyon, they scurried up the slope and back into the rocky recess. The shaft of light fell upon a tall stand of dead brush that stood out from the cliff wall. Entering the sunlight, the two boys cleared a path by crunching the brush down all the way to the back wall. The light fell directly upon the wall and the adjoining foreground.

"There's something chiseled into the rock, where the light is shining," pointed Tammy.

Kneeling down they moved loose rocks out of the way, revealing more of the figure on the wall.

"It's the 'Door' symbol again," realized Bryan.

"This mound of dirt and rock appears to have been put here to hide it," figured Josh.

"Just like what they did to the steps and the platform across the way," recalled Tammy.

"Well, where is the 'Door' then?" questioned Josh. "This cliff is solid rock and the ground under this mound appears to be also."

Bryan looked glum. The fiery glow of the 'Door of the Sun' weakened and began to waver across its counterpart on the canyon wall. How eerie it seemed. The clue to a long lost secret was vanishing away right in front of them—slipping right through their fingers. Bryan turned around and squinted in the direction of the diminishing spot of light. "There she is! There she is!" he pointed hysterically. "There is the real 'Door,' up there!"

"Well I'll be a curly-toed rug rat!" said Josh.

"Truly, it is a '*Door of the Sun*,'" breathed Tammy.

Across the canyon above the steep bluffs was a short plateau about six hundred feet deep, with a vertical wall of dark upthrusted volcanic dikes set back, some being over two hundred feet tall. Near the center and set back even farther the sun shone through a natural arch in the shape of a near-perfect half circle. The light through the 'Door of the Sun' now flickered and was gone.

"Let's grab our stuff and get right over there before someone comes along," directed Bryan.

"The old Indian was right, the 'Door' is above 'the heads of mortal man,' that's why it is impossible to see, except from certain select vantage points," realized Josh.

Moving up the canyon, they found a rough course that zigzagged around the left side of the steep bluffs. Originally, there must have been a trail underneath the boulders and debris, that now occupied the route. The trail was unanimously termed the "Zigzags." Out of breath, they reached the plateau to be greeted by the impressive fiery colored volcanic wall that now loomed up in front of them.

"It's like an outer wall of one of those ancient cities, keeping out all enemies," compared Josh as they paused.

"Quite a mixture of violent geology up here," noted Tammy.

"Rocks are like a history book of the planet. It would be good if we better understood the language," commented Bryan as he pushed on, anxious to get to the gate of that imaginary city.

Following along the wall the 'Door' soon appeared, in a recess about three hundred feet in. As he neared, he mentally gauged it to be about twenty-five feet in width and approximately twenty feet in height. The closer he approached the more boulders he encountered. A few that were extra large, remained stationed near the opening. The arch itself was composed of a volcanic conglomerate. Above the archway, soared the black and red volcanic ridge. Catching his eye along the top of the arch were carved radial lines. Then he recollected the pattern of the symbol, and the window at the Fort. This was the real thing. This definitely was, the real '*Door of the Sun*,' " he told himself again.

Finally the other two adventurers caught up. Josh and Tammy also spotted the radial lines and commented on the boulders and debris that must have at one time blocked the passageway.

"Some of the rock above still looks pretty unstable," additionally noted Josh.

"Door of the Sun"

"Before we step through the time portal, be prepared, who knows what we may find in here," warned Bryan.

Tammy and Josh glanced at each other and then back at Bryan. What was hidden behind these eternal walls?

17

"ORO DE CAÑON"

 gust of wind blew past them through the 'Door.' To their left they could now see the smoke boiling up from the fire. It appeared to be getting closer. Facing the 'Door of the Sun,' Bryan took it all in one more time.

"It's time to go back two hundred years into history," he said as he stepped through.

Josh and Tammy followed Bryan to the other side overlooking a most amazing valley. Red and black volcanic bluffs and lofty granite peaks dominated the eastern skyline. The deep valley appeared to be completely closed off from the outside world. Islands of green vegetation and trees were perched along the rugged slopes and in sections of the valley below. A green ribbon outlining a small stream wound its way down the valley disappearing beyond view. But the thing that boldly stood out before them was the soaring *Obelisk* with its pointed spire. This was beyond all doubt the '*Oro de Cañon*,' the 'Canyon of Gold.'

Bryan looked up at the impressive spire. "There's the point that was in the bottom of the 'Door of the Sun,' " he realized.

"Absolutely amazing. If only we had known the secret of the symbol," understood Josh. The shadow of the Obelisk is projected through the 'Door' at sunrise."

"It was visible only for a few minutes," recalled Tammy.

"We had to do it the hard way," summed up Bryan.

Finding a pathway on the left side, they descended the slope. Part way down, Bryan suddenly put his arm out, warning them of something.

"Tammy, maybe you better close your eyes," he recommended.

"No way! A-ah!" she reacted slapping a hand over her mouth.

There lying on the slope with an out stretched arm was a human skeleton facing up hill.

Bryan glanced at Josh and Tammy. Was this a portent of things to come?

"Come on," tugged Josh as they continued on down.

Nearing the bottom of the grade, the sound of water could be heard. Rounding a bluff, they were confronted by a spectacular cascade of water pouring out of a lens of porous rock.

"Death in paradise," soberly reflected Tammy.

Following the small stream, the remnants of rotted planks gave evidence of some kind of flume. Smoke from the fire temporarily disappeared over the horizon as they dropped further into the canyon. Within a half mile the canyon turned to the left with an immediate change in the rock strata. Nearing the base of the Obelisk, a much darker rock appeared, interlaced with a matrix of quartz veins running wild through out the walls.

"Pinch me if I'm dreamin', this is enough to drive any miner to slobber," stated Josh. He had no way of knowing that this was only the tip of the iceberg.

"I think we're here. What's left of their camp appears to be just ahead. If any of you want to wait here while I look around, feel free to do so," said Bryan.

"I've come this far, I'll go the distance," replied Josh.

"I'm right behind you," was Tammy's reply.

"Okay," gulped Bryan. "Let's do it."

Drawing closer, several mounds of debris appeared, a few pieces of weathered and rotted wood were exposed.

"Must have been lean-tos or something," guessed Tammy.

After a couple hundred feet, mine tunnels began to appear on both sides of the narrowing canyon, driven into the most prominent of the quartz veins. In a couple of the mines, cave-ins were evident. The heavy support beams had been broken like twigs. Tailings were ramped down from the mine entrances. Small seepages ran out of a couple of the mines, eventually finding their way to the creek. Raw ore was piled to one side of the ramps, still undisturbed after all these years.

"Look at this ore," said Josh reaching down to examine a chunk of the weathered quartz.

"Wow!" "This is real gold!" Tammy exclaimed running her fingers over the gold.

"This is extremely rich, better than some museum specimens I've seen," Bryan said excitedly.

The jagged pieces of quartz contained wide veins of glistening gold.

"The search for such riches has driven many a man to his end," stated Josh pocketing a specimen.

"Funny you should mention that," remarked Bryan.

Sighting ahead, the canyon appeared to come to an abrupt end. Blending in with the colorful canyon walls, rock structures now became discernible. They were stacked stone structures and whatever roofs they had, was decayed and fallen in. Wooden beams that had served as window headers, and the stones they supported had also collapsed. The stream that they had been following most of the way emptied itself into a round pond against the east wall. It was about thirty feet in diameter, with no apparent outlet. Above the pond overlooking the settlement about twenty feet up the cliff was another 'Door of the Sun' symbol carved into the rock. One hundred feet beyond the pond and slightly to the left was clustered three stone structures. Built about ten feet up on a rise they overlooked the pond. Behind the stone structures, the reddish canyon walls jumped straight up five hundred feet to meet the horizon.

Josh approached one of the doors of the stone houses.

"No telling what you'll find in there," warned Bryan.

"Little chance it'll be an ice cream bar," Josh replied ducking down to see back in through the debris.

"Don't say that, you're making me drool," said Tammy. "This looks like it could have been used as a stove," she added looking at a rusted hulk of metal lying up against one of the other buildings.

"This last stone structure back here must have been a smelter," guessed Bryan looking through the square opening.

"Whoa! You better come and look at this," called Josh from behind the stone cabin.

Racing around the rock structure, Bryan and Tammy came to a sudden stop. There before them was a deplorable sight. A graveyard. Nine mounds were in two rows with no visible designations.

Tammy gasped for breath. Against the wall in a slight crevice leaned a weathered skeleton.

"The poor fella didn't have anyone to bury him," commented Bryan.

"You think your great-great-grandfather could be buried here?" asked Tammy.

"I really don't know," Bryan responded in a somber tone.

"They must have had a stash for all the gold that was processed," reasoned Josh.

"That makes sense, but where? No doubt it's cleverly hidden nearby," agreed Bryan.

"Maybe inside one of the mines, just like at Crazy Joe's," recalled Tammy.

"If it is, they're too unsafe to enter now," responded Josh.

"Well, there was no guarantee that we would find a treasure trove anyway. I was hoping that I would find out at the very least what happened to my great-great-grandfather. I guess we better think about heading back," commented Bryan.

Bryan sat on the edge of the pond with his thoughts, and waited for the others. He thought of the miners who also must have sat there along the edge of the pool, and tried to imagine what conversations they must have had. The carved symbol of the "Sun" above him seemed to watch over the camp, as it had done in other places. Ripples in the pool caught his attention. Then it struck him. In order for the pool to maintain its level, water had to be going out somewhere, namely subterranean. His eyes followed across the pool to where it met the canyon wall and then up to the 'Door of the Sun.'

"Captain! You are a genius. It takes one to know one," he giggled to himself as a tingle of excitement ran down his spine.

"Who are you talking to down there?" queried Tammy.

"To the Captain."

"I swear, you are going bonkers."

"No, I think I know where his secret hiding place is."

"Where?"

"What are you guys yammering about?" Josh asked drawn by the voices.

"His hiding place is right in there," Bryan pointed.

"In solid rock?" scoffed Josh.

Bryan walked around to the far side of the clear pool dragging a dead limb about ten feet long.

"This water is only about two and a half feet deep along this edge," he said taking off his shoes.

Taking the dead pine limb which had quite a curve to it, he stepped into the water and inched along the cliff wall.

"Now let's see if this will work," said Bryan bending down.

Reaching over and jabbing the branch under the water, its point scraped down the wall into where it became too dark to see. Suddenly there was no more resistance and the branch penetrated back into the unknown. Working the curve of the stick upward, the thickness of the wall did not feel to be very great.

"It has to be hollow on the other side," concluded Bryan.

Josh immediately glanced up at the carving in realization that there could indeed be a connection here. "Tammy, I think Bryan might be on to something. Another door may very well be hidden directly under the symbol."

"Bryan, don't you dare think about ducking under hoping you come up in a pocket of air on the other side. It's too dangerous," warned Tammy rushing over.

In solemn thought they peered into the depths of the underwater passage.

"By the feel of the bottom, it must be about five feet deep, right at the wall," estimated Bryan.

"The solution isn't there, it's up here," announced Tammy.

The boys looked at her, as if to say: "Don't bother us with foolishness."

"All we have to do is dam up the stream and the water should drain down," she continued.

"That won't change the elevation of the pool," countered Bryan. "The outlet elevation is what regulates the pool height, not the upstream water."

"Well, I don't care what you say, I think it will work. Josh give me a hand," she insisted.

"Tammy, I don't see how it will help either," agreed Josh throwing up his hands.

"Stand there if you like," she complained.

"Okay, just to prove you wrong," said Bryan.

Busily they began rolling rocks and moving small logs into place. In fifteen minutes the stream began backing up and just a trickle now reached the pool. After a minute there was no perceivable change. Bryan was about to say: "I told you so."

"Will you look at that!" spoke up Josh. "It's going down."

"How can that be?" said Bryan in disbelief.

"Well! Who was right this time?" triumphed Tammy.

The pool elevation began to drop lower and lower, and soon the top of the cave opening was revealed.

"Just guessing, but the opening looks to be about three and a half feet high," said Josh.

"Just about enough to comfortably duck through," Bryan replied.

"Looks like it's stopping," noticed Tammy.

Tammy was right, it stopped with about eight to ten inches of water in the bottom of the passageway. Fetching their packs, they pulled out their flashlights to check them.

"We don't know how long our flashlights will hold out, so let's keep one in reserve to get us back out," planned Bryan.

Rolling up their pant legs, they were ready. Bryan sloshed into the water and ducked down at the entrance way. Turning on his light, he crept forward. The others slowly followed stepping down into the water. Raising up, Bryan found himself in another pool of water in a high vaulted cavern. His movements echoed throughout the unknown domain. Light radiating through the opening dimly lit up a back wall straight in front of him, about sixty feet away. Stepping forward several steps, the bottom felt unstable under his feet. It seemed as if the muck under his feet was eroding away from under him. He stepped back.

"Josh, hand me that tree limb. There's something going on in here," requested Bryan as he saw Josh peeking in through the opening.

Having retrieved the long branch, Josh watched as Bryan poked around in front of him, and Tammy bugged him to know what was happening.

"There's a bottomless pit out in the center of this pool, or at least it's deeper than I can probe. It must drop straight off," informed Bryan. "Now, over here to the right appears to be a way to get back up on dry ground, but let me poke around some more. You guys wait there."

Checking along the wall on the right side, the floor along there seemed to be solid, and more or less level. Stepping up out of the water, he called for them to come on in, but to stick close to the wall. Flashing the light around, he found that the cavern continued and the overflow from the pool apparently ran in the same direction.

"Hurry up, the cave goes on," coaxed Bryan anxious to continue.

"What an ingenious way to conceal the entrance to a secret hiding place," said Tammy as she stepped out of the pool.

"Oro de Cañon"

"There's your outlet you were talking about," pointed Josh with his flashlight. "Notice how narrow the outlet is at the top."

"Looks like somebody stuck rocks in the narrow slot to regulate the flow or something," said Tammy.

"That's why the pool elevation dropped when water is withheld," understood Bryan. "It works like an inverted weir. The pool elevation can be adjusted in height by restricting the flow in the slot."

"Or by restricting the inflow," reminded Tammy.

"Who would've guessed that they were able to figure such a thing out?" wondered Bryan.

"Me!" reminded Tammy.

Without answering, the boys turned to continue further into the cave. Tammy was very much annoyed with them, but said nothing. Turning the corner, light was pouring in from above.

"This place could be booby-trapped, you know?" warned Josh.

Standing in the shaft of light, they looked up to see a round opening some eighty feet above.

"Save your batteries as much as possible," Bryan recommended.

Leaving the light, the rock strata almost immediately turned dark, basaltic black. And the size and shape of the tunnel went into an immediate metamorphosis compressing down into an oval configuration, twenty feet wide by ten feet high. An increase in downward slope also became noticeable. Though diminished to a trickle, the stream continued to flow down into the unknown depths. The sides of the cave took on a most peculiar aspect, with an odd looking shelf on both sides, and a spine running down the center of the ceiling with ribs radiating down the side walls.

"This is creepy, almost like being inside the body of a prehistoric monster," said Tammy.

"We're inside a lava tube, my guess is we must be working our way under the *Obelisk*," informed Bryan.

205

"Lava tube?" questioned Tammy. "You mean lava flowed through here?"

"Ye-a-ah," acknowledged Bryan.

"This whole thing was molten at one time," explained Josh. "The outer portion cooled first, and inside where we are remained molten. And because it was still in a liquid state it continued to flow downhill leaving a tunnel behind."

"Some of these tubes can be miles long," added Bryan whose voice echoed.

Curving to the left and then to the right the lava tube descended.

"Another tunnel," noted Josh flashing his light up to the right.

The ceiling of which was heavily decorated with long slender lava stalactites. Glancing back down the main tube, it looked to be an eternal vacuum, dark, infinite.

"Let's check it out, a short distance anyway before going on," wisely said Bryan.

Josh went in first, ducking low to avoid the stalactites.

"Somebody has been through here before, look at all the lavacicles that have been broken off," he discovered.

"Fifty percent chance this is the way," concluded Bryan.

"To what?" asked Tammy rhetorically.

The side lava tube ascended a steep grade. They found that most of the so-called lavacicles had been cleared away on the left side.

"I hope there's a restaurant up here, the mention of lavacicles is making my stomach growl," joked Tammy.

After a hundred-foot climb the tunnel leveled off into a large room which split into a lower section that curved away to the right, and an upper section that continued beyond sight.

"Searching every nook and cranny could take forever," complained Josh.

"Yeah, we have to, that is to a reasonable degree," replied Bryan.

On the left side was a rough but adequate way to get up to the upper level.

"If you want to, wait here. Turn your light off till I get back," suggested Bryan.

"Okay! but hurry," agreed Josh.

As Bryan crept up to the upper level, he could hear them whispering and occasionally a word or two would float up to him. The room tapered upward and in the dim beam of light it appeared to end in a solid wall. Swinging the light from one side to the other, the back wall was visibly rough and irregular with no openings or markings. But one section looked somehow different. "Na," he told himself. Turning to leave, Bryan caught himself and decided to look anyway. "That's strange, this wall is made up of individual stones, it's not solid."

On each side of an eight-foot section there was solid rock. Putting his hand over the cracks, he could feel air being drawn through. He called for the others to come on up. Spotting a broken three-foot section of lavacicle lying on the floor, he tried loosening a couple of the rocks by prying in the cracks.

"Give me a hand Josh, with these rocks. I think there's a passageway hidden behind here."

"How can you tell?"

"Put your hands over the cracks."

"Air! Air is moving through them," he realized. "What are we waiting for, let's open this puppy up."

Packed in as tight as they were, the first rocks came out with much difficulty, revealing another layer of rock behind. Bryan took the shaft of lava rock and beat it against the rocks in the back. Suddenly one of the rocks fell out and a blast of air began whistling through the opening with extreme velocity.

"Good grief! What could be causing this terrible draft?" wondered Tammy.

"I think we've opened a can of worms," replied Josh.

They could feel the intensity of the wind growing at their backs. It seemed to eat away at the breach in the wall. Another rock broke loose, then another and another. Finally in a thunderous roar the whole wall blew-in and crashed in a heap. The most dreadful howling and moaning sound now came to them from somewhere ahead, through the opening.

Without saying a word about this whole astonishing event, they crept over the rubble into a gallery that led upward. As the intimidating wind helped to push them along, the howling grew louder. Almost immediately they entered a labyrinth of interconnecting tunnels so large, that their puny beams could not traverse it. Bryan suddenly put his arms out stopping Josh and Tammy in their tracks.

"What's up?" they asked.

"There's nothing but a big black void out in front of us," informed Bryan. "And unless you can fly we're not going anywhere."

The air flow descended into a dark abyss that was just in front of them. But this was not the source of the howling, it still came from somewhere beyond.

"Can you guys shine your lights along this right side?" requested Bryan.

"It looks like a ledge along the wall," realized Josh.

"Is it safe?" questioned Tammy.

"I believe so," replied Josh flashing his light along the ledge.

"Let's go slow," suggested Bryan.

Tammy nervously clutched the back of Josh's shirt, as they cautiously worked their way along the wall. Dim light now could be seen coming through an irregular opening ahead. The wind currents reversed, and now blew against them as they moved away from the abyss. The tone of the howling deepened as they approached the opening.

Stepping through, it was like they had stumbled upon some kind of lost world. The wary adventurers were momentarily stunned by all the sights and sounds that now simultaneously manifested themselves. A cavern vaulting hundreds of feet above, now engulfed them. Light poured in through volcanic vents high along the exterior walls, pinpointing the source of the mournful sound as it wailed through the ancient orifices.

Their gaze lowered to note the return of the gold rich quartz matrix spider-webbed throughout the walls. In some places voids in the strata revealed quartz crystals that gaped like skeletal teeth. No longer needing light they switched off their flashlights and proceeded along a wall that brought them out to the edge of the main floor of the cavern. Stepping down about two feet onto the sunken floor they noted areas stained from seepage. Rounding a corner, a stack of rotted timbers came into view. And further around to the right was what appeared to have been a cooking site for the miners.

"Beyond doubt, this has to be the place that we've been looking for," concluded Bryan.

"Back in there," pointed Josh. "Is that what I think it is? Veins of gold?"

Drawing closer, the amazing truth of the question was verified. Four tunnels had been driven into the most prominent veins, penetrating only about five to eight feet into the rock.

"This is unreal, this vein is nearly half a foot thick," breathed Tammy. "I didn't know gold could be found like this."

"Rarely," answered Bryan. "But this is beyond anything even the legends have alluded to."

"The rich ore we saw outside is just a tease compared to this," added Josh.

"This cave was probably discovered later," thought Tammy.

"One thing is for sure, they didn't get very far before they were shut down," stated Josh.

"Somewhere in here also could be a stash of smelted gold," said Bryan working his way around to the left.

Drifting toward the miners camp, Josh noticed a marking on the floor that was being illuminated by a shaft of light.

"It could be some kind of solar clock. Look at the tick marks along the line," guessed Tammy.

"And look at this, it would seem to be a miniature 'Sun' further along the line," noticed Josh.

"As the sun swings around to the west, the light should move along this line and shine on the symbol. Matter of fact, that could happen in just a few minutes, if my guess is right," figured Tammy.

"But what would it mean if it does?" questioned Josh.

"I don't know, just wait and see," she replied shrugging her shoulders.

In the meantime, venturing over to the cook site, they found stacked rocks and the remnants of rotted timbers. Black smudged rocks indicated the location of the fire pit that must have been used for the preparation of food.

"Not much to look at, broken pottery and a few relics," said Josh surveying the scene.

"Let's try prying some of the loose gold out of the veins," suggested Tammy.

"Okay, but first I want to check the floor clock again," replied Josh.

Approaching the primitive solar clock, they could see that the light had indeed moved along the line and was now encroaching on the "Sun" symbol.

"Bryan!" called Josh.

"Yo!" he replied from across the cavern.

"Come look at this."

"What did you find?" asked Bryan approaching.

"This crudely carved line on the floor seems to be a solar clock of some kind, but notice in particular the 'Sun' symbol that the sunlight is just about ready to touch," pointed out Josh.

Bryan squatted down for a closer look.

"Something must be ready to happen," thought Tammy.

Suddenly, Bryan and Tammy's eyes met.

"Are you thinking what I'm thinking?" asked Bryan jumping up.

"Maybe so."

"What? Did I miss something?" asked Josh feeling left out.

"You dummy, don't you get it, it's all part of the pattern," explained Tammy sweeping back her bedraggled hair.

"Pattern?"

"Yes, remember when the sun shone through the 'Door of the Sun,' this morning? What did it shine on?" she continued, edging away.

"The wall, with the—" His eyes lit up. "Okay, I get it, but how do we know where to look?"

"Just look around!"

"Over here!" came the call from Bryan.

Rushing over Josh found Bryan and Tammy staring up at a blank sunlit wall.

"Any symbols or anything?" he asked.

"No, but I think this is another false wall," replied Bryan feeling the cracks in the rock.

"If it is, they sure took care to fit these rocks together and to make them flush with one another along the front face," observed Tammy.

"Josh, let's find out, grab this rock over here and we'll use it as a battering ram," suggested Bryan.

The first blow bounced off. But with the second, the wall seemed to give. They looked at each other and gave it all they had. Two rocks turned inward. Another blow pushed the rocks out through the back.

"It is a manmade wall," said Tammy trying to peek through.

The boys continued to chip away at the upper corners of the hole. Finally a V shaped wedge of the wall fell away and the sunlight poured through.

"I must be dreaming!" exclaimed Bryan.

"Oooh-wee! This must be the granddaddy of them all," said Tammy.

Josh was absolutely speechless. There before them again appeared the *'Door of the Sun,'* brilliant, glorious, carved into a vein of solid gold nearly four feet across. The width of the vein flared out, as it descended through the floor down into the unknown depths. A resurgence of the moaning wind finally brought them back to consciousness.

"Could it be possible that the whole base, the foundation of the *Obelisk* or at least part of it is solid gold?" speculated Bryan.

"Gold is heavy, it would sink to the bottom," commented Josh.

"These could be like filaments that were drawn up into the neck of this volcanic pinnacle," reasoned Tammy.

"It blows me away to think, that just below our feet, could be more gold than in Fort Knox or even in circulation around the world today," said Bryan.

"This is—what dreams are made of," stated Josh.

Climbing through the breach, they followed the wall that contained the golden 'Sun' around to the left, to come into a dark room. Clicking on their flashlights, they now realized that they had finally come to the end of the trail. Crudely formed gold bars about eight inches long were compactly stacked along the right side. Rotted leather pouches containing gold dust had dumped their contents on the floor. Old trunks laid in pieces along the left side.

"What's that back there," questioned Tammy spotting something in the dim light.

A large square shaped rock came into view toward the back of the room.

"Look at this. A layer of gold bars has been laid across the top of this rock like a table top," observed Josh.

"A satchel," declared Bryan.

"It's sitting there almost like its waiting for someone to come and get it," commented Tammy.

"Hold the light steady," asked Bryan unfolding the heavily oiled leather pouch. With the skill of a surgeon he opened the fragile satchel. Peering inside he reached in and pulled out a small leather bound book. Looking at the binding, it appeared that a section in the rear of the book had been removed.

"It's a diary," recognized Tammy.

"It's cross-written. Down the page as normal and then turned sideways and written over the top the other way," noticed Josh

"Jackpot! This may be worth more than gold," said Bryan. "What's this? There's something hard inside the back cover."

"Oro de Cañon"

Examining the edges Bryan felt a fold along the bottom edge. By reaching under the fold he was able to push the object out. An odd shaped chunk of metal appeared.

"Wait!" exclaimed Bryan rubbing it on his shirt to brush off the deteriorating leather. Etched lines now were distinguishable.

"The 'Sun!' Could this be the— Wait one minute, there's one way to find out," said Bryan digging through his pockets for something. Finally he pulled out the medallion. Placing the two together they interlocked.

"The second half, you found the other half of the medallion," realized Josh.

"It forms a complete sun now," observed Tammy.

"The sun shines again, after two hundred years," said Bryan.

"This definitely confirms that this was Captain Camino's gold mine and that he was here," said Josh. "But what happened to him?"

"Maybe only the diary can answer our questions," replied Bryan.

"And don't forget about his wife, the daughter of an Indian chief," reminded Tammy.

"This vault and the tunnel leading to the cavern were sealed off from the outside, whoever did it, probably being the Captain himself, may have taken a quantity of the gold with him," guessed Bryan. "But anyway, the diary should give us the answers."

"Say, what else is in the satchel?" questioned Tammy as she reached inside. "Hey, look, there are three gold bars!"

"How interesting; almost like we were expected," commented Bryan. "Each of you take one. You've certainty earned them."

The wind moaned again, creating an eerie effect.

"Is that smoke I'm seeing?" questioned Josh.

"It certainly is! The fire must be getting close," realized Bryan. "I'd forgotten all about it."

Re-entering the main cavern, they found smoke swirling down through the volcanic vents.

"We better slide out of here," said Josh.

Bryan made sure that he had the diary and medallion safely tucked away. Before leaving the vault, reaching the far side of the cavern, Bryan stopped to peer back at the golden "Door of the Sun," now dimmed in the smoke filtered sunlight, one last time.

Ducking down through the lava tubes and back up into the chamber that contained the pool, they discovered that the water level had risen. The opening to the outside was still there, but it was definitely smaller.

"Well, it appears we'll have to get a little bit wetter this time," said Bryan sloshing into the pool. "Remember, stay against the wall."

Stooping down low they soon popped back out into the open, to find blowing smoke and ashes raining down everywhere.

"The fire must be just over the ridge or up on top," declared Josh.

"Let's finish releasing the water to hide the entrance again, before we go," said Bryan picking up his pack and heading up to where they had constructed their temporary dam.

Having accomplished that, they headed back up canyon, toward the 'Door.' As they hurried along the edge of the creek, Tammy could still hear the eerie moan coming from high above them near the summit of the Obelisk. Looking back as they climbed the slope, flames were now visibly leaping up from the ridge top that overlooked the 'Canyon of Gold.'

An angry, coppery sun shone through the blowing clouds of smoke. Coughing, they finally made it to the portal that would take them to the outside world. They glanced back at the smoky valley one more time before passing through the 'Door.' From the edge of the plateau, the main canyon below was visibly free of smoke but clouds of smoke were now blowing up over the top. They began their descent along the edge of the bluffs, when suddenly shots rang out. Bullets whizzed passed them ricocheting on the cliffs behind.

"What the heck!" exclaimed Josh as they hit the ground.

"Quick, behind these boulders," barked Bryan.

"I didn't see anyone down there, did you? They could be hiding anywhere down below," said Josh breathing heavy as he slumped against the rock.

"Look's like we're trapped," concluded Bryan.

Tammy's dark eye's had a cold stare. She seemed to be more frightened tan anytime before.

"Come on, let's crawl back up to the 'Door of the Sun,' that'll be our best defense," said Bryan coaxing them on.

It took them what seemed an eternity to crawl on their bellies back into the notch. Bracing up against the south wall, they slid back through the smoky opening.

"It's just a matter of time, before they find their way up here," realized Josh.

"With them blocking us in and the fire raging at our backs, how can we possibly escape?" worried Tammy.

"Don't worry, we can easily hide in amongst these rock formations. If they pass through here and proceed down into the canyon, that'll allow us to make an exit," encouraged Bryan. He glanced at the rugged volcanic extrusions that ran along the back of the cliff. In reality he realized it would not be that simple, but a little interjection of hope wouldn't hurt. In the meantime he had to think of a real plan.

"The fire and the smoke may get us first," coughed Josh.

Fixing their attention on the fire, it was definitely intensifying as it roared up the slope, leaping as it topped out on the far ridge, sending thick clouds of black and gray smoke southerly across the canyon.

"Somehow this is all so ironic. Here we are trapped just as Captain Camino and his men were, two hundred years ago. They say history repeats itself, you know," pondered Bryan.

"But what details does history actually paint? Did the Captain escape, or was he a victim like so many of his men? Will we also be victims of the 'Valley of Gold?' " questioned Josh.

"One thing is for sure, I'm not giving up without a fight," said Bryan. "We can't shoot back, but maybe as a last resort we can fashion some clubs out of some of these juniper boughs."

After finding a secure place for Tammy to hide, they took their station on each side of the 'Door' and waited. Bryan's imagination drifted back to that other battle that must have raged here two hundred years before. He could almost hear the war-crys of the Indians, the arrows whizzing through the air and the yell of the Captain's men.

"The fire is burning toward us along the ridge," pointed Josh, bringing Bryan back to the present.

"Hmm, so it is, but that'll have to wait. We have a more pressing problem."

At that moment, two men armed with rifles appeared rounding the corner. Stopping they pointed in their direction. As Josh edged over to get a better look, his foot slipped out from under him and he tumbled into the entryway. Instantaneously one of the two men spotted Josh, pointing. Spontaneously, they brought their guns up to a ready stance. Josh scrambled back to his position, red-faced and flustered.

"Great! There goes any advantage of surprise that we may have had," said Bryan.

"You kids, get out here! We'll give you two minutes, then we're coming in after you," came the call from one of the men. "And to show you we mean business—"

Boom! They fired off a gun shot into the rocks south of the entrance.

"I don't trust 'em," said Josh.

"They're probably the same two guys we've seen before. No matter, we can't just sit back and let them take control."

"I'm game."

"That's the spirit, we'll send 'em for a loop, if they try anything."

After the two minutes had expired, the two men began their approach. Bryan and Josh held their clubs in readiness.

Tammy's head popped up to see what was happening. Josh waved her back down.

"This is it," silently mouthed Bryan as they neared.

After all that had happened was this to be the end of the road?

18

MORE THAN LEGEND

T he silence was broken by loud yells and the demand for someone to put their guns down. Bryan and Josh peeked around the corner to see the two bad guys with their hands raised over their heads, and their guns on the ground. They were surrounded by a number of other men.

"Who are they?" asked Josh.

"One of them looks like my dad."

"Are you sure?"

"Looks like the Sheriff, too."

"Bryan! It's safe now," came the call from one of the men.

"Come on, Josh and Tammy, it is my dad!"

Venturing out, two men wearing cowboy hats approached. His father ran up and they hugged each other.

"I don't know if you understand the gravity of your situation here?" his father said finally.

"Yes, for the most part."

"Well, the main thing is that you're all safe. Josh, your mother is really worried about you two. She'll feel better after we radio down and give her the good news," continued Mr. Anderson.

"Say, it's Mr. Krasnik," noticed Bryan as the Sheriff's men turned them around and put handcuffs on their wrists.

"Apparently so," replied his dad.

"I guess we had him pegged right," said Josh.

More Than Legend

By a flash of memory, Bryan recalled the bandage on his teacher's forehead. And he realized that it was just before that when the Professor was run off the road. But anyway it was water under the bridge now. "Oh, by the way, Dad, do you see the lines carved into the archway back in there?"

"Yeah, I think so."

"Well, this is, believe it or not the way into the legendary 'Canyon of Gold,' " revealed Bryan. "And I have what I believe to be Captain Camino's diary to prove it, besides all the other evidence we've discovered."

"You wouldn't believe the things we've seen," burst in Tammy speaking excitedly.

"Really? I can't wait to hear all the details," Mr. Anderson replied. "But right now, we have to handle these guys, put out the fire, and get everyone home."

"That looks like a firefighter down there, talking on a walkie-talkie," pointed out Josh.

"That's right, because of the rugged terrain they couldn't parachute in, so they hired me to bring them and their equipment in on hoof. As well as the Sheriff and his party, trying to find you and catch up with these gun-slinging crazies," he explained.

A group of firefighters began to gather at the head of the canyon, dressed in their distinctive garb of khaki shirts, green hard hats, and red handkerchiefs.

"Bryan, there's someone here who wants to see you," informed his father with a gleam in his eye.

"Who?"

"Your mother."

"She's here?"

"That's right, she insisted on coming up, after I called her to see if she had any idea where you had disappeared to."

"Where is she?"

"Down by the horses," directed his dad.

Hurrying down the plateau, he could see her standing by the horses looking up in his direction. Spotting Bryan, she waved and started walking over to meet him. As he descended, a large plane roared over the crest and banked to the east, releasing its load of red fire retardant on the ridge to the northeast. Passing the group of firefighters he couldn't help but notice the variety of tools they carried: double bit axes, pulaskis, brush hooks, shovels, and mcleods.

"Are you all right?" as she gave him a big hug.

"I'm fine."

"Did you hurt your arm?"

"Oh, no, nothing serious."

"Apparently, you were serious when you said you were hot on the trail of your great-great-grandfather, and it appears that others were too."

"Yeah, it all seemed to come together right here," replied Bryan, still somewhat surprised that she was really here. "We didn't find the Captain, but we did find some of his gold, a diary and— Look at this, the second half of the gold medallion."

"This is amazing. It fits together and forms a complete sun," she observed holding it in her hand.

"Mom, I'm really surprised you're here," stated Bryan in a serious tone.

"I was so worried about you. Your father called me after he returned home and found you and the pickup missing, as well as Josh and his cousin. He found the address book open to my number, so he assumed you may have called me and that I would know something. Of course I told your Dad, just what you had told me, how you were following up on the clues to the Captain's hidden gold mine. I guess that's when it all clicked. Right after the conversation that we had on the phone, Rosa told me her uncle suddenly became very ill and she needed to leave immediately. This was the first that I'd ever heard of this uncle. But anyway, more than an hour later someone in a strange gray vehicle picked her up out front on the main road. I thought it strange but nothing sunk in at the time."

"So it was Rosa, who was listening in on us," realized Bryan.

"I believe so. Did your dad, say anything about me, or us?" she questioned after a pause.

"Uh, no, why?"

"Well, after your visit, I started thinking about things. Like, how it used to be with us, and the truth about your great-great-grandmother, the Captain's Indian wife. It all kind of sunk home. Beyond the animosity that had been created some years ago, the truth is she wasn't personally responsible for his death at all. But she actually remained loyally by his side to the very end. All of this made me think that perhaps I've been wrong, for leaving and not working things out. I guess, what I'm trying to say is, if you and your dad want me back, I would like to get together again."

"Really, and leave the ranch?"

"Since you and your dad are as stubborn as your mules, I guess so."

"That's great Mom, this is better than finding any gold mine," he joyously replied.

From behind came a rustling sound out of the bushes.

"Touching story Ma'am. I've got you two covered. Don't turn around," came a gruff voice from behind. "Now hand me that gold medallion and the diary."

Bryan caught a glimpse of a man with long dark hair. Could this be Dark Shadow, one of those assigned by Indian tradition to be watching over this place? And for an instant out of the corner of his eye he thought he glimpsed a second person. The Sheriff's party was now making their way down the hill.

"Hurry up, fast!" was the demand.

Before they could respond a loud roar was heard from the direction of the 'Canyon of Gold.' Noticing that the man was temporarily distracted, Bryan whipped around and knocked the gun out of his hand and sent it flying up into the rocks.

Bryan's mother immediately began waving her arms and calling for help. As they ran for safety, Bryan finally got a good look at the man as he scrambled for the gun. He wore a pair of ragged jeans, a blue flannel shirt, and a gray headband. Running up canyon to where the firefighters had assembled earlier, they

221

found no one there. But some of the Sheriff's party had seen their plea for help and were hurrying down. At the same time a pall of dust could be seen blowing over the volcanic crest, indicating a landslide must have occured. Guns drawn, the men worked their way cautiously past their location. After a couple of minutes there was a yell indicating that they had caught their man.

Bryan turned around to see what was happening, just as the deputies holding the first two prisoners and his Dad reached their position. Josh and Tammy soon followed.

First the Sheriff reappeared, then three of his men led the culprit toward them.

"Now we'll find out who's behind all this," said Josh.

As they drew more closely, it was apparent that this was not the mysterious Indian known as Dark Shadow. This man was shorter. Both, Mr. Krasnik and his partner glanced at each other, and seemed to have a blank expression on their faces as they brought this man up. But there was something about his face that seemed familiar.

"Okay! Buddy! Who are you?" asked the Sheriff as he frisked him to make doubly sure he wasn't concealing any weapons. As he checked the man's legs, Tammy spotted something that she had seen before.

"Look, he has the footprint with the small squares that we've seen up and down the river, especially up on the North Fork," she pointed out.

"North Fork! Ah ha! You must be one of those that I've been trying to catch up with, causing a lot of ruckus up there," concluded the Sheriff. "I'm no spring chicken to go running around these mountains chasing after gold crazy people anymore. Now who are you? Fess up!"

The unknown man who had all the appearances of a local Indian refused to speak. He pulled at the restraints tied around his wrists.

More Than Legend

"What in thunderation! There's something phony going on here," continued the Sheriff as he circled around him looking him over. "This isn't your real hair."

Pulling backwards on his hair, it came off. Bryan and his father gasped. It was Professor Burke.

"Professor Burke! Were you the one behind this whole thing all along?" asked Bryan still surprised.

"He's the one that hired us," confessed Mr. Krasnik probably hoping to lessen their plight.

"Yeah, and they turned on me," finally spoke up the Professor.

Then Bryan remembered the blood on the roadway and the Professor's initial wound that he tried to hide, it all made sense now.

"Well, it's all over now. Anyway, the fire caused a massive rock slide that has sealed off the gold mines. Unless you know another way in?" wondered Mr. Anderson glancing at his son.

Bryan stepped next to his dad. "No, I don't believe there is, but I was hoping by finding the mine, it would have saved our home from those vultures. I saw the letter you threw in the trash," replied Bryan.

"I know, but the main thing now is that you've come through this safe. To put your trust in riches is a futile thing. We'll work something out," he encouraged.

"But dad, you should have seen the size of the gold veins it was extraordinary," revealed Bryan under his breath.

"All right! Come out with your hands up!" yelled one of the deputies drawing his gun.

Everyone was caught off guard by this new advent. Directly behind them among some bushes was a group of boulders, and apparently someone else was hiding back there.

"Come on, you can't escape, come out slowly," continued the Deputy.

Finally a pair of hands emerged out from behind the rocks and then a head and a body. Mrs. Anderson's face went white as she realized who it was.

"Rosa! You! You're a part of this?" she exclaimed.

"Don't look so surprised, I have a right to that gold just as much as you," Rosa fired back.

Bryan's mother knew all too well what she meant.

"Boy, they're sure coming out of the woodwork," chuckled the Sheriff.

After things settled back down, the men set about getting ready for the return trip. The Sheriff was anxious to get the prisoners back, and the sooner he started the better, even though there wasn't much of the day left. Bryan's father had to stay for at least two more days and bring the fire crew back. Everyone else was to return with the Sheriff's posse.

For Bryan, seeing his mother and father holding hands with that look in their eye once again, made all things worthwhile.

Noticing Tammy sitting by herself, Bryan felt he should at least say something positive after all the things she had been through. Approaching, it appeared she was examining an injury on her foot.

"Did you get hurt?"

"No, just a scraped ankle," she answered looking up. "Oh, your arm, sit down here and let me look at it," she insisted, still feeling a little responsible for his injury. "Hmm, it'll still need some doctoring when we get home, but it should be okay."

"Thanks Doc'. Say, is that a tan I see on your arms and face?"

"Oh, before I forget," she responded, ignoring his observation, "here take this. It's my gold bar that we brought out of the cavern. It may help save your home," she offered.

"Tammy, no. We faced the dangers together. It's only right that we share what we found together, but I appreciate your offer. Besides, I think I've found something more important," he replied indicating his mom and dad.

She smiled. "Despite your being so ornery at times, I'm still happy for you," she said gazing up into his eyes.

Bryan caught a little sparkle in her eye as their eyes briefly met. An unexplained ripple went through him. Somehow he felt different toward her. A feeling that was strange to him and disturbing. Bryan unconsciously pulled his arm back to himself, which Tammy had been holding onto all through their conversation.

"You want to meet my mom and dad?" asked Bryan.

"Yes, I would love to," she responded getting up.

In the meantime preparations were being made to ready the pack train for the return trip. Equipment and food for the fire fighters was being unloaded to make room for the extra passengers that would be going back down. Tammy and Bryan's mom seemed to really hit it off and soon walked off continuing in their conversation.

"You know," spoke up Bryan's father lookin around, "I believe at one time that I had come down through here many years ago."

"Wow, if that was true, you were only a thirty minute walk from millions in gold just sitting there," replied Bryan.

"And at the same time we had to struggle to make ends meet. Apparently it was not time for the secret to be revealed," replied Mr. Anderson.

"But now, it seems that all things have come back together, in the past and in the present," reflected Bryan.

As the procession began down the trail via the north end of the canyon, Bryan swung around and waved back at his dad. And then he looked one last time at the valley, where the 'Door of the Sun' had so prominently displayed itself that morning, and up to the plateau as he recalled once again, sights and wonders that few have ever seen, nor may see again. As he straightened in the saddle, something caught his eye. It was the silhouette of a man on the far horizon. He was tall with long flowing hair. In an instant he was gone. Bryan knew who it was. And for that one and the others that had been bound by tradition, it was the end of an era.

More Than Legend

In the week that followed, Bryan was busily moving his mother's belongings, including all her painting supplies up from the ranch. He was excited by their new arrangements.

He recalled his grandfather's, off the cuff reaction: "It's about time—senseless women anyway!"

Bryan was still revisited from time to time by the black cloud of realization, that it was in the grip of his hand to save the day, but he had failed.

Bringing his thoughts back to the present, his mother was bending over boxes, and selecting items in her endeavor to redecorate the house. She had put Gus in charge of the day to day operations at the ranch, but would run the business end of things from up there.

Tammy returned to the city soon after they had returned from the mountains, declaring she had enough of the mountains to last her a long, long time. But it was not until later that she realized that some profound changes had come over her. She smiled at the memories of that summer, and kept them close to her heart.

And as for Josh, he was more preoccupied with getting his Jeep back on the road more than anything else.

In the quiet of the evenings, Mrs. Anderson began the task of translating the diary that did prove to be the Captain's. He signed it: "The Journal of Captain Maximo Camino." She knew enough Spanish to feel qualified to make a good rendering. It took a great deal of concentration to read the crisscross written pages. But due to deterioration, many of the passages were found illegible.

Gradually the true story unfolded giving credence to what was called legend:

April 20, 1792
... with Carlos, we penetrated one day's march
up river and have found signs of flake in the clear,

reflective waters. I have called this river Aurora. On the right fork we have found even more color.

April 21
While hunting in a side canyon I heard a scream. Running upstream to investigate, found Indian woman cornered by large grizzly. Killed bear but almost lost my arm in the fight. Spent two days in camp nursing my wound.

April 23
After awakening from a troublesome sleep, found a basket of food. We suspect the Indians have paid us a visit.
April 24
We have resumed our prospecting but have the feeling we are being watched....
April 29
Morning ... two Indian braves appear in camp out of nowhere. By their sign language I perceive they want us to follow, but Carlos is afraid of their intentions. After showing we had little interest in the matter, five more braves joined them and escorted us a mile up the river to their summer camp. There must have been upwards of one hundred souls in their base camp. A group of Indians some with head dresses awaited our arrival. The man who appeared to be the Chief began talking with his hands, it made no sense to me. Finally, he brought a young woman to me and joined our hands, it proved to be the one I saved from the bear and the Chief's own daughter. I was made to believe that she would go with me and that she was willing. One brave appeared to be in disagreement with the situation and there were a number of young braves standing with him. It seemed that I was being used to resolve a domestic problem, perhaps an unwilling bride. I thought best to decline, but under the circumstances I dared not make any

false moves. The three of us finally returned to camp and sat in silence for a long time as if we were in a stupor.

May 2
... returned from an excursion up side canyon. The Indian woman had not left, she even prepared a meal for us. By taking a feather from her head dress, she communicated that her name was White Feather.

June 15
Have met with much disappointment, only finding minor deposits. White Feather has made me understand that further up in the mountains there is a place that has much gold but snow will prevent journey for about half of a moon.

July 2
... on canyon wall we notice paintings of birds. White Feather says they are from an ancient people, long ago.... Entered a narrow gorge, a dangerous place during a mountain storm.

July 3
Entered hidden valley through a grand archway and found extensive formations of exposed gold. A dark giant watches over the valley, an impressive volcanic spire. Indians believe the mountain winds dwell up here in among these rocks. A natural stream at the head of the valley will be a great asset in our operations.... Found that the stream goes into an underground cave. Must explore later.

August 10
Began mining into the most prominent veins.... Have brought fifteen men, all sworn to secrecy.

August 20
Commander has agreed with secret plan....

October 2
Established low land base camp, below forks of river. The men have come to call this place Metallic City due to the tool and blacksmithing ... White Feather has been my constant companion all summer, she has never hinted that she wanted to go back to her people and continues to work hard without complaint. I must admit I am growing fond of her.
November 9
Winter has come to the high country, a wet blanket of snow fell last night. Numerous horse tails beckon another storm. I have decided to shut down this year's operation in the Oro de Cañon.... Moved men and gold down today to Metallic City. Quartz vein has proved barren. ... will use tunnel as intermediate storage until tunnels at Rancho are complete.
November 16
Arrived at Rancho.... Decided that we should get married, but found out that in the eyes of the Indians we already have been all this time.

Bryan looked up from the last page. "Mom, what could this be referring to, 'until tunnels at Rancho are complete?' Are there any tunnels down there?"

"Not that I've ever heard of or seen," she replied.

"And what could this 'secret plan' with the Commander be all about?"

"I don't know, but maybe there will be more said about that as I get more written out in the next couple of days."

More Than Legend

The last twilight of day was flickering as his dad now drove in returning from the county seat. Clamoring in through the doorway, his facial expression gave no hint of how things went.

"Well, we got exactly, $660.29 for the gold," he finally announced.

"That'll help," Mrs. Anderson said encouragingly. "Oh, by the way in today's mail we received the notice from the County Assessors Office, giving us thirty days to pay up or they would have to begin the legal process to—well you know."

"Well great! We're up against it now, and looks like we're going to fall short, even with the extra money from the Forest Service."

There was a long pause.

"Tell you what, I'm going to sell my two show horses at the ranch," Mrs. Anderson announced.

"Mom, you love those horses," protested Bryan.

"I know, but horses can be replaced."

"There's got to be another way," Mr. Anderson insisted.

Bryan thought to himself, maybe there is. Pressing his mother to complete the diary, he felt the answer may lay hidden in its pages. Anxiously the next day he began pouring over the next section:

March 4, 1793
... main tunnel completed through to cliff, enlarging of chamber should only take ten more days and the connecting tunnel to the Fort should begin....

April 10
... First shipment of gold placed in chamber. Word has been sent that Alverado's ship will not arrive until July.

May 15
Due to mild winter, have moved up schedule on

*commencement of mining.... White Feather is heavy
with child but will not be left behind.*

June 9

*Operations renewed at Oro de Cañon, small
contingent left at Metallic....*

June 15

*White Feather had a visit today by two braves,
and a young woman that proved to be her sister.
Word has it that there is growing trouble between her
people. The young brave, Walks Tall, has drawn
many young braves to his side. They have spoken out
against the strangers, that have grown in number,
threatening their way of life and have talked of
attacking and removing the scourge. The chief is in
disagreement with this, and that which would lead to
his own daughter's demise.... I have decided to arm
the men as a precaution.*

July 1

*... shipment sent down to Metallic City. Indians
have been watching our every move.... Have
prepared a map and markings just in case we should
fail to return to the Rancho.*

August 10

*Running Fawn, my wife's sister has arrived to
help deliver the baby and brings news, that agitation
among her people grows.... Have explored water
tunnel, followed subterranean breeze into large
cavern discovering veins one to two varas wide. In
the act of opening up the restricted passageway, we
have somehow altered the air currents and now there
is a moaning sound that pervades the mountain. The
miners no doubt will refuse to work with that awful
sound. Will probably have to seal the passage during
work periods. Indian belief would have us understand
we have disturbed the great mountain winds, thereby
bringing about some kind of vengeance upon us.*

More Than Legend

August 20
... son born late this evening. Mother doing fine.

August 21
Sent shipment down today. Also moved operations into cavern.... Found a way to set the stream flow so it covers cave entrance....

August 28
... two men wounded during last shipment. Indians on renegade.... Second ship has not arrived, must be problems in Mexico.

September 11
... Mexican Federals have attacked the Fort and burned some of the buildings at the Rancho.... Gold in chamber secure. I have my doubts the ship will ever come, everything in Mexico must have blown wide open.

September 25
We have been surrounded by Indians, they will not let us leave the canyon to get fresh supplies. We have ceased mining and are concentrating on defending our position and rationing food....

October 2
The Chief and a small party forcibly entered the valley to plead to his daughter that she and the baby should leave, before it is too late. White Feather refused, but it was agreed that the child should be taken to safety. He left with a heavy heart.... Four hours later a wounded Indian from the Chief's own party returned to the valley, reporting they had been ambushed by renegades from their own tribe. Apparently the same ones that have us surrounded. Most of the party had perished, even the Chief. However, Running Fawn hid and apparently has

escaped with the child.... they have driven us back
from the Door of the Sun, and have closed us in by
rolling boulders into the entry way.

"Woo! my heart is pounding," said Bryan getting to the end of what his mother had written to date.

"I'm almost afraid to read on," she replied while rinsing dishes.

"According to this, Mom, there is a tunnel that leads over to the cliffs and perhaps one to the Fort as well. So maybe, there is gold still stored in the 'chamber.' "

"That could be, but I don't have a clue as to where to look," she confessed.

"Well," laughed Mr. Anderson over hearing them. "We could get a backhoe and dig a trench across that side of the house till we find it."

"I hope that's not necessary," she replied.

"The logical place would be out of the basement," thought Bryan.

"I guess we could drive down tomorrow and have a look," said his dad. "And if you want Josh to tag along, he can come too."

"I'll check and see, but I think a pack of wild horses couldn't keep him away, " gladly responded Bryan.

"Okay, and I'll fix a picnic lunch," announced Mrs. Anderson.

Early next morning, after picking up Josh, they headed down across the San Joaquin Valley toward the low hazy Coast Range far in the distance.

Arriving, Bryan's parents first checked on things around the ranch, while the boys eagerly began their investigation. They circled the house looking for subtle depressions in the ground and walked out toward the bluffs, but found nothing.

They next headed back to the house and stopped at the head of a short flight of stone steps. Which led down to a set of rusted iron doors that once gave access to the basement.

"Josh, I wonder if there ever had been another building out here, about where we're standing?" wondered Bryan.

"Well who'd know? Your mom?"

"Possibly. What I'm thinking, is that they could have unloaded the animals inside some kind of stable. From there they could move the gold directly into the basement and into a tunnel."

Stepping into the house, they spotted Bryan's mother sitting at a desk going through some papers, and his dad standing over by the family paintings. He was mentioning something about how he had forgotten what the Captain looked like.

Asking his mother about the possibility of a pre-existing building on the south side of the house, she had to stop and think for a few seconds. She then recollected that at one time, someone had made a reference to a shed or outbuilding.

"Dad, do you want to help us look in the basement?"

"Sure," Bryan's father agreed joining the boys as they descended into the dimly lit basement. "Let's check for hollow walls," he suggested.

Following that suggestion they began banging on the walls.

"These walls are made of stone and mortar, and have been laid flat," observed Mr. Anderson as he scraped a crevice with his pocket knife. "Even if it was hollow, we wouldn't be able to hear it."

"Well Bryan, this is a familiar situation to us. What have we learned from the Captain's previous inventions?" recalled Josh.

"Yeah, it's probably looking at us in the face, right now. The most obvious thing would be a 'Door of the Sun' symbol, if we can find one."

"Nothing obvious anywhere, just stones laid in level courses throughout the walls," commented Josh. "Maybe the access was outside, underneath the old building, being covered with boards or hay or something."

"Maybe it's not staring us in the face, but instead it's right under our noses," said Mr. Anderson.

"Under our noses?" repeated Bryan looking down at the dirty stone floor.

"Let me go find a broom," said Josh disappearing up the stairs.

"There appears to be some white quartz mixed in with the other stones," pointed out Bryan's dad, squatting down to get a better look. "Quartz is not native to this area, so it had to be brought over from the foothills."

"Or from the 'Oro de Cañon,' " thought Bryan.

Josh began sweeping from the stairway toward the south wall, stirring up a dust storm. Coughing his head off he finally stopped.

"Hey! look here, the shape made by the quartz," noticed Josh.

"It is, the 'Sun!' and it is facing toward the back wall," realized Bryan.

Out of its base, where the *Obelisk* was depicted was a pathway of quartz disappearing under the dirt.

"Let's see where this quartz vein leads," said Mr. Anderson.

Josh continued his sweeping across the floor, tracing the manmade quartz vein to the wall just to the right of the iron doors. Following up the wall about a foot and a half, the quartz trail ended at a stone set in the wall.

"What do we do now?" asked Josh.

"Try moving the stone," suggested Mr. Anderson.

"It's coming out," said Josh pulling on it.

"Pull it all the way out," said Bryan's father helping him shimmy it out.

"It's hollow back in there and pitch dark," said Bryan looking through the hole.

"I'll find a flashlight," said Mr. Anderson hurrying up the stairs.

"Josh, I think we found it!" excitedly declared Bryan.

"I wonder, what could still be in here?"

Returning with the light, and stooping down, Bryan's father shined the light into the dark void. "It looks like some kind of rusted metal latch."

"Here, let me push on it with the broom handle and see what happens," said Josh.

Pushing on it, there was a definite click, and then a terrible high-pitched screeching sound of scraping metal coming from below them. Wham! A section of the floor dropped out from under Josh sending him plummeting into the dark depths below.

"Josh, are you all right?" called Bryan.

There was a silent pause.

"O-o-oh. I think so. The wind got knocked out of me. I'm still in one piece. Say, how about a ladder and some light down here," echoed Josh's voice.

"Don't move, we'll be right back," said Mr. Anderson.

"What on earth was that noise?" Bryan's mother demanded, coming part way down the stairs.

"It was from an old trap door that we discovered. Josh has fallen into a tunnel or something," replied Bryan.

"We need a ladder and more light," added Bryan's dad.

"Oh my! There's a ladder and some kerosene lanterns out in the barn," she replied.

Returning Bryan's dad lowered the ladder down to Josh, and he firmly set the feet. Climbing down with a lit lantern his father went first. Bryan quickly followed carrying a lantern also. His mother fumed and fussed at the top of the ladder, she was apprehensive about going down into the old tunnel, but curiosity would not leave her alone.

"Looks safe enough, Andrea, it should be okay, its been standing up all these years," said her husband, using the flashlight to check out the ceiling.

"All right, but I reserve the right to change my mind," she said grinning.

As they proceeded, the yellow light from the kerosene lanterns was so dim, that the flame itself was about all that could be seen. The floor seemed to slope downward. After about eight hundred feet small pools of water began to show up.

"We must be getting close to sea level," thought Bryan.

"Yeah, but is the tide in or out? We'll have to make sure we don't get into a spot where we'll be trapped," cautioned his father.

"What's this, someone notched the shape of a side tunnel into the wall," noticed Josh.

"I bet this was to be the tunnel to the Fort," replied Bryan.

"Look here, rock strata," observed Mr. Anderson holding up the lantern.

"We must be going under the bluffs," commented his wife.

"It shouldn't be too much further then," figured Bryan.

It seemed that the height of the tunnel began to shrink and the floor was now covered with fine sand. Waves could now be heard crashing just ahead, echoing with a clamoring boom. Ducking lower, the tunnel suddenly opened into a large room.

"This must be the 'chamber,' " thought Bryan, his voice echoing.

The sound of splashing water came from the darkness ahead. Stepping forward, they could now see a large pool of churning ocean water that surged and splattered upon the surrounding rocks.

"Look, there's a round hole leading out, under the water," pointed Mr. Anderson.

A dim green light could be seen under the turbulent water. Flashing a light along the wall just above the opening, the remnants of an old iron door could be made out.

No one spoke as they scoured the room wall to wall and out to the edge of the water, but nothing was found. Disappointment showed on everyone's face.

"One thing is for sure, this proves the accuracy of the Captain's diary," commented Mr. Anderson on a positive note.

"Let's get back, this place feels like its closing in on me, if you know what I mean," said Bryan's mom.

Bryan glanced back to where the tunnel entered the room, noting that its height was about two feet shorter than it was further up.

"Now wait a minute," said Bryan. "This is not the original ground we're standing on. Look at the doorway, how short it is."

"Sand must have accumulated in here all these years," agreed his mom without getting the import.

Suddenly, the realization hit Josh, and he started digging down into the sand. Bryan jumped in and helped him scoop it away. Just over a foot down they hit something hard.

"Looks like bricks," said Josh.

"Bricks?" Mrs. Anderson questioned.

"We need more light down here," said Bryan.

"Yeah, they're bricks all right," said Bryan's father excitedly.

"Bricks, what are you talking about?" his wife demanded.

"Gold bricks!" he answered.

"Here Dad, take this one, go pay the taxes and buy yourself a new pickup with the rest," said Bryan. "Ye-e ha! We found it, Mom, it's still here!"

"I can't believe it, all this time, right under our very noses," she replied.

Bryan's mom and dad hugged each other then they all hugged.

"Come on, let's get back to the sunshine," she coaxed wiping the tears out of her eyes.

Pulling two more bars out of the hole, the boys soon followed them back to the ladder.

"Wait a minute Josh, I have one more thing to do," said Bryan climbing off the ladder.

Searching through the paintings in the corner, he pulled out the one of White Feather.

"I can see where you get your good looks," observed Josh.

"She really was beautiful, and that was also true of her loyalty, a quality that's not always inherited."

More Than Legend

It was now the last week of summer vacation, as Bryan gazed into a crackling campfire on a family camp out. Being drawn into the restful flames, he fell into reminiscence of all that had happened that summer.

He remembered looking down at the El Rancho from the bluffs with new eyes, to see how the Captain had even laid out the ranch to match the general pattern of the 'Door of the Sun.' " The main ranch house was located in the central position of the "Sun." The Fort interestingly was in the relational scheme of things occupying the symbolic place of the *Obelisk*, where the map was hidden.

Whatever did happen to the Captain and White Feather he pondered? Only a few more passages were entered into the diary. As he recollected, their principal hope was to escape through the lava tubes, but it was a small chance. Only two others decided to take that chance and go with them. It would seem foolish to stay and starve to death, unless there was another wrinkle to the story. Nevertheless the last entry was dated October 9, 1793 and as he recalled these were the vital passages:

> *This is my final entry. We are preparing to leave tomorrow. We should be successful in finding a breach in the lava tunnel, which I believe we will, due to the fact that a constant breeze blows through them. Our course will strike southeast over an unnamed pass to a place White Feather calls Whispering Valley.... We should not be followed there, as it is in Paiute country. It has plenty of water and good game. The elevation is low enough to miss the first snows, if they should come.... Must be hot springs in the area.... We have to descend to the desert side of the mountains near the Lake of the Monache. We will try to circle around the southern tip of the range and return to the Rancho if I do not run into Federal soldiers looking to arrest me.... I am not out foxed yet, I have conceived one more plan.*

More Than Legend

Will mark the trail from the Monache to Whispering Valley. At the Valley will leave instructions containing details to follow a reverse trail back into the mines and a copy of my continuing journal.... To the reader of this journal: The legacy I leave is an inheritance, and I hereby claim it in behalf of my son and his heirs, that to which you see here, and in and about the Canyon of Gold. Let this journal bear witness to this fact.

Captain Maximo Camino
October 9, 1793

Bryan again pondered the nagging question, as he threw a stick into the fire, what did become of the Captain and White Feather? It appears they did not return to the 'Canyon,' or to the Rancho. Did they even make it to the place called Whispering Valley, or to Mono Lake as it is now called? Maybe he was arrested as a revolutionary, as he thought was possible, or perhaps the Paiutes may have even taken a dislike to him.

As Bryan looked up into the starry expanse that vaulted over the majestic peaks and the Purple Hills, it all seemed to mesh together to form a grand architecture. Perhaps it really wasn't the mountains that called him. Maybe it was something higher.

Stirring the fire, a flurry of sparks scurried heavenward. In the final analysis, that summer had been—*More Than Legend.*

During the long winter that ensued, the unknown days of Captain Camino still bothered him. Sitting at his desk he poured over numerous maps, trying to figure out where this fabled Whispering Valley could be, and the possible routes that he may have used to cross the Sierra and descend into the Mono Basin. There were at least two or three strong possibilities. As the rain beat on the window and the wind blew, he stared out thinking of the high mountain passes and the wind that whispered through them calling the Captain's name. Someday he was determined to visit them.

More Than Legend

On spring vacation, the two boys pulled into Josh's driveway noticing a strange car and a couple of well-dressed women standing nearby, talking with Josh's mother.

"Who is that with your mom?" asked Bryan.

"What? Where's your eyes, that's Tammy and her mom."

"No way, that's not your brat cousin is it?"

"Here she comes now, see for yourself."

"Hi Josh, Bryan," she said greeting them with a smile and a sparkle in her eye.

Bryan was speechless, his mouth hung open.

"What's the occasion, you're all dolled up with fancy hair, high heels, and that frilly dress?" inquired Josh.

"A friend of my mom's got married, we were in the ceremony. We were bride's maids. I guess we'll be staying over for two or three days. Bryan! Why are you staring at me that way?" she blushed.

"Oh, I, I guess I must have just been thinking about something else," Bryan stammered trying to act nonchalant.

"I see you have your packs, where are you guys going?" she asked.

"We're back on the trail of the Captain," answered Josh.

"We have a couple of clues we want to check out," added Bryan.

"Clues? Give me ten minutes to change, you can't leave without me," she said running toward the house holding her skirt. Speechless the boys stared at each other.

Watch for
The Sequel – "Indian Sky"

After two years the paths of Bryan, Josh, and Tammy had strayed. Yet ultimately they would be drawn back together, as the search into the mystery that was Captain Camino continues, and an inevitable romance blossoms.

Join them in their search, as Yosemite's beauty comes alive, from the foot of the Great Tissiack to the gleaming peaks of the high country.

The discovery of events that could rewrite the history of the American West is also part of the tangled web that leads East and into the Southwest.

But who was the crazed man at Deadman Creek? What drove him? What had he seen?

And there was the "Indian song," a story about the "beginning time." Woven into the song was what appeared to be a cryptic message. Was the Captain again showing them the way?

The adventure continues.